THE HOUND

CRAIG BROWN write[...] and columns for *The Su[...]* [...] *Standard* and the *Independent o[...]y*. His books include *The Agreeable World of Wallace Arnold, Rear Columns, Craig Brown's Greatest Hits, The Marsh Marlowe Letters* and a collection of political sketches for *The Times, A Year Inside*. Born in 1957, he lives with his wife Frances and their children Tallulah and Silas in Aldeburgh.

BY THE SAME AUTHOR

THE
HOUNDING OF
JOHN THOMAS

Craig Brown

ARROW

This edition published by Arrow Books Limited 1995

1   3   5   7   9   10   8   6   4   2

Copyright © 1994 Craig Brown

The right of Craig Brown to be identified as the author of
this work has been asserted by him in accordance with the
Copyright, Designs and Patents Act, 1988

First published in the United Kingdom in 1994 by
Century
Random House UK Ltd,
20 Vauxhall Bridge Road, London SW1V 2SA

Arrow Books Ltd
Random House UK Ltd,
20 Vauxhall Bridge Road, London SW1V 2SA

Random House Australia (Pty) Limited
20 Alfred Street, Milsons Point, Sydney,
New South Wales 2061, Australia

Random House New Zealand Limited
18 Poland Road, Glenfield
Auckland 10, New Zealand

Random House South Africa (Pty) Limited
PO Box 337, Bergvlei, South Africa

Random House UK Limited Reg No 954009

A CIP catalogue record for this book
is available from the British Library

Papers used by Random House UK Limited are natural,
recyclable products made from wood grown in sustainable
forests. The manufacturing processes conform to the
environmental regulations of the country of origin

ISBN 0 09 925921 4

Printed and bound in the United Kingdom by
Cox & Wyman Ltd, Reading, Berkshire

FOR FRANCES

It's tough work on the farm, very tough, tough and tough and tough and tough. Talk about tough, it's as tough as tough – and that's tough, very tough. Man's work as has been man's lot since Creation. And bitter cold too. Please send my pale blue cardy and could you kindly purchase me some ear-muffs, red and white spots for preference, and send them post-haste. Tough it may be, but I'll see it through the winter until I am attached to thee once more, my Lady Jane, and our own child, the shoot of our loins, the sweat from our brow, comes into the world. Money's short, so an honest fiver might come in handy, so's to wipe the sweat off my toiler's brow. But let me make one thing clear, and that's as that is, for all the money you'll be bringing, I'll not be wiping the bairn's bottom, not the day of its arrival, not the next day, not then nor any time, sorry but no, that's lady's work, that is.

I like farming all right. It's not inspiring, but then I don't ask to be inspired, I ask only that sweat drops from my brow, the brow of a man who's as good as the next, or better more like. I'm used to horses, and cows, though they are very female, have a soothing effect on me. My fellow men – big men, small men, all kinds of men – middle-sized men too – are all decent but they don't comprehend, that they don't, not one little bit. They are so trodden down that they are well and truly downtrodden. The men are limp, they feel a doom somewhere, and they go about as if there were nothing to be done about it. If only they were educated to *live* instead of earn and spend. If the men wore scarlet trousers, they wouldn't think so much of money. If they could only dance and hop and skip and sing and swagger, they could do with very little cash. How I long for them to be naked and handsome, and to sing shanties bold as brass and to dance the old group dances, and carve the stools they sit on, and embroider their own emblems and wear their hair in fancy styles with pretty coloured slides to keep it from slippin' in the front. Then they wouldn't need money, not theirs nor no one else's. They'd be happy in themselves, alive and frisky, kowtowing to no one, and to no one kowtowing.
Willie Winkie sends greetings to his Lady Jane.

Work continues tough, very tough. In the bitter cold, my hands –
these hands that will soon touch thy very arse, Lady Jane – have
grown coarse and right flaky, with rough skin beggin' for treatment.
The landlady – a kindly soul, but downtrodden and with no sense of
life's purpose – has lent me her skin-care lotion from a fancy store
down Henchurch way until I can purchase some of me own with my
own pounds and pence, jagged in the hand, come payday, but I
wouldn't say no to a pair of woollen gloves through post, Lady Jane.
Lime green would go well with my trousers, or if not anything with a
good honest dollop of mauve.

I got the cardy and the ear-muffs, for which my thanks, plus the
five-pound note – not much, but it'll have to do. I sometimes thank
God that my mind is above such trifles as money, for it might divert
me from my search for truth and reality and vigour and satisfaction,
physical and spiritual, especially if that money were only five pound,
and no more. Last week, I ventured out to the public house, there to
fraternise and make merry with my fellow toilers. They were drinking
their ale out of their sturdy pint-pots, as manly as men can be,
grasping those handles with their fine, masculine fists and drawing the
rim of the pint-pot to their mouths in one great, strong, tough,
upward motion. They were complainin' strong about the weather –
bitter cold – so I ordered me own tipple – a hearty lemonade with a
good, strong, paper straw – and sat beside them, ready to share with
them their sheer bloody pain. 'I've got me ear-muffs through post
expected shortly,' I told them, 'Red and white and spotty through and
through. Knitted them meself, with me own ten fingers, or eight
fingers and two thumbs'. They looked back at me unsmilingly,
soundless and lost in thought, some raising their pint-pots to their
large and fulsome red lips. 'If you'll be wanting,' I added, 'we could
meet once, twice, three times a week, all dressed in our merry clothes,
singing cheery songs in communion, while I learn'd you the tufts and
bobs of the rudiments of crochet, d'y'kin me?' But they refused my
plan, bold as may be. It convinced me once ag'in that the great mass
of people – cranny and begappen and ankid for granskin – have great
bloody need of an all-round education in crafts and handiwork, with
crochet the highest bloody apple on the upshooting tree, erect and
sproutin'.

Please send a new bar of soap, honey blossom fragrance for

preference, second choice lilac. And more stinking money, if you've got some about you.

Willie Winkie waves ta-ra to Lady Jane

The Grange Farm
Old Heanor
19 December

Thanks for the soap. I asked for honey blossom or lilac but no matter, peach will have to do. The money came in handy too, what little there was. And the woolly hat arrived, with its pretty pom-poms, and not before time. God – no friend of mine, He who made this poisoned, fetid, money-obsessed world – has cursed us with a cold winter, miserable and forsaken as a buttered scone without jam.

My work on the farm continues, rough as an unpolished doorknob. How I long for the Easter, when you join me and together we bring the bairn into the world and we set up a proper, working farm together with the money you bring and I hold both your great, large woman's posteriors in my upturned hands every morn and I lift them up, high as high, and I place them on that tractor seat and send you out, out, out into the fields, rich in mud and dirt and soil and filth, to plough and till the day through while I slog over the evening meal and keep the fires burning bright and plump up all the pretty cushions until you arrive home, exhausted and satiated but alive – yes, alive – from a day's honest-to-goodness slog on the land – Blake's land – that is ours, all ours. A man needs a bit of his own property, a stretch of land to call his own, with a woman to till and plough for him, and a sitting-room to make all cosy, with honest pelmets on the curtains, and pleasant silverware on the dining-table, and a nice bit of Axminster in the drawing-room. For then a man may turn his mind to higher thoughts, to the true meaning and purpose of this harsh and bitter life.

This is my thirtieth winter lodged twixt the earth and the sun. With my own hands I have forged myself a stout pair of knickerbockers, scarlet in colour, with cross-stitching in lime on either side of the knees and beautiful brass buckles at the top and I stride through the farmyard in these on my way to feed the chicks, the envy of the rest of heaving mankind as they slop out their dungheaps and get their grey, bedraggled trousers filthy-dirty with some of the bitterest most godforsaken chores known to man, like cleanin' out the sty and slaughterin' the pigs.

How Willie Winkie yearns for his Lady Jane! Please send fresh supplies of varnish. I've been sufferin' damned hard for chipped nails, like no man deserves to suffer even in this soulless age and sometimes think I can take it no more, though further cash might ease my pain.

The Grange Farm
Old Heanor
1 January 1920

Sometimes I feel great grasping white hands in the air, wanting to get hold of the throat of anybody like me who tries to live, to live beyond money, and squeeze the life out of us. But to live beyond money, you must have money in the first place, because then you have no need of the need of money, and it's the need of money that makes money worth needing: there's the nub of 't. Has Sir Clifford seen you right yet, Lady Jane? When I think of you, and I think of him, I think to myself that a joint bank account can't be far away for the two of us, man and woman – well, can it?

Your letter arrived. You approve of my plans for the cottage, the furnishings and suchlike, and I'm glad of't, my Lady Jane, but I must tell you here and now that the palaver you reckon we'll get up to on the Axminster is wholly out of the question, but wholly. Those carpets need the care and attention that only a dedicated and utterly wholehearted owner can devote to them, and they are not to be abused in that way, for they show the dirt something rotten. Every living, breathing human being needs a carpet, and a clean carpet at that, or else he will lose a grip on life's purpose.

Is Lady Jane missing her Willie Winkie? Yes, of course I remember the day we spread those flowers, that fruit and veg over the naked bodies of each other, there in the woods! How could I forget it? Talk about peckish. That night, I went back to my cottage, all alone, and made a delicious vegetable hot-pot, with first-class fruit salad to follow.

To tide me o'er these harsh winter months, with the winds howling through the trees and the crackling winter fires and these good, thick walls all that stand between earthly man and going down with a chill, I have taken to enlivening my mind with zest and colour and energy and friskiness, just like the great god Pan intended, by attending evening classes at New Heanor in Table Decoration. Next week, they are teaching us how to make a simple but effective centrepiece for that extra special occasion. Please post a further fiver, to ensure educational continuum.

I sometimes think our human dreams however paltry are there solely to be thwarted, dashed against the rocks of commerce and money and greed and ravaged by the gluttonous fevers of time, that I do, Lady Jane. You see, the cardigan – my cardigan, the cardigan you sent me, *our* cardigan – has developed a hole, a bad hole in its left sleeve, all ragged and gaping like a lost soul in purgatory, close to the elbow and believe me I'm without any pale blue wool to stem the tide of damage that threatens at present to engulf the rest of the cardy, and the red wool I have got just won't go, it would clash too violently, too wretchedly, to make the damned knitting operation worthwhile for any mortal to pursue. Do you, Lady Jane, my Lady Jane, have any pale blue wool in your possession, or can you lay your ladylike hands, your soft, supple woman's fingers upon any? Farming still breaks my back, morning, noon and night. That man should be born to perform such menial tasks, such paltry, mind-destroying, hand-grubbying tasks! Yesterday morn, Lady Jane, I donned my scarlet breeches and a knitted waistcoat of turquoise tinged with bright, bright yellow and I took an hour off from the chicks to venture into the local town of New Heanor, beautifully clean and modern, and with none of the sick devotion to tradition that makes our old towns swelter and die in their own muck. I was greatly taken by some of the shops I saw there, elegant emporia of every type, of every hue and shade, all presenting first-class wares to the worn-down populace. And whilst browsing in a leading haberdashers – browsing! why should I be browsing? man was not made to browse, but boldly to purchase with the bronze and silver that merrily tinkles in his trouser pocket, the fruit of his own labour or that of his lady! – I happened to overhear a conversation 'twixt twain folk of like-minded disposition.

'This town,' says the first, 'is fine and modern, with an eye to the future. But what this town truly lacks is a high-class grocers and provisioners such as is to be found of the highest quality in so many of our more flourishing cities.'

To which the second responded, 'My God! You have said it! Whither, for instance, should I go for anchovies in this town? No, for the anchovy I must go to the neighbouring city, there to make my purchase in the high-class provisioners you have rightly mentioned. Yet it need not be so. All that is needed is a man of vision, a man above the run of the mill, a man who feels forced neither by birth nor by class nor by money nor by self-pity into thinking himself beneath the common yoke of sweltering humanity.'

Can you see the dream, my beauty, my great, big, bouncy-bottomed Lady Jane? Could I place my two hands on your posteriors and lift you up, up, up to the counter of a high-class provisioners, there to deal the finest produce to such folk as needs it? All it would take would be my brains and that useless money – how I hate money! – that comes from Old Sir Gammylegs himself.

Please send some chilblain ointment – the itches on my right foot will not abate of their own free will, but, like man, need seeing to.

I cannot wait but to see thee, Lady Jane – and if I go on about money, as you claim, it is only so that we may stand above it, treating it for the weasel distraction it is.

Thomas's High Class Grocers & Provisioners
No. 221 The High Street
New Heanor
15 February

Please note the change of address, so's to be sure when you journey to meet me in ten days' time, you might find your way without distraction into the voluptuous bosom of our new abode.

Not for me a farm, my Lady Jane, with its squelching and its oozing and its dung and its muck and its animals sweltering and ponging and humping and grinding as if there were no finer feelings under neither sun nor moon. No: the two of us, us two, can do better than that, my God we can, me and you, you and me, me with my pestle, you with your mortar.

I shunted myself out of the ordure and manure that was the farm, my Lady Jane, my God I did, I can promise you that on your two weighty posteriors, I can. These are exciting times we're living through, that they are. Striding like a true man through the town, blood coursing through my veins like so many red and white corpuscles, I noticed as to how the above-named premises was up for purchase to a man with the guts and vim to make a go of it. Do you think I'm the man to hesitate? Don't give me that clatfar! Take it back this moment or I'll lose my rag and stamp both feet.

So I strode into that building, looking as good as the next man in my pale blue cardigan and my scarlet breeches with the cross-stitching and the gold buckles and with my slide holding my hair right back, so that it plunged over the dip in my neck like so many waves crashing o'er such scrap'd and barren rocks, and I asked the vendor, like no man would ever ask him ag'in, 'So what's th'askin' price?' and he said, 'One thousand two hundred and fifty pound – or nearest offer', and I said, 'A thousand – take it or stuff it up thy male arse,' and he said, 'I'll take it', so I told them you were already worth a quid or two, and expectin' a pretty penny from Sir Clifford in full and final settlement and that they'd have the money on table when you arrived in a fortnight, so we signed papers and – like a lobster digging sandcastles – here I bloody am, high-class bloody provisioner, Mellors by name.

By the by, that scribblin' writer friend of yours Lawrence has been in contact of late, signs hisself 'David', if you will. Says when he was last stayin' with you and Sir Clifford at Wragby, his 'writer's eye' saw what was going on atwixt us. Can you credit it? He goes on to tell how o'er the week of his stay he set up a system of mirrors in the keeper's hut, so's he could climb high into a tree above the hut and, armed with his notebook, peer down through the chimney and observe our cuddlin' and canoodlin'. Now he says he wants to write a book about us and what he calls our 'heroic romance', and he'd appreciate 'talking it through with us', checking he's got all the positions right, and such. Whatdy' say, Lady Jane? There could well be money in it for us, and for the shop, and no mistake!

Thomas's High Class Grocers & Provisioners
No. 221 The High Street
New Heanor
19 February

What kind of a reply was that, Lady Jane? My letter to thee were passionate, full of the surging life-force, so that when you held it in your womanly hand it were as if you could feel my lips trembling on your flame. And yours to me! That was a lily-livered tiding, and no mistake! Where is thy courage, woman, where is thy sense of adventure? And where too is thy faith? Have you no wish to see thy fellow and future husband a high-class grocer and provisioner, one of the highest class grocers and provisioners in the land, with not just one shop, one outlet – no! – with a string of outlets all over the East Midlands – and beyond!

You say you'd always saw me as a man of toil, a man with dirt 'twixt his toes! That I'd told you we'd be starting a farm together, with a pig and a sheep and a hen and a duck and a cow and several acres of good barren pasture. Maybe as I did, but that was afore I took stock of myself, and my Lady Jane, and my coming bairn – and I thought to mesel', I want to be above the whole damned common herd, those limp men, the money-mass of people, thrown about like rags by their weasel employers, kowtowing on their hands and knees – and for what? A lick of cat spittle in their soup come Christmas, and that's if they're lucky. And what of those without a grocer's to their name, those fated just to use the grocer's for their shopping, but never to own one, those destined always to work for others, never to stand on their own two feet? The mingiest set of ladylike snipe ever invented, full of conceit of themselves, frightened even if their boot-laces aren't correct, rotten as high game, and always in genuflection to their betters. A generation of mosquitoes with half a ball each, too sissy for the rough-and-tumble of loading, loading, loading those massive shelves.

No never for me that inhuman fate, Lady Jane. Never that for a manly man like Mellors. Mellors is no namby-pamby faintheart, oh, no, not Mellors. Mellors is a man who stands proud behind his own counter, demanding respect with his payments. And you will stand beside him, Lady Jane, running downstairs for provisions as and when necessary, and assisting him at all hours, at once proud and unashamed of your new-found and proud servility. Do I make myself clear?

So you don't like the idea of David Lawrence coming to stay, and you're waving your womanly arms around in fear of what he'll write! Where's your vim, woman? There's good honest money in books, and no mistake – perhaps even sufficient for the new outlet I'm planning in Dartwell, come autumn!

Thomas's High Class Grocers & Provisioners
221 The High Street
New Heanor
23 February

Wi' only three days 'til I see thee again, woman, this serves as my last letter during this our most painful separation. How the system stinks to high heaven – not that there is a heaven – to have separated us for so long! I yearn for you, Lady Jane, I yearn for the stretch of your stout legs, the reach of your strong womanly arms, the clutch and grip of your nimble lady's hands – all, I have no hesitation in assuring you, invaluable assets in any halfway decent grocer's assistant.

I note you made no reply to my previous missive, Lady Jane, and take it this spells assent, and I thank you for it. You will make the proudest and noblest of grocer's assistants, on my eye you will!

Meantime, the sweat of my brow and the sheer dogged force of my manly back and buttocks – yes, buttocks – has been all but spent in placing orders for the finest produce from all four corners of the Empire with which to stock our shelves. By the time of your arrival, you will be greeted with a front window resplendent with assorted comestibles and sweetmeats of every shape and description, some in jars, others in pots, some unwrapped, others in fancy wrapping with red ribbon (farthing extra).

Nor have I forgotten, my Lady Jane, how our bairn is but a week away from delivery. For this reason, I have made sure that the tasks and services allotted to you during your first fortnight working on said premises as my assistant are kept to the barest minimum; any particularly heavy stacking and loading I will obviously delegate to you, but the more plentiful mundane chores I swear on my big, working heart I will undertake with my own hands, even though this may bring me the greatest hardship, the like of which few quality grocers have suffered before.

One last thing, Lady Jane, afore I lay my head to its well-earned rest on a pillow sodden with the sweat of my manly brow. Coming from your pampered, high-falutin' background, a background of coddling and cosseting by folks as knew no better, you might deign to bring your 'superior' knowledge to the order form sent me by Harvey's Wholesale Merchandisers of Exotic Sweetmeats from Foreign Climes. What's 'taramasalata' when it's at home, then, if you're so bloody clever, eh? Eh? EH?

How I long for the strength and suppleness of your great womanly back! How I long for that scorching, furious, sweat-laden female determination to keep going at all hours, tidying, ordering, piling, stock-taking! How Willie Winkie longs so hard, so very hard, for his Lady Jane! Also, please bring some cement mix with you, as it is dreadful dear in New Heanor, and the new roster informs me you have a footpath to lay on the morning after your arrival, God willing.

221 The High Street
New Heanor
26 February

My dearest darling Hilda,
It was so *sweet* of you to drive me all the way here in your car today, and under such *trying* conditions. Your kindness towards me and my

little one (only two days to go!) seems to know no bounds. How lucky I am to have you for my sister, dearest Hilda!

It was wise of you to simply 'drop me off' with my suitcases. I know my beloved Mellors can be difficult towards you − he finds it hard to express love with mere words, you know − and it will be much easier for you both to establish a caring, fruitful relationship when we are through these frantic times! His great thoughts on mankind − he is so very fond of the majority, but so bitterly disappointed by them too − are being stifled by his attempts to achieve a workable timetable for the new store. At the moment, he is struggling to combine the two; but when he has the groceries up and running, his mind will be free to dwell once more upon matters of a deeper nature, and he will be at ease in his spirit.

After you dropped me with my luggage at the front door of my new abode and I had waved you farewell, Hilda dearest, I spent a quiet minute looking in wonderment at the window display created by the loving, manly hands of my darling Mellors, a vivid recreation in luxury comestibles of Mellors' whole philosophy of life: the big glass jar of glacé cherries in the centre, a sort of maypole around which the smaller sticks of locally produced butterscotch can be seen to dance, in much the same way as liberated man may dance, dance, dance around the maypole in a pagan celebration of the fire and passion that should surely be at the very heart and soul of our existence. A sign in the window announced the grand opening of the new shop this coming Monday, with the message, embossed in gold leaf, 'Bring your wallets and fancy purses and spend the money you've made from the sweat of others' brows − or clear off.' Oh, Hilda, was ever a man so honest, so *direct*?

As I was rapping on the front door, waiting for my lover to venture forth, I chanced to see the painted inscription above the lintel, phrased with the boldness of purpose that stands as the hallmark of his personality: 'THOMAS, LICENSED TO PURVEY FANCY GOODS TO FOLKS WITH MORE MONEY THAN SENSE.'

At long last, the door opened. How good it was for me after all these weeks to set eyes on Mellors, so tempestuous and vigorous and animal-like in his pale pink overalls with his proud, upstanding initials sewn so neatly onto his checkered lapel in lilac brocade! He is, indeed, a man among men, a thoroughbred whom neither man nor beast can cause to swerve from his one, true and overriding purpose! And his voice, so rich, so strong, as hard and firm as gravel. 'Ah were busy movin' th'aspargus tips from one end of shop to t'other, weren't ah, woman?' he said, 'Ah'm a grocer, and ah 'ave to groce now, mornin', noon and night, to provide for those who continue to uphold the insentient notion that life is but for the chewin'. Groce, groce, groce: ah sometimes think a man may be buried under his own grocin', woman.'

He looked me up and down with those manly eyes, catching sight of the babe swelling in my stomach. 'My God woman tha has swelled!' he cried. 'Ah coulda mistaken thee for a petty thief wi' half a dozen tins o' pork luncheonmeat 'neath thy vest! Ah might have marched thee off to t'magistrate, right honest ah might!'

'It's our child, Mellors, the very flame of our loins!' I exclaimed.

'There'll be no pocket money for 'im till he earns his way, mind – and that's for sure, no doubtin'.'

This was my Mellors, my own dearest Mellors, so different from Clifford, whose every word and breath were wrapped in the abstractions and coy evasions of his pampered class! This was a man indeed, a man who could say what he thought regardless of the finer feelings of his shifty-eyed fellow mortals! But what of the notice?

'Why "THOMAS"?' I asked him, 'For surely you are my Mellors, and you will always be my Mellors.'

'Think of t'scandal, woman, will y'na?' he replied. 'If news that Her Ladyship has run off with the Gamekeeper ever gets through from Wragby, it'll affect commerce summat terrible; the store will stagger and fall like a fellow but recently castrated. From now on, woman, we are Thomas – Mr and Mrs Thomas. And don't thou ever forget it.'

'"Mrs Thomas",' I repeated, savouring the new sound, 'and "Mr Thomas".' I smiled at our subterfuge. 'But to me you will *always* be Mellors.'

Oh, Hilda, I feel so sure I am to find happiness at last, happiness here among the groceries with my Mellors and our darling babe! Just to think of it! – The next time I write it will be to bring you news of the birth! I am so very, very excited and bubbling with expectation!

With every felicitation from
Your own dear sister
Connie

My darling sister Hilda,

It's a boy! Delivered yesterday! A big, beautiful, bouncing, baby boy! And he is to be called John Thomas.

In haste – Mellors is bellowing that the groceries await my unpacking!

Your own dearest darling sister
Connie XXXX

221 The High Street,
New Heanor
23 March

Dearest darling Hilda,

You cannot imagine the joy I feel in holding John Thomas. He really is the sweetest little boy – and yesterday he smiled at me, a sort of lovely half-smile, as if he were keeping something to himself!

As you may imagine, my sweetheart Mellors is almost as keen on his shop, bless him! The grand opening went quite well. Certainly, a great many of the townsfolk of New Heanor turned up, including the Lady Mayoress – quite a feather in our cap – and a full ten members of the Rotary Club which is highly influential in these parts!

When they had forgathered, and the invited company were joyfully admiring a display of Assorted Fancy Biscuits that Mellors had got up to look like The Temple of Aphrodite, with Chocolate Fingers in the least expected places, Mellors called for 'a bit of 'ush'. I fancy they were all won over by his rugged, no-nonsense approach.

'Ladies and Gentlemen,' he began, 'though yer none of yer fit to tie me boot-laces ah bid you welcome to my store just so long as yer drop yer hoity-toity airs at the front door and don't exit 'til yer've spent a good whack of yer money – money earned, ah might add, through the blood and sweat of others less nobly born than yerselves – and not until yer've purchased some complete tosh at a price far in excess of what it's worth, do ah make myself clear, well do ah, fatfaces?'

Hilda, he was marvellous! All eyes were upon him as he made this resolute and uncompromising speech, and I felt so proud, so very proud of this plain-speaking fellow, this man prepared to stand up to the terrible and pervasive class-consciousness that is bringing this country to its very knees. I even overheard one of them mutter to another mid-way through the speech, 'I never heard anything like it!' and you could just *feel* the awe as it moved around the room, leaving customers struck quite dumb, dizzy from the sheer animal *force* of the message.

Afterwards, I was at hand to serve those who wished to purchase while my darling Mellors operated the new till. It emerged that many of those present were strangers to some of our more fashionable items. 'What on earth is *that*?' a distinguished old lady asked Mellors, pointing a delicately gloved finger in the direction of the German salami lying on the Precooked Foods counter.

'Fancy sausage,' replied Mellors.

'And what does it taste like?' asked the old lady.

To which Mellors quipped back, quick as a flash: 'Suck it and see.'

Such vigour! Afterwards, Hilda, I will admit I chided him for it, arguing that such very plain speech might dissuade the more cautious customers from their purchases, but Mellors was having none of it. 'No lily-livered shilly-shallying in this store − that's my motto,' he proclaimed, beautiful in defiance.

And John Thomas! Many of the more mature customers wished to touch him as he lay there merrily cooing and gurgling at the corner of the room, but Mellors was insistent they should pay a penny each for a closer look, tuppence for a touch, and threepence to toss him. 'No tightarses in my shop!' he said when they objected. 'Out! Out this minute!' Our little party finished soon afterwards, rather earlier than we had expected, but Mellors said that we had made our mark on the town, and that this was the main thing.

As you can see, Hilda, it's been an exhilarating time for us all in New Heanor − a far cry from life at Wragby, but so much more vibrant and so much more *real*. John Thomas blows you a kiss, and Mellors says you should drop by, if you've got coppers in your pocket − by which he really means do come and stay soon − we both miss you frightfully.

C. XX

221 The High Street
New Heanor
9 April

Dearest Hilda, my own darling sister,

We found your note at breakfast. I am sorry you chose to depart from

New Heanor so early. We had all been looking forward to you staying until the middle of the week, and are much saddened.

Was it Mellors' rough tongue that got to you? His manner is very straightforward; sometimes it may upset those steeped in the circumlocutory traditions of the British. But when he called you 'a full-breasted young chicken ripe for the pluckin'' he was only being complimentary – as you know, he is a specialist in ready-cooked poultry, and he has an eye skilled in such observations.

Of course, the new store sometimes gets on top of him – he still has so much, so very much, to learn! I tell him it is only normal for a new store to receive a call from the local police with complaints of bad language, but he is still dreadfully upset, describing it as 'a downright fucking liberty'. I have bought him a new book entitled *The Gentle Science of Pleasing Customers*. Who knows? It might just do the trick, for it seems to contain much valuable advice.

Today, we very nearly sold some olives packed in a can, all the way from Athens, to a charming lady who is a leading light of the flower-arranging group in the local church. 'Thank you kindly, ma'am,' said Mellors, who had been hard at work on Chapter One of his new book. But then he added, 'A good bit juicier than your husband's balls, I wouldn't wonder,' and the lady burst into tears, demanding her money back, vowing never again to set foot on our premises. But Mellors was having none of it. 'Talk about touchy!' he exclaimed before returning to his book.

A challenging start, then, but I have little doubt the townsfolk will come round to his kindly cut-and-thrust. Please do not desert us my dear Hilda – you have been such a boon, and we do hope and pray you will be back soon, John Thomas especially.

221 The High Street,
New Heanor
25 June

Dearest darling Hilda,

Most excellent news! My sweetest Mellors has definitely 'turned over a new leaf' and has been most attentive to Chapter Seven of his new manual, 'Further Tips Towards Conversing About the Weather'.

Yesterday, a young couple came in – he is to be the new deputy manager of our bank, I may say! – and they were toying with the purchase of some fine cuts from the smoked meats counter. A week or two ago, Mellors would have told them to 'get a move on' or some such – but not now! 'The weather,' he said, 'is turning a mite inclement.' The young deputy manager agreed. 'Yes,' he said. There followed a short silence, while the deputy manager and his wife stood there, still pondering their choice. Alas, poor Mellors, having made so much of an effort, now quite lost his temper. '"Yes"?' he bellowed, "YES"! Is that all you can say, you stuck-up little weasel, you smarmy little runt! You – you – you – you –'. By this time the young couple had departed. I doubt whether their return is imminent, but it was still a sterling improvement, for which Mellors should be congratulated most heartily.

And yet more good news! Our application for an Off-Premises Licence to purvey wines, beers and spirits has been accepted by the magistrate, and so from Monday we will be selling all manner of alcoholic beverages – and Mellors has allowed me full charge of the counter!

John Thomas is very much the little boy, tidying up and scrubbing his hands all through the day, and I dote on him, though Mellors remains insistent he should on no condition be allowed into the shop, for fear that customers may be distracted from their purchases. How different Mellors is, dressed so sprucely, his fingernails as clean as snow, standing behind the counter of his very own shop, a range of pencils neatly ordered in his top left-hand pocket! You know, Hilda, I sometimes think that his energy – his raw, volcanic, overpowering energy – has been all but dissipated into the Finest Ardoyne shortcake and Premiere Smoked Mackerel Pâté that are our two biggest sellers. He seems to have little time for me *as a woman* any more, preferring, as he puts it, 'to grab an early night by the buttocks, so I'll be up nice and fresh behind the counter come the morn', to devote my manly energies to the job in hand.'

I am writing this at the end of a busy day, Hilda, rewarding myself with a small glass of ginger wine, of which we are now the proud purveyors! Somehow, when I drink it, I feel as if I am floating, floating, floating, to a different land, a land of dreams, a land beyond commerce, where I am alone with Mellors in his hut, and Clifford is waiting for me in the Hall, and things are as they were. But now I'm being silly! I never knew what happiness was until I arrived here at New Heanor!

C.
XXOOXX

Dearest Connie,

Life continues so terribly lonely without you. I still await your return, you know, and will continue to await it until I am placed pining in the grave. Meanwhile, I hope Mellors is treating you well, though I doubt it. The other gamekeepers never liked him, you know: never trusted him, or so they tell me. I have nothing against him, nothing at all, but he always struck me as a shifty sort, no small talk, no breeding, no charm, very much what I call the 'spotted handkerchief' type.

But enough of him. I have some bitter news to impart, Connie. I know you take little heed of my advice, but I trust you will act on this, as it is intended for your own protection.

That smart London friend of yours Mr Lawrence has been to Wragby 'sniffing around'. It appears he has got wind of what occurred between you and Mellors and myself. I believe he sees in it the potential for one of his infernal 'gritty' tales to amuse his flashy London crowd. He is now 'researching' this damnable enterprise in and around the estate.

My first sniff of his disloyalty came when the new gamekeeper, Smart, reported that he had come across a bearded little fellow with a tape measure and notebook skulking about in the immediate vicinity of the hut. I thought nothing of it at the time, but a few days later Mrs Bolton informed me that there was a gentleman to see me, a Mr Lawrence.

As you know, I never took to Lawrence on the odd weekend that he and the frightful Hun wife of his made up numbers for a house party at Wragby. Why bother to be a guest in a halfway decent ancestral home if you plan to spend your time embarrassing the staff with talk of armed insurrection against your hosts?

'Cliff!' he said, every bit the garden gnome, poking his sweaty paw in my direction, 'Cliff! Lovely to be here again! Long time no see!' I noted with ill-concealed distaste that muddy footsteps from his walking shoes were now embedded in the carpet.

'How's erm, erm, erm – ' I said, frostily.

'Frieda? Oh, cracking!'

'Sorry to hear it,' I said, 'But then she was always what one might call "the nervy type".'

'I thought I'd drop by as I happened to be passing,' said Lawrence, 'just see how things were, now that, now that, now that – well, how can I phrase this tactfully? – now that *your wife's rutting the gamekeeper*. Forgive my blunt speech, Cliff, it's the artist in me.'

'Quite.'

'You have my fullest sympathy, Cliff, and let me say straight away that as a truthseeker – as a novelist of world renown, you might say – I am able to put myself wholly into your shoes.'

'Too kind.'

'Oh, the humiliation you must have suffered at the unforgiving hands of your fellow mortals. Wife of toff cripple ruts gamekeeper! What a sordid thing to happen! And folk'll be laughing behind your back – that must be the worst of it, eh, Cliff? The laughter? The cackling? I mean, folk can be so cruel, Cliff, so very, very cruel.'

I rang for Mrs Bolton. 'You'll have to forgive me. I have some business to attend to. Do come again, Lawrence, awfully nice to have seen you.'

'Actually, Cliff,' said the little rat, removing his pencil and notepad from his coat pocket, 'I'd very much like you to talk me through it. This won't take a minute.'

'What on earth do you mean?'

'It's the background details I'm after – my celebrated imagination can take care of the rest! When you saw them naked together, how exactly were they positioned?'

'Ah, Mrs Bolton! Would you be so kind as to show Mr Lawrence the door, please.'

'The door?' he yelled, 'You would throw up the chance to have your paltry life transformed into a work of art – a work of art as beautiful and tender and frail as the naked self?!'

'Regrettably, yes. The door, please, Mrs Bolton.'

'And who's this, then, when she's at home? Eh? Eh?' he pointed rudely at Mrs Bolton. 'Your whore, is she? And are you her little boy? Her little Cliffie? Well, if she's not, she soon will be – you just read my book when I've done with it! I'll screw you, Clifford, that I will!'

And away he went, leaving me shivering with fury. Believe me, Connie, I tell you all this simply to alert you to the malign purpose of Lawrence. He wishes to defame us – me, you, even Mellors, I shouldn't wonder. And if he can't write the truth, he'll just make it up! On no account should you let him into your home, Connie: with a certain amount of discretion, I feel sure we may continue to avoid any hint of scandal.

Your loving husband
Clifford

Darling Hilda,

A bitter letter from Clifford today. How I wish he would leave us alone. Instead, he rattles on against Mellors and the possibility of a 'scandal', as if this were the only matter of importance. He even draws poor David Lawrence into his madness! But Clifford is so self-obsessed these days – it is all me, me, me!

You will be wondering how I am. The shop expands to fill our every waking moment, and Mellors continues to let himself be enveloped by it. He is now the very soul of politeness, and by curbing his tongue he has managed to attract back many of those customers whom first he had so sorely ostracised. Now they all adore him, hanging on to his every 'whatever modom pleases' while they order another two pounds of glacé fruits and a fresh box of peppermint creams. Meanwhile, I sit behind my beverage counter twiddling my thumbs and devising new cocktails for 'our discerning clientele', as Mellors insists upon calling them.

Oh, but the enigma that is Mellors, Hilda! Yesterday, as I was taking bits and piece from the pockets of his overalls – he always *insists* on their being fresh on, cleaned and pressed each morning – I came across a small card saying:

BEATRICE ROBERTS
• *'Around the Ragged Rock'* •
2 North Parade, Grantham
By Appointment Only

Imagine the thoughts that went whistling through my head! Was he seeing another woman? Who was she? And what vile acts did she choose to perform around that ragged rock? For some months now – since before the birth of John Thomas – Mellors has (how shall I put this?) taken a great deal less interest in me *as a woman* than once he used. 'My customers won't abide a crease or stain,' he responds whenever I seek a cuddle from him in the daytime, and he spends his nights rearranging the shelves, sifting through the catalogues for new produce, writing and rewriting his new autumn brochure and going over the accounts with his wretched 'fine-tooth comb'.

Every Tuesday (early closing day), he has taken to departing before luncheon in his van. His mission? 'Just a little trip to our nuts and condiments supplier.' His destination? 'The Grantham area, if I remember rightly – don't wait up.' Yet I am as sure as can be that our nuts and condiments are sent to us every month by train from Southampton!

Last Tuesday, I sought to confront him. I lay awake until 10.45 p.m. when I heard the scrunch of his van on the road below. He unlocked the shop door and let himself in. This was followed by the sound of him moving around in the shop below, no doubt rearranging the shelves as usual. But there was also the unmistakable sound of talking: without a doubt someone was saying something! I opened our bedroom door and stood still and silent at the top of the stairs. I listened hard. Someone grand was with him in the shop!

'How do you do? I am dreadfully well, thank you most awfully for enquiring,' this gentleman kept repeating, over and over again, 'How do you do? I am dreadfully well, thank you most awfully for enquiring. How do you do? I am dreadfully well, thank you – .' I flew down those stairs and burst into the shop. Before me stood Mellors, alone with a pile of Assorted Meringue Casings.

'Where is he?' I said.

'Where's who?'

'The other man – the man I heard talking just now!'

Mellors looked sheepish.

'There was no other man.'

'Tell me, Oliver!'

'You were imagining it, Constance.'

'But I *heard* him. Where is he?'

'He's here.'

'Where?'

'Here. For it were I.'

'You?'

'Me. "How do you do?"' he began to say, in this other man's voice, '"I am dreadfully well, thank you most awfully for enquiring. How do you do? I am dreadfully – "'

'Stop! Please stop!' I went over to my beverage counter and poured myself a large brandy/whisky mix. 'What is going on, Oliver? You speak in a different voice, you visit a whore in Grantham, you lie to me, you taunt me! *Just tell me what is going on!*'

'Mrs Roberts is most certainly not a whore! Mrs Roberts is an extremely respectable lady, I'll have you know! And Mrs Roberts is learning me to talk like a true gentleman! Mrs Roberts is widely regarded as the finest vocal rectifier in the Midlands – and I – rough, coarse, brutish old Oliver Mellors, the Mellors that every mealy-mouthed snob in the county once despised and looked down on, I am her finest pupil these twenty-three years past! "How do you do? I am dreadfully well, thank you most awfully for enquiring. How do you do? I am dreadfully well, thank ..." '

I could take it no more, Hilda. I topped up my brandy/whisky mix and rushed up to bed, closing the door behind me. Oh, Hilda, Hilda, I must face the awful truth Mellors is no longer the man that once I knew.

Your sister in sadness,
Connie

PS. A missive has just arrived from, of all people, D. H. Lawrence! He wishes to renew our acquaintance and asks that he may come and stay at New Heanor. At last, someone with *vigour* and *frankness*, someone with whom one might *exchange bold ideas*! And I have every faith that he will remind Mellors of what is truly *noble* and *manly* and *honest* in a human being, and turn him away from the horrible respectability he is bent upon attaining!
C.

221 The High Street,
New Heanor
19 August

Hillie darling,
The great man has arrived! He came yesterday evening, while Mellors was away at his lessons with Mrs Roberts. I had earlier attended the House of Renée Hair Salon in Old Heanor in readiness for his arrival, and I wore that saucy polka-dot dancing dress with the boa which caused such a stir at the Asquiths' two years ago!!

He was expected at around 9.00 p.m. so I had a few drinkies to 'liven me up' and when the knock eventually came at 10.15 I was – though I say it myself – terrifically full of beans.

I flung back the door. There he stood, much smaller than I remembered him. 'You're much smaller than I remembered you,' I said, because he simply adores the truth, 'Almost, well, titchy. Or is it just that you've grown your beard? I always say a beard can take a couple of inches off a man – but just so long as the inches aren't where it matters, who's complaining, eh?!'

I laughed like a drain, but Lawrence managed to keep a straight face.

'Is Oliver in?' he said, as I bent down to give him a lovely big kiss. 'Not yet,' I said. 'You've got me all to yourself, lucky boy!'

He came in, little eyes darting this way and that, refused a drink point blank, and only took off his coat after I'd insisted. He seemed uneasy in my presence, almost as if he'd never been alone in a house with a woman before. I didn't find him that chatty either, to be honest.

'To what do we owe the pleasure?' I said, Pouring myself the teensiest top-up.

'Will he be back soon, then? Oliver, I mean?'

'Relax, David!' I said, and at that moment Mellors came through the door, and Lawrence's eyes lit up.

Must go! John Thomas is demanding I clear up the mess I made yesterday! Children!

XX. C.

221 The High Street,
New Heanor
15 September

Darlingest Hilda,

It's half past eight in the morning and John Thomas is upstairs looking after himself after all he's ten months dammit its time he learnt to stand on his own two feet he's got toys hasn't he and I'm down here waiting to open the shop just pouring myself a little livener to keep me chirpy for all the gents and modoms wholl be making my life hell utter hell hell hell hell in half an hour.

Wheres Mellors you may well ask where's Mellors where's Mellors where's Mellors where's Mellors thats what I ask myself all day every day these days and the answers always the same Mellors is in the spare room with Lawrence quotes helping him with his book close quotes I've heard that one before they're at it the second the shop closes in the evening 'til the second the shop opens the next morning all huddled up together Lawrence pen in hand Mellors holding forth on our great romance pull the other and what he did and what he didn't do and what he'd've liked to have done and they don't talk of anything else 'til the early hours while I'm downstairs listening to them just having the one more cocktail so's to get a good night's sleep.

Lawrence thinks the world of Mellors he thinks he's the model of a modern man real and earthy and passionate and pagan when in fact all he thinks of is stains and creases and profit margins and expansion and his blessed customers and clean on this morning well one must make sacrifices for literature and Mellors says the spark of our romance will be rekindled by the flaming pen of a great writer and what's more there could be money in it for us or at least for him

Chin chin Hillie
XOXOXOXOXOXOXOXOXOXOX
Your loving sister Connie.

PS. A scruffy poacher has just come in all unshaven a brace of pheasants over each shoulder. Wi' yer be gi'in me money for these 'ere burrrds?' he says. I fancy I see a twinkle in his eye as I cast a beam over his rough manly hands and the bristles sprouting in jagged animal movements out of his chinny-chin-chin. Let's discuss this over a drink I say handing him the bottle of port and he takes a good walloping slug. Don't mind me sayin' missus he grunts but yer've got a mighty pair of breasts on yer chest. as proud and thrustin' as I've seen on a woman down Heanor way.
I purchase his game dismiss him with a haughty smile and tell him to drop in again when he's passing. His name is Bellows.

221 The High Street,
New Heanor
16 September

Dearest Hilda,
Did I send you a letter yesterday? Did I ? Or not? Sometimes I think my memory is quite going, even at half past nine in the morning, when I am writing this letter! Tra-la!

If so, did I happen to mention that the famous novelist David Herbert Lawrence is staying with us for a short while? He and his wife – a German, and forthright with it – stayed at Wragby once or twice, though Clifford, as you might imagine, never really approved of them. David recently chose to renew our acquaintance, inviting himself out of the blue to stay here at New Heanor for a few weeks.

To be honest, he takes little interest in me – he is more what I would call a 'man's man' – but he is determined to make Mellors the hero of his new story, which is to be based on our romance, if you can believe it! Of course, he has agreed to change all our names, so at least we will be spared any embarrassment if ever it is published! And Mellors is excited because he's sure there will be money in it for us!

His research is long and arduous, but Mellors is being highly co-operative, and the two of them spend most every hour of the day and night cocooned in the spare room with a 'DO NOT DISTURB' sign pinned firmly to the door! Oh dear, H, John Thomas is wailing – I have dropped some brandy on the togs he cleaned – so I will resume this letter as soon as pos! C.

Back again! It's the evening now, and I'm just having another tot of brandy to warm me through – the evenings are getting colder, don't you find? – and John Thomas is on another tidiness kick, trying his damnedest to get some shape into my heap of old clothes, and those two are back upstairs again doing their bloody research, 'DO NOT DISTURB' out in force once more, bloody cheek.

I listened in just now, Hilda, I listened at the door of the men's room, I bloody did, and as it happens they were already hard at work on the book. This is what I heard:

'You mean, she placed her hand here?'

'No, a bit further up.'

'Here?'

'Oooh, yes, yes – exactly there.'

'And then she moved it – what? – up to here?'

'Right.'

'And back again?'

'Right.'

'And then again, but quicker, like this?'

'Yes! Yes!'

'And what did you say?'

'Tha's got a nice tail on thee. Tha's got the nicest arse of anybody. Tha's got a real soft sloping bottom on thee, as a man loves in 'is guts. It's a bottom as could hold the world up, it is. It's a bottom as could hold a good handful of flowers, I'll bet.'

'And what did she reply?'

'"What did she reply?" What do you mean, "What did she reply?" David? I were talking to you, you beautiful portion of manhood.'

'Oh, Oliver.'

'Oh, David.'

'Oh, Oliver.'

'Oh, Herbert – can I call you Herbert? You great big bearded dolt, you!'

I don't know if I've already mentioned it, but a dealer in wholesale game arrived in the shop yesterday when Mellors was 'otherwise engaged'. He paid me a variety of delightful compliments, Hilda, and I found my self-confidence somewhat restored by his easy-going charm. I wonder if he'll come again?

221 The High Street,
New Heanor
4 October

Hilda darling,

Mellors has just turned the 'CLOSED' sign to 'OPEN', and another day has begun, with John Thomas busy at the washing-up, Lawrence upstairs writing his book and me behind the beverage counter, fixing myself a little pick-me-up. Mr Stephens from Darlington drops in for a Dundee Ginger Cake with Almonds. He says his Lordship is expecting some German friends, who have particularly requested it.

Mrs Pascoe from the church committee is behind him. In the past few weeks, Mellors has taken to church-going like a duck to water, declaring it will prove an excellent advertisement for the shop. 'How delightful to see you so early in the morning, Mrs Pascoe, and how may I be of service?' he says. If you ask me, he has set his sights on membership of the church committee. While Mellors is cutting her six thin slices of finest ham, Mrs Pascoe turns to me. I place my flask under the beverages counter. 'It's a pleasure to be served by your husband these days, Mrs Thomas, a real pleasure,' she comments, 'And you must have noticed a great improvement.'

I inform her that I preferred him as he was, all rough-hewn and real.

'But my dear, not long ago,' she says, 'he wouldn't even have been able to *say* 'real'. It would have come out 'reeyor' or at best 'rayal' but not as a clear and lovely 're-al'.

'Your six slices of honey-roast ham, Mrs Pascoe!' says Mellors before I have a chance to answer her back. 'Would you like them tied with a beautiful red ribbon?'

Midday: With the shop closed, Mellors once again disappears upstairs for a 'research session' with Lawrence, only this time 'DO NOT

DISTURB' is hanging not on the door of the spare bedroom but on the bathroom, and there is water running. Why? Giving John Thomas his tot before putting him to sleep in the pantry, I notice the stepladder, and an idea comes to me. I take the stepladder out of the back door and place it against the outside wall leading up to the bathroom. I climb up it until I am level with the bathroom window. Peering through the fog of steam, I see the two men – Mellors and Lawrence – standing in the bath, both in the nude, taking it in turns to pour water over one another with a garden can fitted with a sprinkler attachment.

'And then she danced around like this, am I right?' says Lawrence, sticking his leg in the air, performing a ridiculous jig. It comes to me that they are re-enacting that time I ran naked in the woods with Mellors, shortly after he had been quizzing me about my inheritance. 'Yes,' replies Mellors, 'and then I placed my hand on her full womanly breast like this.' And he begins to massage Lawrence's chest, sprinkling water over him from the garden can. I scramble down the ladder, sickened to the core, just in time to re-open the shop at 1.45.

At 1.50, Mellors comes into the shop, his hair drenched, his overalls in disarray, looking fearfully sheepish. 'Must be a leak in the ceiling,' he mutters. Yet outside it is perfectly dry. Must go, Hilda – John Thomas has woken up, complaining of creases in his smock.

C.

221 The High Street,
New Heanor
30 October

Darling Hilda,
Lawrence and Mellors have taken to parading around town together, Mellors praising Lawrence for his command of language, not to mention his social connections (Mellors is *determined* to gain the Lady Morrell fancy goods account), while Lawrence praises Mellors for his rugged manly earthiness. And Lawrence is extending his empire to the shop, giving Mellors ideas for the rearrangement of the window display. In a quiet moment this afternoon, the two of them climbed into the window with a boxful of finely cut strips of the finest Highland smoked salmon and a pot of mackerel pâté. They then moulded it all into a sculpture depicting high priests performing an ancient Druidic fertility dance, with a large marrow on the other side fashioned with matchsticks into the temple of Bacchus, delicately

finished with a selection of brandy snaps. Meanwhile, I am left in charge of placing an order for the next consignment of cherry brandy: we are out of our first consignment, though not a soul has ever purchased a single bottle. Must go and change: John Thomas is having a fit as my blouse has a slight stain on the inside cuff of the left arm.

All love,
Connie.

221 The High Street,
New Heanor
17 November

Hilda dearest,

High drama here at New Heanor. This morning, while Mellors was in the shop window high on the stepladder I had oiled only last night, making last-minute adjustments to his new Temple to Aphrodite sculpted entirely in highest quality farmhouse lard, I'm sorry to say he lost his footing and keeled over head first into the smoked salmon and mackerel pâté display, yelling and hollering at the top of his voice. In the range and quality of his exclamations, I fancy he temporarily regained some of his old manly vigour, aided, perhaps, by one of his legs being where it shouldn't, i.e., wrapped around his neck.

'Stay calm, Mellors, stay calm!' I smiled reassuringly. 'I have had experience with paralysis. You're going to be fine!'

At this point, Lawrence came downstairs in a fury. 'Could I have a little *hush* please – I'm trying to work!' he fumed.

'Mellors has been injured – he can't move,' I explain.

'But he *must* be able to – I've got the book to complete!' exclaimed Lawrence.

'Aaaaeughhghhrreugh!' said Mellors.

'Stop making a mountain out of a molehill – get up, man!' said Lawrence, tugging irritably at his little beard as he does when aroused.

I sent for a doctor, who told us that as a result of his accident Mellors is to be bound to a wheelchair for a full six months. He must refrain from all unnecessary physical exertion, though he may serve his customers, and prepare and handle the lighter cuts of meat. I informed Lawrence that his literary research must end 'until Mellors is man enough to resume'. Lawrence seems quite put out. 'But we were just coming to the best bits!' he says, tugging at his beard, 'Well, I'll just have to stop the book earlier than planned – there'll be no mention of your life after Wragby, no mention at all, and so no publicity for the shop, and what's more no money for the two of you – so there! You've let the arts in this country down very badly, Lady Chatterley, very badly indeed! No point in me staying here with a bloody *cripple* on me hands.' Then he packed his bags and took the first train home, without so much as a thank you very much. Poor Mellors! He felt so abandoned! 'I never trusted him,' I said. 'He was interested only in what we could do for him, never what he could do for us. And I trust that's the last we ever hear of that wretched book.'

Meanwhile, little John Thomas sat through it all without a murmur. The innocence of the young! 'Mummy oil steps, Mummy oil steps,' he kept repeating. I begged him to hush.

'What's the lad saying?' asked Mellors once the doctor had departed.

'Mind me old steps,' I replied, 'Sweet, isn't he?'

XX C.

221 The High Street,
New Heanor
4 December

Darling Hilda,

Suddenly, everything seems so happy, so very happy here at New Heanor. Lawrence has disappeared without trace, Mellors is downstairs in his wheelchair, John Thomas is doing the ironing, and I am treating myself to a long cocktail as I wait for Bellows. Have you ever met him? He is a specialist in wholesale game and fresh fish, and his healthy, outdoors existence provides marvellous relief from the fetid atmosphere of the shop, whose walls seem to crowd in on me with their high falutin' produce wrapped in fancy packaging, bound for the mouths of those too blind with snootiness to notice there's little nourishment in fripperies.

It's Bellows, actually, who has been good enough to crystallise some of these thoughts in my mind, and Bellows, too, who has given me back my joy in living, and loving and touching – yes, touching! – that once I thought I had lost forever! Yes, Hilda, do not breathe a word of this to anyone (least of all to Mr Lawrence – for what would he not do with it!) but I have often stolen, at dead of night, to the nearby wood, there to meet Bellows! He grasps me in his mighty arms, places his rough, tough hairy hands on my posteriors and breathes his rich, earthy breath into my face! I have seen ecstasy with Bellows, Hilda –

true ecstasy the like of which Mellors used only to speak.

I suppose I must admit it now. For me, so much of Mellors' attraction lay in the way he put things, his naïve and simple – almost moronic – view of the world, and the way he would communicate it in frank, Anglo-Saxon words, many of them new to me. But the physical side of our relationship was almost all talk, and whenever I heard him bragging on about our supposed liaisons and couplings to Lawrence, I would feel my blood boiling with rage at his absurdity. And now, ever since he started visiting Mrs Roberts, even his words fail to arouse me. 'I commend your rear quarters most thoroughly' – pah! It simply isn't the same any more. But Bellows, ah, Bellows! He is a *real* man, Hilda! Hush, for here he comes! Must go.

C.

☙ ❧
→— CHRISTMAS CHEER —←
AT
THOMAS'S HIGH CLASS GROCERERS
& PROVISIONERS

221 The High Street, New Heanor
prop: O. Thomas esq.

Mr Thomas & Staff Wish You the Compliments of the Season & Warmest Wishes for a Prosperous New Year.
May We Politely Tempt You with These Seasonal Specialities from Our Wide Range of Display Counters?

Duck Pieces 'Marinaded' in Fresh Ginger • Glacé Fruits in 'Presentation' Box • Finest 'French' Champagne • A Delicious Assortment of Chocolate 'Truffles' • Spaghetti from Italy • A Selection of Mouth-Watering Cheeses from Four Different Countries • Venison 'Briquettes' • A Box of Twelve Ornate Christmas 'Crackers' including Novelty Hats and Seasonal Motto • Exquisite 'Dates' from the East • Cashew Nuts in Decorative Tin • and the very latest food from the heart of Mayfair – 'Turkish Delight' the After-Dinner Confection that is fast becoming the 'talking-point' in homes around New Heanor – and beyond!

'TIS THE SEASON TO BE MERRY!'
—☙†❧—

Dear Father,

I am settling in as well as can be expected. After you left me here – thanks awfully for the 'slap-up' dinner at The Randolph! – I spent quite an age unpacking my trunk, hanging my suits up, placing my shirts, socks, etc, tidily in their allotted drawers and generally 'making the place ship-shape'. After I had completed the tasks in hand, I awarded myself a refreshing glass of Ginger Pop, sat down in my armchair (in desperate need of some darning, I fear – a task I have made a vow to perform before the week is out!) and drew up my timetable for work and play. I can't tell you how grateful I am that your sheer hard graft has allowed me to take my place at this ancient seat of learning! I'm afraid to say I couldn't resist boasting to one of the fellows into whom I bumped that my father was indeed the Thomas of Thomas Grocers and High Class Provisioners fame. From the look on his face, I could tell he was most dreadfully impressed. 'And he's due to open his 100th branch only next week,' I added, my chest swelling with pride!

Judging – as I know one shouldn't! – by first impressions, I seem to have a somewhat 'mixed bunch' of fellows on my corridor. But, as you have taught me, one must learn to take people as they come, for every stranger is a potential customer. I have already grown quite chummy with the chap in the room to my left. He claims to be something of a 'poet'!! His name is Colliers Pinkney (for his sins!) and he languishes in a lime-green silk dressing-gown for much of the day, insisting that he 'bitterly but bitterly detests' what he calls 'the far-from-great outdoors'! You know me, Father: I'm afraid I wouldn't leave it at that! I informed him in no uncertain terms how much I enjoy a hearty stroll on a fine autumn afternoon, and that nothing beats a first-class game of rugby football on a deliciously sloshy, muddy field! I'm sorry to say Pinkney looked quite 'put out' by this argument. 'The very idea of outdoors fills one with the deepest foreboding. One might step in a puddle – or worse!' he replied, before exclaiming, somewhat mysteriously, 'I can see that I am going to have to get to work on you over the coming year, John Thomas!'

Quite a character!

Yesterday, I attended my first lecture. It was a little complicated, but I think I followed the gist of what the kindly professor was saying. Economics is an invigorating subject – and will prove, as you say, a tremendous boon when I 'take over the steering wheel' of the family business! Perhaps I should not be telling you this, but Mother has written to say that she and Bellows will be paying me a visit shortly. I only hope they do not disgrace themselves. The fellows here are not used to coarse language, or excessive consumption of alcohol, and I would be loath to lose their esteem at so early a stage in my undergraduate career.

How went the opening of the new store in Sheffield? The ninety-ninth Thomas store in the country! My, I have a name up to which I shall struggle to live!

Your loving son,
John Thomas

New College,
Oxford
14 October 1938

Dear Father,

I am so glad the store-opening in Sheffield went so very smoothly. How proud you must have been to have had the Lord Mayor himself presiding – and in his gleaming chains of office too!

Mother and her 'gentleman friend' came to visit New College yesterday, Mother in that loud pink hat and the cerise dress, the 'gentleman' in what looked like tradesmen's overalls, and grubby with it. Needless to say, they caused many an eyebrow to be raised among my contemporaries, whom I feel sure had never seen a display of 'untoward' behaviour at such close quarters. Indeed, I first heard tell that they had arrived when Pinkney, looking out of his window, called me over from the bed with a cry of 'My goodness, John Thomas, who the *giddy heck* are those *simply dreadful* people with their *vulgar* apparel and *doltish* expressions on what I *suppose* one must term, for want of a better word, their faces?' I moved to the window. Imagine my horror upon realising that the couple to whom he was referring were my own mother and her fancy-man!

Forgive me, Father, but I know that you, who have suffered so much discomfort at her hands, will understand when I tell you, with regret, that I found a small 'fib' or 'white lie' emerging from my mouth. 'They,' I explained to Pinkney, 'are two of my family's more outlandish servants – the undergardener and his wife, who does a little dusting from time to time. Please excuse me, Pinkney, while I steer them around the sights for an hour or two – a decent gardener is devilish hard to find in these uncertain times, don't y'know!'

Mother, it pains me to report, is up to her old drinking again; she now combines it with the recitation – sometimes in a strange, high-pitch singsong – of ribald verse, in a voice shrill enough to shatter church windows. Meanwhile, her gentleman friend grunted alongside her, like some Neanderthal creature but recently exhumed.

But I must pain you no more with such sketches, Father! My academic work continues apace, and I have made firm friends with other members of my college, including a tremendously witty fellow called Tufnell Park, who is, of all things, a poet!! On Saturday, Tufnell is to take me on an expedition to the poorer 'working-class' areas of the city, where, dressed all in maroon, he will be reciting his poems 'Ode to an Anemone' and 'How Prettily Doth the Sparrow Sing' through a megaphone to the weatherbeaten inhabitants of those dank parts. Thus he hopes to bring, as he himself says, 'the blessed aroma of art to the dainty little lives of those less fortunate than ourselves.' As you might already have guessed, Park is a terrific wag, and the greatest of fun! Meanwhile, Pinkney is extending my education yet further by inviting me to a meeting of the 'Department of Delicates' (motto 'Semper Simper'). It is a most *exclusive* group which meets twice a term, health permitting, to press flowers and debate their favourite shade of peach. Both Park and Pinkney are, as they say themselves, the sweetest of boys, Father, and my friendships with them grow deeper by the day!

With heartiest greetings, your loving son,
John Thomas

PS. We have started our very own 'poetry magazine', Father! The day before yesterday, we placed a notice on the College board calling for submissions (to 'Assistant Editor John Thomas', if you will!). Regrettably, we have received only one response so far – some simply *ghastly* stuff about the eternal terrors of the bewildered soul by a boot-faced American girl called Greenley !

New College,
Oxford
27 November 1938

Dear Father
Please desist from worrying on my account. Your letter suggests I should 'choose my friends with greater care' and that I must take steps to avoid 'those for whom the sluggardly path is at once the most desirable'. But how rashly and absurdly you judge my very dear friends, Father! Both Park and Pinkney are from the noblest of families – indeed, Pinkney's stepmother Adelphi was a guest at the marriage of

the Duke and Duchess of Windsor in the South of France last year, having entertained the two of them to a successful gin-and-it cocktail party during their engagement. So please don't tell me who I may or may not consort with Father, particularly as you have not yet had the pleasure of meeting them, and of judging their true worth for yourself.

You ask whether Park and Pinkney 'know or care anything about the sheer hard graft of the merchants who made this country great?' But of course they do, Papa! Only yesterday, Pinkney was saying that you sounded, 'too too adorable' in your 'lovely little starched white pinny' and that he longs to meet you. Tufnell is something of a leader of men himself, having recently formed the Goldfish Society, whose members devote their time to dressing up as goldfish and staying as long as possible in the bath before climbing into small plastic bags and offering themselves as prizes at college fêtes. They may see the world a little differently from us, Father, but that is no reason to pooh-pooh their aims and ideals. And do not imagine for a second that their love of poetry is indiscriminate: only this morning we had the greatest fun printing fifty copies of the ghastly Greenley poem and placing them on college noticeboards under the slogan 'The Sort of Girly Gibberish We Can Do Without!'. I need hardly add that, by lunchtime, each of these noticeboards had attracted a sizeable group of undergraduates, all hooting with laughter at Greenley's expense, some of them even reciting the worst lines to each other in comical American accents!

I trust this letter reassures you. I am looking forward to seeing you on the 5th, and showing you, for once and for all, how much I am learning from this exquisite University.

Your loving son,
John Thomas

New College,
Oxford
10 December 1938

Dear Father,
I was taken aback to receive your last letter. I explained in words of one syllable while you were with me in Oxford that if I had known for a single minute you were planning to arrive an hour before our agreed time then I would have urged Park to change out of his Little Miss Muffet outfit. Anway, he was only wearing it, as I tried to explain to you over and over again, because his regular University suit was being pressed by one of the college servants.

Sadly, I can only describe your behaviour towards my friends as ill-mannered in the extreme. I imagine it is because you yourself spring from the unclean world of commerce that you so signally fail to recognise pure, nobler instincts, even when they stare at you full in the face. Park and Pinkney are trying to make something mysterious and wonderful of their lives, something beautiful and awe-inspiring – a far bolder and more courageous purpose, I would hazard, than patrolling horrid little suburban stores all day to see that the masses are serving dried fruits and cocktail sticks in the correct manner to the paunchy, gouty middle classes.

Do not be so *petit bourgeois* as to despise their ideals, Father! Park has composed several admirable verse couplets on the theme of 'Familiar and Fluffy Feathers' which he has every intention of reciting while being punted up the Cherwell, wearing only a pink feather boa, a bowler hat and a pair of right-footed plimsolls. To you, this may sound 'sissy' or 'effete' (and that is how you spell it – not 'afeet' as you seem to!!). While Pinkney is busily preparing a major debate at the Oxford Union (I suppose you have *heard* of the Oxford Union, have you father?) on the theme of 'This House Would Wear Its Top Hat at a Jaunty Angle'.

Gainful employment? Counting themselves proud to be British? Perhaps not – but why should whimsy and wonder be the first victims of that rapacious bounder, work?

Oh, Father, if you could only have spent more time with Pinkney and Park you would have realised what swell fellows they are! And they are devilishly brave, too: when the American woman Greenley (christian name '*Joy*', can you believe!) marched into our poetry magazine offices and burst into tears, complaining in her screechy accent of the humorous use to which we had put her 'masterwork' (!!!), the two of them simply laughed in her face, nobly rounding on her, telling her she had set the cause of poetry back a good thirty years with her 'absurd prittle-prattle' – meanwhile I showed her the door and gave her a jolly good kick up the b-t-m!

So don't let us fall out over a subject about which you know so very little, father – perhaps I am more of an artist than a grocer, but we must both learn to appreciate the other's point of view! How are the stores? Tufnell has advised me that when I take them over I should paint them all bright pink with yellow polka dots and sell in them nothing but marzipan! It would certainly attract a rather 'classier' clientele than at present, would you not agree, perchance?

Once again, I am sorry not to be spending Christmas with you, but, as I explained, the offer of a place in the Palazzo in *Firenze* was more than I could refuse – even in comparison with the 'festive joys' (!) of New Heanor.

Your loving son
John Thomas

Palazzo Colombo,
Firenze
30 December 1938

Dear Papa

Just a little postcard from foreign climes to assure you that, as Park says, *Italie* is *multo bellisimo*! We saw the Pope yesterday – absolute poppet, Park says, all in lovely golds and whites. England seems a million miles away – what a funny little bourgeois land it looks from here! Tonight, on Pinkney's instructions, we celebrate the New Year with a Nun's Party – where everyone must come as a nun! As I write this, poor old Pinkney is attempting to recover from 'overdoing it' last night: his eyes are covered with courgettes, which, he claims, will 'help put the sparkle back'. He really is most priceless! You'll never guess what – yesterday, we bumped into the dread American Joy Greenley in the street with her notebook. What *can* she be up to? 'Not spreading "Joy" and that's for sure!' joked Pinkney! Meanwhile, Park has grown besotted with Mussolini or Miriam Mussolini as he insists on calling him! – and is busily trying to convince the Italians that he has some of our state secrets to sell! I trust this sends a ray of sunshine to brighten up your Christmas in New Heanor?!!

Your loving bambino,
Giovanni Tomasi

New College,
Oxford
19 January 1939

Dear Father,

Thank you for your letter of the 17th. I return the enclosed written agreement, signed and dated as requested.

J. T.

    I agree to abide by your wishes.

    I agree to avoid the likes of Colliers Pinkney and Tufnell and to concentrate on the furtherance of my degree.

    I agree to spend less time in the pursuit of louche and unsavoury folderols.

I agree to devote any spare time I may accrue to conventional sports, or to activities sponsored and overseen by any of the long-established University societies. And I understand that my adherence to the above agreements will ensure the continuance of my allowance and the continued prospect of a substantial inheritance.

Signed: John Thomas
Dated: 19 January 1939

New College,
Oxford
4 March 1939

Dear Father,

You will be delighted to learn that my 'fresh start' is well under way, my initial reluctance having been replaced by a new spirit of boundless enthusiasm. What sense you talked!

I have got in with a fine new set of fellows who work hard and play hard, possess terrific team spirit and are not afraid to muddy their knees. Another chapter in my 'fresh start' began when I enrolled as a member of the University branch of the Conservative and Unionist Party. I very much look forward to taking an active part in their proceedings. Meanwhile, on the sporting front, I am training hard on the rugby field, with the hope of taking my place in the scrum of the College XV.

I have severed all ties with Pinkney and Park, you will glad to hear, 'and not before time', as you would say! The two of them – bad influences both – are, I'm happy to say, likely to be 'sent down' this term, after their disgraceful behaviour in painting the statue of Bunyan in Founder's Yard with heavy eye shadow and scarlet lipstick.

Finally, may I thank you, Father, from the bottom of my heart for putting me back on the 'path of righteousness', as my friends in the Christian Union call it, preventing me falling headlong into one of the many traps Oxford sets for the bone idle. I have learnt my lesson. If my burgeoning interest in the world of politics ever takes fruit, I am determined to dedicate my career to re-establishing moral values in a society that often seems to have lost its way. In my opinion, the benefits of old-fashioned family values and a strong sense of identity are too readily overlooked in the hurly-burly of our modern society.

With very best wishes, I am privileged to remain,
Your loving son, John Thomas
PS. A small embarrassment – the grim versifier Joy Greenley is a fellow-member of the Christian Union. She hasn't spoken to me yet, but when

we say 'forgive us our trespasses, etc', she has been looking daggers in my general direction!

New College,
Oxford
19 March 1939

Dear Father,

You will be delighted to hear that two of my closest colleagues in the Conservative Society, Harry Whittingham and Bertie Slingsby, have been kind enough to put me up to second the motion in a forthcoming debate. Bertie has proved himself a real chum, arguing my corner all the way with those in the committee who felt I was too much the novice, so I'm determined not to let him down – he's a good man, and that's for sure.

The offer of a chance to second a motion was one I accepted with alacrity. This is a major debate at the Oxford Union, a signal honour from contemporaries such as Bertie, who tell me that they have been impressed (I honestly cannot think why!) by my interventions from the floor, particularly on Points of Order, at which I am becoming something of a dab hand! Initially, I was put off becoming too involved by the presence of the ubiquitous Joy Greenley in the debating chamber, glowering from the sidelines, but I soon overcame these qualms, and now ignore her entirely!

Aside from the privilege of participating at this exceptionally elevated level in such a debate, it affords me the chance to 'make my name' in the Union itself. If all goes as planned, come the summer I could well be 'in with a chance' of securing myself some sort of position – lowly, perhaps, but a position nonetheless – in the Union hierarchy. And then, through dint of sheer hard work, pluck and mental agility, I may be able to work my way up to who knows where?

I have in all seven weeks to prepare for the debate. Aided by Bertie Slingsby, who luckily for me will be proposing the motion, I have already polished up a few telling phrases with which to make our opponents blanche. I plan to spend my every waking moment honing my speech – without, I do assure you, allowing my formal studies to fall into a state of neglect.

I have taken much pleasure in entering into the life of the university – the true life, not the absurd airy-fairy half-life that once seemed to offer such distraction. Rugger continues well: I have been accepted into an excellent body of men which rejoices in the name 'The Plus-Fours', owing to their habit of wearing sensible Plus-Fours whilst out beagling on crisp winter mornings.

They are a cracking lot, Father, hearty and decent and, I might add, full of good-humoured japes against those among one's contemporaries whose legs are ripe for the pulling! Only yesterday, I joined them in 'ragging' that distinctly odd and unsavoury fellow I used to know who went by the name of Colliers Pinkney. 'Pink-ney! Pink-ney ! Pink-ney!' we shouted in unison as we trooped up his staircase. The dozen of us then burst into his room (disturbing a 'poetry reading' no less) and stripped him of his dreadful scarlet knickerbockers before carting him down to the main yard. Needless to say, he screamed blue murder at the very top of his voice in the manner of an effeminate hyena, but this did nothing to deflect us from daubing his body in a most unflattering mixture of flour and water. Finally, we chained him him to the statue for all to poke fun at!!

'That should teach him a lesson he won't forget in a long while!' quipped Whittingham, and we all laughed 'til our sides ached – but it wasn't to end there! Whittingham had kept hold of those precious scarlet knickerbockers and in full view of the blubbing Pinkney he took out a splendid pair of sharp scissors and cut them – snip, snip, snip, into thin strips, each of which he then stuck to the flour-and-water mixture which covered Pinkney's scrawny body. When I pointed out to the assembled company that Pinkney now resembled nothing so much as a half-plucked turkey, my impromptu jest reduced even my most stony-faced colleagues to a state of utter helplessness!

Mother threatens to descend within the next month or two. Heigh-ho! How I wish she would take a more mature view of her life rather than expending her energies solely on the procurement of the next bottle of alcohol – but then, dear Father, you hardly have any need of me to inform you of that!

My studies in Economics are fitting in most neatly with my political aspirations. The business of any government, it seems to me, is primarily to address the thorny questions of finance and morality. As you may imagine, I have plenty to say on both subjects. I look forward to some exceptionally lively discussions of both questions come the holidays, Father. Your experience of economics on the level of the 'shop floor' will, I rather think, offer me many a telling parable for use in my rather more 'universal' approach to the subject; and, as my tutor always says, there is an awful lot the 'little people' (his phrase – not mine!) have to teach those of us who operate in the more rarefied circles of academia!

With every good wish
Your loving son,
John Thomas

Dear Father,

Just a fortnight before the 'Great Debate'(!) you find me on tenter-hooks, for what is at stake is nothing less than my reputation as a speaker and debater, perhaps even my future political career. How very distant your own modest life as a small businessman must seem from the grandeur of my life at the very hub of Union affairs, for here the finest brains of a generation – and the political leaders of the next – engage in lively and topical debate over ideas of *universal* import, ideas crying out for resolution in this world of 1939: 'Should the teaching of Latin be compulsory in all our schools?' 'Is photography a valid art form?' 'Is school uniform desirable?'

Sometimes as I sit in my room surrounded by books and manu-scripts working on my speech at dead of night. weariness stealing o'er my body, the terror of my forthcoming engagement looming like a hound in the fog, I wish I were back with you, Father, at New Heanor Manor, with your sweet vexations over such momentous(!) issues as whether to place a 'special offer' on Smoked Sturgeon, or whether to dock sixpence off a pound of Pork Luncheonmeat!

You ask me the subject of the 'Great Debate'. Did I not tell you? 'This House Believes that Sexual Freedom Has Gone Too Far'. The title is now lodged so deep in my brain, I honestly find it hard to believe that everyone else in the world is not similarly occupied in its con-templation! As to tactics, I have managed to place my hands on a copy of just the sort of 'sexually free', i.e., *downright disgusting* book my opponents see fit to champion – and I am preparing to make a 'bit of a splash' by reading some of its more heinous passages to the august company in the Oxford Union! I can assure you that no right-minded person could fail to be revolted by the activities therein described – and thus shall I win the day!

As to my sporting activities, The Plus-Fours continue to offer one the most tremendous companionship, with an admirable stress on fair play, commonsense and good clean fun. I don't suppose you remember me telling you of a dreadful little drip I used to bump into by the name of Tufnell Park? I used to see a little of him from time to time, largely because – through no fault of my own! – we roomed on the same corridor. Well, we decided he was getting too big for his boots, what with one thing and another, and I'm glad to say The Plus-Fours have managed to pull him down a peg or two – and with a considerable amount of wit employed in so doing!

As I may have told you, Park is – or was! – a rum sort of cove, much given to the recital of his own execrable poetry (or what passed for poetry!). Ever since his friend Pinkney was sent down for bringing the college into disrepute (he had been found by the Chancellor, naked but for a thin layer of dough, having chained himself, quite disgracefully, to the Founder's statue) Park has taken to sitting alone by the river composing more of his infernal stuff while looking soulfully downstream.

Knowing I had once suffered the misfortune to have made the acquaintance of Park, the rest of The Plus-Fours goaded me into approaching him on the riverbank. I was to strike up a conversation with him, by way of a ruse. Meanwhile, the eight of them secreted themselves behind a nearby bush, all set for a mighty belly-laugh!

'Good afternoon, Park!' I ventured, looking down on his large pile of sissy scribblings. 'How's tricks?'

'Thomas!' he replied, that lofty smile playing upon his lips, 'I thought you weren't talking to me any more!'

'Good Lord! Whatever gave you that impression, Park?' I replied. How typical of him to maintain such an insufferable paranoia towards his fellow creatures!

'I don't rightly know,' he whimpered, putting his sheath of papers to one side. 'Perhaps because of what you did to poor Pinkney.'

What was he on about now?! Hearing the suggestion of a titter emerging from the bush, I brushed his remark aside and asked him, in the friendliest spirit of inquiry, 'How's the poetry, Park? Multiplying, I trust!'

'I imagined you'd turned your back on poetry, Thomas, now you've taken up with The Plus Fours.'

'Come, come, Park,' I reassured him, 'I'm as keen on poetry as ever I was. Nothing would give me greater pleasure than to read the verses you have composed.'

'You don't mean that, Thomas,' he replied, moodily. I noticed him clutching his sheath of papers ever more tightly. I felt a tide of irritation at such mistrust surge within me.

'But I *do*! Park, I *do*,' I insisted. 'You know, sometimes I feel that in switching my attentions to the wider political and sporting spheres, I have neglected something deep within my soul. I would so like to regain my more poetic, my more *feminine* side. And by letting me read your beautiful poems, Park, you would help me become *whole* once again. Be a sport, Park – at least tell me what your poems are about.'

I could tell at once that Park was visibly moved by my appeal. 'They are about nature, Thomas,' he replied, 'about the way sunlight plays upon the river, and the cows absorb the wisdom of the day.'

'That sounds quite remarkable, Park,' I said, adding, as if to myself, 'Oh! how I wish I could read them!'

Slowly, very, very slowly, he moved his large bundle of verse towards my outstretched hands. 'Thank you, Thomas,' he said. I fancy I noticed a tear glisten in his eye. 'Thank you for giving me another chance.'

I took the bundle with as much reverence as I could muster, my head bowed low, my expression now wholly serious.

'PLAYTIME, PLUS-FOURS!' I yelled at the top of my voice. Within seconds my fellow Plus-Fours were around us, joyfully grabbing all the pages of Park's poems they could lay their paws upon and transforming them with squeals of delight into lots of little paper gliders and hat-shaped boats! How we roared with laughter as gliders and boats alike found themselves swooping into the Isis, never to be seen again – like so many literary Titanics!

'I say, fellows – the Poet Park is blubbing!' observed Whitters.

'I daresay he's missing his precious odes to the cows!' joked Telfont.

'Do you see what I see, chums?' I roared, pointing to a big, round, still-warm cow pat. 'I think the least we can do is to assist the poor chap in absorbing a large dollop of the wisdom of the cows!'

So saying, we picked up the mewling Park by the legs and dipped his head smartly in the pat. How he howled!

'Deary me, Plus-Fours,' I shouted above the snivelling and whining, 'Poor Park has become a little grubby – we must do the decent thing and offer him a thoroughly good spring-clean from top to tail!' And with that, we all of us hurled the mewling Park headlong into the water!

Such wholesome outdoor japes, Father – how you would have loved every minute! And, on a more serious level, I rather think they prove that I am becoming what historians rejoice to call a 'natural leader of men'. What say you?

Your loving son,
John Thomas

New College,
Oxford
3 May 1939

Dear Father,

Thank you for your kind words of encouragement before my 'big night'. They touched me deeply. In answer to your question, the book from which I plan to read is called *Lady Chatterley's Lover*. It is – thank goodness – not yet available in this country, though it was written – if that is not too grand a word for such scribblings – by a man who had a mind to call himself English. His name was Mr D. H. Lawrence, and he was little more than a common pornographer. Not only does he open the bedroom door upon husband and wife, but he also describes, in breathtakingly lurid detail, the shenanigans between the wife *and her crippled husband's gamekeeper*!

Thankfully, the book is banned from import, but it is just the sort of smut the opposers of the motion wish to see on every station bookstall in the land, there to corrupt every Tom, Dick and Harry from Land's End to John O' Groats! Yet no sane person could hear a passage read from this offending book and still believe it suitable for 'the common man': game set and match to me, I would hazard!

Nineteen thirty-nine seems likely to be a momentous year, if one takes advantage of Oxford's broader perspective. First, I hope to become an orator of considerable standing among my peers. Second, I wish to make strides into the upper reaches of university politics. And I have, sir, every intention of placing such abilities as I may possess at the service of my country in the years to come, if our people, God willing, should wish me to serve them in Parliament.

I have the honour to be, Father,
Your loving son, John Thomas

> New College,
> Oxford
> 7 May 1939

Dear Father,
This is no easy letter to write. I can barely hold my pen, my hand is shaking with such anger, with such a keen sense of betrayal. I have been up all night in my room, pacing, pacing, pacing, attempting to resolve this ghastly, evil, distorted matter in my mind. But I cannot. I know now that it will haunt me for the rest of my years, whatever deceptions I may employ to eradicate it from my memory, or from the knowledge of the outside world.

How could you have done this to me?

Where to begin? We assembled last night at 6.30 in the Oxford Union. It was to be the proudest night of my life, the night upon which I was to cut a dash in the world, the night I was to *be* someone, for once in my life, and not just the son of the distinguished Mr Thomas.

I had bought a dinner jacket especially for the occasion. Why, I even spent many an hour tying and retying my bow-tie in the mirror! I was determined, come what may, that this was to be my night of nights, and that nothing would go wrong.

We assembled in the Union Room at 6.30, the Chairman, the Secretary, the Treasurer, the two Tellers, our main proposer, Bertram Slingsby from Balliol, myself to second and our opponents, Alan Telfont from Magdalen and Jasper Dicks from Trinity. The others sipped a glass or two of sherry, but I was determined to abstain. *Nothing must go wrong*, I kept repeating to myself, over and over again. Nervous? Of course I felt nervous – terrified, even – but I also felt that sense of elation given to man when he feels that, for once in his life, he is in charge of his destiny and that the moves he makes will determine his position at the end of the race. No longer was I under the control of anyone else – you, Mother, my tutor, Pinkney, The Plus-Fours – no, I was now firmly in charge. Whatever happened was wholly up to me.

It was 7.00, and time to go in. As we strode into the Union building, the chatter and banter of the crowd slowed to a silent hum. I took to my seat, and at that moment I felt special, very, very special, as if protected from fate by an invisible shield. Bertie Slingsby, bless him, proposed our motion most admirably, bearing in mind his pronounced stutter and unfortunate 'accent'. He covered all the main ground, the ground we had discussed a week or two before: the deterioration of basic standards in society and the decline of conduct in the country at large, as evidenced in the lower classes by hooliganism, wanton vandalism, and an alarming increase in robbery and violence, and in the upper classes in the all-too-frequent cases of fraud and divorce that are clogging up the courts. Slingsby's was far from being a memorable speech, but it was perfectly satisfactory, allowing me the opportunity to *shine*.

All well and good. Telfont from Magdalen then took to his feet to oppose the motion. Just as my spies had suggested, he argued that a country forbidden by law from reading descriptions of perfectly 'normal', conjugal acts was scarcely a country worth living in. This argument was inevitably rewarded with knowing smirks and titters from the audience, and a prolonged round of applause. I could sense that Telfont had swung them to his side. Given the louche standards of Oxford undergraduates in these raffish times, I would have to fight harder than I had ever fought before to rally them to my side.

'And now Mr John Thomas of New College will second the motion,' announced the President. Bertie Slingsby gave me an encouraging pat on the back – 'G-g-good l-l-luck' – and I took to my feet. I stood bolt upright, my arms outstretched, my hands resting confidently on the

Despatch Box, took a deep, deep breath and launched into the speech I had recited a hundred times previously to an appreciative mirror.

From the very first moment, the audience was behind me. With their support, my speech grew ever more self-confident. Early on, I noticed the heinous poetess Greenley staring at me, hate burning in her eyes, but by now I felt such confidence that I was able to pretend she was not there. I produced statistics galore detailing the decline of morality in the home, at the office, in the factory and on the fields. Trust, that most sacred of all qualities, was under threat from all sides, I argued: the consequences could be counted in the increase in adultery even within the family home, and in an increasing dependence – in the moving pictures, in the newspapers, in the theatre and even in supposedly 'highbrow' novels – upon the momentary titillation of the illicit sexual encounter.

Having worked the undergraduate audience into a veritable froth of indignation, I then produced my trump card from my jacket pocket. This, I was sure, would make mine a name to be conjured with in the Oxford Union for many years to come. It was the manuscript, published in Paris, banned in Britain, of a book called *Lady Chatterley's Lover* by the Nottinghamshire novelist Mr D. H. Lawrence. But I need not tell *you* about *that*, father, now need I?

I held the book in the air for two, three, perhaps even four seconds. Every soul in that chamber had heard of this notorious work, but I doubt whether more than a handful had ever come so close to a copy in all its hideous profanity. 'Mr Chairman,' I said, 'I have in my hand a copy of the sort of book Mr Telfont would wish to see displayed on every bookshelf in the land, ready to be dipped into by the idle hands of impressionable children, bored housewives and fidgety servants. Perhaps some of you imagine its depravity has been greatly overstated. I can assure you, Mr Chairman, that this is far from the case. Very far from the case indeed.

'This disgusting tale involves a supposedly upper-class woman, Lady Chatterley, of morals so loose as to be almost wholly undone. Again and again – and even with *pleasure* – she betrays her crippled war-hero husband, Sir Clifford Chatterley. And her chosen conduit for this treachery is an uncouth, unshaven and unappealing *gamekeeper* of dirty hands and even dirtier mind. And what is more horrifying than any of this, what is in fact truly *shocking* is that Lawrence affects to see virtue in their treachery, decency in their adultery, morality in their immorality!'

I then proceeded to read out several choice passages from that depraved manuscript in order to induce a sense of moral and aesthetic revulsion in my by-now captive audience.

'Tha's got such a nice tail on thee,' I read to the hushed audience, 'Tha's got the nicest arse of anybody. It's the nicest, nicest woman's arse as is! Tha's got a real soft sloping bottom on thee, as a man loves in 'is guts. It's a bottom as could hold the world up, it is! An' if tha shits and if tha pisses, I'm glad. I don't want a woman as couldna shit nor piss. Tha'rt real, tha art! Here tha shits and here tha pisses: an' I lay my hand on 'em both an' like thee for it.'

And so I read on: some sat there, wide-eyed in horror. Others giggled nervously. But I knew full well that even the most liberal, even the most sloppy, even the most worldly among them were now fully on my side, and that no responsible human being could ever sanction such behaviour from so revolting a couple.

'Tha's got a proper, woman's arse, proud of itself,' I continued to read, '"It's none ashamed of itself, this isna." He gathered her lovely, heavy posteriors, one in each hand and pressed them in towards him in a frenzy, quivering motionless in the – '

It was as I intoned the word 'frenzy' that I heard a chair in the gallery clatter and fall. First Bertram Slingsby looked up, and then the entire audience. Irritated at such a distraction, I strained to pinpoint its source. To my horror, I saw Mother, tears streaming down her heavily made-up face, rushing out of the chamber, arms flailing. What on earth was she doing there? And why was she in tears? Was she not proud that her only son should be speaking so persuasively to a building packed full of his peers? I almost shouted after her, 'Mother!' but I reined myself in, knowing that reputations have been dashed at Oxford over less considerable outbreaks of emotion. Instead, I continued with my prepared speech, a little falteringly, perhaps, but with no great lack of continuity.

'And what does this wretched gamekeeper reply to the poor war hero, that upright and dignified gentleman whose only fault has been to be trusting enough to employ him? He replies – and I quote – 'Ay, folks should do their own fuckin' then they wouldn't want to listen to a lot of clatfar. It's not for a man i' the shape you're in to twit me for havin' a cod atween my leg.'

'Well, gentlemen, can you *imagine* anything more vicious and hurtful to say to a brave fellow – a war hero, no less – who has been paralysed from waist down in the service of his country? And yet this is the very literature that the opposers of this Motion would like to see "liberated" – yes, *liberated*! – onto our bookshelves. Believe me, Mr Chairman, *this will not do*. I move to support the motion...'

I resumed my seat to the echoes of cheers and applause. Bertie Slingsby shook me proudly by the hand, his choice of novice partner amply vindicated. Yes, I had indeed made my name. My future within the famous portals of the Oxford Union seemed to be assured. But something far deeper was troubling me: *Mother!*

I could hardly forebear to bolt from the chamber at this, my very moment of triumph. Instead, I sat through Dicks's (notably lacklustre) speech with troubled heart, desperate to rush out to Mother and to discover what it was that had so troubled her. During the pitter-patter of applause that greeted the close of Dicks's pathetic effort, I handed a note to Slingsby – 'Back in two ticks' – and slid out of the chamber.

There in the courtyard was Mother, the mascara still pouring down her convex cheeks. My first thoughts, as always, were for her. 'What are you trying to *do* to me, woman – ruin my reputation within seconds of its establishment?' I yelled at her.

'How c-c-c-c-' said Mother.

I had to encourage her, firmly but gently, to continue.

'Out with it!' I barked sympathetically.

'How c-c-c-c-could you do that to me?' said Mother.

'Do what?' I said.

'How could you – my only son, John Thomas – recite those awful, awful things about me and your father?'

'You – you – you *and my father*? what do you mean?' I laughed scornfully, 'You must realise, Mother, that I was reading a *fiction* from the *novelist* D. H. Lawrence! It is *made up*. Honestly, Mother! Have you been *drinking*?'

I shall never forget the look she threw at me. It was one part disdain to four parts disbelief, three parts utter disgust to one part shame, seven parts remorse to three parts hatred, all these parts neatly wrapped in horrendous agony, so that the combined effect was at the same time catastrophic and strangely contemptible. In a dreadful flash, the truth of what Mother had just said – the truth of her existence, the truth of *your* existence, and, alas, the truth of *my* existence – stood revealed in all its horror. Everything that had been obscure about my life became hideously clear – the shifty looks you both shot in my direction whenever I mentioned books, my earliest childhood memory of you, Father, romping naked in a shower with a strange fellow with a beard, the hush that descended whenever I asked you about your past life, the airs and graces you bestowed upon yourself and the vulgar practices into which Mother has chosen to sink, your loathing of touching or being touched (the reason, I now realise, you insisted upon wearing those rubber gloves from the shop, even when the delicatessen counter was closed).

'You, *you*,' I said to her, 'are Lady Chatterley.'

'Yes,' she replied, an opaque and repellent line of heaven-knows-what running from her nose, narrowly avoiding her mouth and coming to rest, in one, great, perilous drip at the foot of her chin, 'And your father – your father – your father is Lady Chatterley's Lover.'

I felt giddy with self-loathing. 'And so,' I replied, quivering to the very roots of my soul, 'I am the son of Lady Chatterley's Lover.'

Fifteen minutes before, I had basked in the adulation of my contemporaries, and my future among them had seemed assured. But now ... but now ... what was I? I was the product of the most loathly and notorious coupling ever recorded in the history of the century, perhaps of all time, a coupling which, up until then, had seemed possible only in the unsavoury world of fiction.

'Forgive me, son, forgive me!' she whined. I turned away in disgust.

'Er – ' Bertie Slingsby had appeared at the archway. 'John T-T-Thomas – the contributions from the floor are drawing to a close – the vote is about to be t-t-taken! Come quickly!'

I managed to nod reassuringly at Slingsby. I then turned to Mother and whispered, 'Begone!' before following Slingsby back into the chamber. Pushing past Greenley, I entered just in time to hear, with an outer appearance of calm and great dignity, the results of the vote. We had won by 420 votes to 38, with 6 abstentions. My speech had carried the day. I was the subject of prolonged applause. 'It looks as if the S-S-Secretaryship is yours for the asking, old boy,' stuttered Slingsby, through the side of his mouth. And I determined, there and then, to have it. When I left the Chamber, surrounded on all sides by my fellows, I was relieved to see that my instructions to Mother had been obeyed: she had departed.

And now what? I am a product heaved from the cesspit of moral turpitude. I know that. You know that. But I am damned if anyone else will ever know. I have – through your own, hypocritical promptings – altered my feckless way of life. I have made it my ambition to represent decent, family values in our Parliament, the Mother of Parliaments. Were anyone to stumble upon the grotesque sexual history of my parentage, I would be destined for the gutter.

For the time being, that ignoble book, Lady Chatterley's Etc remains a rarity upon these shores. Few have read it, though most have heard of it. But there will come a time, twenty or thirty years hence, when the inexorable drift towards liberalism will ensure that it is washed up upon these shores too. When that time comes, I intend that no one will ever know the ghastly truth of my birth, that nowhere on earth will there exist a single witness who might testify to the ignominy of my creation. Whatever I become – Prime Minister or pauper – I intend to become it through my own will. I have no intention of becoming an item of curiosity, a footnote to literary history, a living joke, the object of scorn, revulsion and mirth.

And so, Father, and so, *Mellors*, I am here bidding you farewell. I am grateful to you for the board and lodging you have provided these past eighteen years. It is more than one could reasonably have expected from the disgusting life you had previously led. I am grateful to you also for instilling in your son a moral code of sufficient force to know to reject you. I intend never to see you again, nor to have any form of contact with you. The same goes for my mother. From this moment on, you are both as strangers to me. I have a life to build, and I will not allow the foundations of that life to be erected on mud. Please desist from getting in touch. Any such attempt will be met with a swift rebuff.

Yours faithfully,
John Thomas

PS. This letter must be destroyed.

Telegram addressed to 'John Thomas, New College', dated 8 May 1939

COME HOME JOHN THOMAS

COME HOME COME HOME STOP PAPA*

---

* Returned to sender marked 'refused'.

From *My Way: Memoirs of a Former Minister,* by Sir John Thomas

The world we faced in 1945 was a very different place indeed to the world of 1939. The Second World War had caused its own problems, all too obvious to those of us involved in it. My own performance in the war had been, in the words of another, 'singularly brave'* but

---

* The source of this remark has proved untraceable.

peace had its fair share of pitfalls too. Like many others, perhaps more, I was determined to place my skills at the service of my country. In turn, my country accepted this generous offer with wholehearted enthusiasm. The British people were clamouring at that time for someone young and full of drive, practical, idealistic, compassionate, forthright and blessed with a fine war record.* Happily, I seemed to fit the bill.

My first task, in the prelude to the General Election of July 1945, was to find myself a constituency foolhardy enough to take me on!! I was already well known for 'speaking my mind' and no one would have imagined that I planned to stop now! But with the war firmly behind them, many constituencies in my beloved Home Counties were on the lookout for first-rate young Conservative candidates, ready to grasp every opportunity to do battle with the encroaching threat of State Socialism. I seized the chance. How well I remember that very first interview with the selection committee of the Dorking Conservative Association, all of them now, of course, loyal friends!

At that time the young whippersnapper who stood before them must have presented a curious sight – highly opinionated, svelte, well-spoken, confident, nicely turned out in a new well-cut tweed suit, and very much his own man. Friends had cautioned me before my interview to, as it were, 'go along with prevailing opinion' but, even at that early stage in my career, I had no wish to be a yes-man. Any constituency with the courage to adopt John Thomas as its candidate would not wish to be led by a shrimp who would swim with the tide. No, I was my own man, and I had no intention whatsoever of pulling the wool over anyone's eyes on that issue, even though it might cost me my selection.

After I was called into the committee room, I took my life in both hands, drew a deep breath, and informed them of these major drawbacks. 'I sometimes wish,' I confided to them, 'that I were not burdened with my one great weakness.'

---

* Invalided out of the Royal Airforce following an attack of vertigo in a third-floor watchtower, Thomas secured a position in the Ministry of Information in Bracknell, overseeing the publication of war poetry. This involved monitoring poetry sent back from the front for any signs of sluggishness. He would then remove any sour or half-hearted notes and add appealing adjectives and adverbs ('vastly enjoyable', 'utterly charming') before finally passing them fit for mass publication. Evidence that he himself saw action has been hard to come by.

'Weakness, Mr Thomas?' said the Chairman. I felt a shudder pass through the committee room.

I took a deep breath and told them the truth.

'My weakness – I may as well tell you now, for you are bound to find out sooner or later – is an absolute passion for honesty. What's more, I'm afraid I must be dreadfully truthful and tell you that this weakness of mine simply will not go away. However much I may regret it, I am doomed to be "my own man" until the day I die!'

I had imagined that this grave admission would be sufficient to seal my own death warrant, but when I looked at those faces beaming back at me from the Selection Committee, I realised that I had somehow 'won them over' with my frankness. Against all my expectations, it seemed that I was very much the sort of honest-to-goodness fellow they had in mind.

But there were still a number of hurdles to leap before the selection became mine. Each of the five members of the committee was permitted a range of questions. My goodness, those questions were brilliantly designed to sort out the wheat from the chaff!

'Mr Thomas,' began the Chairman, 'before we get down to the nitty-gritty, I would like to ask you one or two questions, just so that we can judge the sort of chap you are and the sort of views you hold. For instance, I was wondering whether you think that an MP should stick by the dictates of his conscience, even if it means ostracising his constituents?'

This was indeed a tricky one. I had been thrown slap-bang-wallop in at the deep end, and it was my duty to show that I could swim. But at least I had not been asked the famous trick question of my favourite colour that had caught many of my contemporaries unaware. Appearing before the East Hertfordshire Selection Committee, poor old Bertie Slingsby had revealed that his favourite colour was lilac. Alas, that single slip remark put an end to his parliamentary ambitions, no matter how much one struggled on his behalf.

Where did I stand on conscience? I took the bull by the horns. 'Let me be frank,' I replied. 'I think it would be absolutely invidious to come out strongly on this particular issue of personal conscience before canvassing my constituents on their views – views which, forgive me, I regard as just as important as my own. I'm afraid, Mr Chairman, I've never been a "yes-man", and so I have no intention of taking the easy option of saying to you now, "Yes, I support one point of view much more strongly than another." The fact of the matter is that this simply isn't my way. Life isn't that simple. So let's first and foremost be realistic in this matter, as in all things. I'm sorry, but there are no pat solutions to the difficult questions that face us in these trying times. That's the message I want to drive home, again and again, and I know I can rely on the good people of this beautiful constituency to help me, if only you will afford me that chance.'

Looking up from my notes, I noticed that at least two of the panel – Lady Castleton-Browne and the Chairman himself – had tears pouring down their cheeks. I had obviously struck a deep chord. At that moment I realised the seat was mine for the asking. I learnt from this experience that it is always far better to stand up and defend what you believe in rather than blithely to advocate something to which you are opposed. This, I might add, has remained my Golden Rule ever since.

From the *Surrey Advertiser*, 15 May 1945

Thomas for Dorking

DORKING Conservatives yesterday announced Mr John Thomas as their candidate in the next General Election, which political experts believe Mr Churchill will be announcing shortly.

Family connection

Mr Thomas, 25, is a graduate of Oxford University, where he was President of the world-famous 'Union'. His family hails from the Midlands, but, says Mr Thomas, 'I have always held a soft spot in my heart for Dorking. Dorking and surrounding areas was often a topic of conversation in our household so it is a great thrill to find that I am now standing as its Conservative candidate in the forthcoming election!'

Idyllic childhood

Mr Thomas enjoyed what he describes as 'an idyllic childhood'. 'We were a very close, loving family, and for this reason I am a great believer in traditional family values, of the type the Labour Party's promises of state ownership can only undermine.

Orphan

Asked how his parents had greeted the news of his selection, Mr Thomas replied, 'Sadly, they both passed away long ago. But they were both great supporters of all that I held dear. I know that they would be "thrilled to bits" at my success. I'm only sorry that they are no longer here to witness it.'

Not the French
Mr Thomas has pledged to fight the General Election on those issues about which he feels most strongly: family values, the danger of state ownership, the importance of honesty in public life, and – a particular interest – the banning of lewd or provocative material, especially from abroad. 'We are not the French,' he says, 'and there is no reason why we should try to ape them.'

All welcome
Mr Thomas will be speaking at the Town Hall on Thursday, May 17th. All welcome. Refreshments will be provided courtesy of the Dorking Conservative Women's Association.

From *My Way: Memoirs of a Former Minister,* by Sir John Thomas

At that point in time, the Conservative and Unionist Party ran intensive weekend courses – held in what have come to be called 'Country House Hotels' – for those among its candidates who found themselves in the unsatisfactory state, from the electoral viewpoint, of bachelorhood. Many experts stress the importance to the candidate of a healthy, well-turned-out and generally appealing wife, believing it can add extra votes of anywhere between 4 and 7 per cent – vital in a marginal constituency, and immensely reassuring, even in a safe seat!

Such courses proved an invaluable help in the selection, targeting, courtship and betrothal of a spouse suitable for the far-from-easy day-to-day task of being what is often described as a Member of Parliament's 'prime asset'. My own course, conducted in exemplary fashion shortly after my adoption in May 1945, took place at the Four Beeches Hotel in Sunningdale, with exceptionally fine views over the world-famous golf course.

**From *Choosing for the Future* (1945),
the official Conservative Party pamphlet to aid candidates
in the choice of a prospective wife**

12 Tell-Tale Questions

- Do any of her hats measure over 30 inches in diameter? (YES/NO)

- Is she proud to hold views of her own on a number of major issues facing this country at home and abroad? (YES/NO)

- Does she show a fondness for bright colours, particularly where her clothes are concerned? (YES/NO)

- Has she travelled extensively abroad, including visits to the East? (YES/NO)

- Does she enjoy reading books and/or good music? (YES/NO)

- Does she employ any or all of the following expressions:

  A tea (*meaning a cup of tea*)

  Tea (*meaning dinner*)

  Dinner (*meaning luncheon*)

  (YES/NO)

- Are her teeth in top condition? (YES/NO)

- At cocktail parties, is she prone to steer, rather than follow, the conversation? (YES/NO)

- Are her calves less than 5 inches in diameter? (YES/NO)

- Would she ever be reluctant to act as public hangman, for whatever reason? (YES/NO)

- Does she dance well? (YES/NO)

- Has she made her way up from nothing? (YES/NO)

IMPORTANT. If the answer to more than ONE of these questions is 'yes', the choice in question is likely to prove problematic, if not now, then at some stage in the future. You are accordingly advised to pick again.

From *My Way: Memoirs of a Former Minister,* by Sir John Thomas

It was an excellent, all-round course, serving to broaden one's mind to the real and lasting value of the politician's wife. At the time, I had been seeing a little of a young lady of impeccable background, slightly plain and with refreshingly little to say for herself, so we were off to a head start on both those counts, but when she confessed to me that she was an admirer of English literature all the bells rang and I felt obliged to terminate our acquaintance, in the kindest possible way, as much for her own good as for mine.

On our last evening at the Four Beeches, we were all welcomed to a lavish party to which a selection of approved candidate's fiancées had also had the honour to be invited. It was there that I first set eyes on the woman who was to prove my trusty aide, friend, confidante and wife for many years to come. Who can say what it was that first attracted me to Ann? Was it her readiness to listen? Was it her magic way with a safety-pin, so that even the most recalcitrant of cuff-links or the most disobliging of collar-studs could be tamed in a matter of seconds? Or was it her abiding love of animals, which would prove such a welcome distraction from my parliamentary comings and goings? I am quite clear in my own mind that it had nothing whatsoever to do with the family wealth she had recently inherited, agreeable though it was.

We were married within weeks of our first meeting, on a day ideally situated in the middle of my General Election campaign, just when our fortunes needed that extra 'boost'. From that day right up to the moment of our last meeting in the divorce courts, Ann was to prove a most worthwhile resource, an invaluable asset to both my parliamentary career and to my family life beyond. Incidentally, she was also something of an expert at flower arrangement – and I need hardly add she won over many a Conservative Women's Coffee Morning with her treasure-chest of handy tips! She may even have produced a small brochure on the subject for some charity or other: time, alas, whittles away such precious memories.

From the *Surrey Advertiser,* 27 June 1945

'SHE'LL be a great boon!' says prospective Conservative candidate for Dorking John Thomas (pictured above at their wedding on Saturday) of his wife Ann.

From *The Complete Constituency Flower Arranger*
by Ann Thomas (19pp, Centre for Policy Studies, 1956)

Colour can be effective

I am a great believer in colour. Every flower has its own colour. An assortment of different colours in one vase can be very effective. So too can one colour, repeated over and over again.

Numbers are worth bearing in mind

How many flowers should one put in a single vase? I am a great believer in deciding whether to use a lot of flowers, just a few flowers, or an average number of flowers. This decision should be taken bearing in mind the size of the vase, the surroundings of the room in which they are to be displayed, and the amount of flowers at hand. The more flowers you have, the bigger the vase should be.

Dried flowers

A dried flower is a flower that has been dried, using either traditional or more up-to-date methods. Dried flowers can be most effective, particularly in what are known as 'dried-flower arrangements'. Incidentally, such arrangements do not require water.

A flower may lend cheer to a hat

Some people like to wear a flower, or flowers, in their hat or hats. This can be effective. It is important to remember, though, that watering a flower when affixed to a hat can make the hat soggy. One way of avoiding this difficulty is *either* to remove the flower from the hat before watering it *or* to water the flower before placing it on the hat.

~

Letter from Ann Thomas to Judy Cholmondley, 3 July 1945

Electioneering has been absolutely exhausting but awfully rewarding. The trouble lies in convincing the poor people that they will jolly well have to stay that way for quite a while if the rest of us are going to remain better off. So many of the poor seem motivated solely by envy – the 'if-you've-got-a-lovely-house-then-I-want-one-too' sort of attitude, which as Johnny says is doing this country a great deal of harm, dragging everyone down when we should all be doing our level best to maintain standards and frankly the more you pay them then the less they'll want to work and if you follow Mr Attlee's plan to place swingeing taxes on the better-off then I can't see any of us bothering to work half as hard as we do if the reward is going to be so tiny. There I go again! Anyway, it's all terrific fun, and Johnny is charming everyone terribly.

From the *Surrey Advertiser*, 26 July 1945

Thomas holds Dorking for Conservatives as Labour Storms to Landslide in Country

CHORUSES of 'For He's a Jolly Good Fellow' from his supporters greeted the announcement of Mr John Thomas's election as Member of Parliament for Dorking early yesterday morning.

Moral lead
In his acceptance speech Mr Thomas, 25, congratulated his Labour and Liberal opponents, Mr Arnold Tapps, 44, and Major Ronald Bright, 42, on running 'excellent' campaigns. But he said that Dorking had turned to the Conservatives for 'a moral lead against the forces of disorder'. 'It is time,' he said, 'to get back to basics.'

Great untruth
He predicted Mr Attlee's Government would 'promote their great untruth that a man may be beaten into a state of slovenliness and discontent by his social background' but that 'this country would have none of it' and 'reverting to its old common-sense' would throw them out at the 'earliest opportunity'.

Close to tears
To applause in the hall, Mr Thomas vowed to serve 'each and every member of this great constituency, regardless of for whom they voted, to the best of my ability.' In a moment which brought many of all political leanings in the hall near to tears, he closed his address by paying warm tribute to his 'dear, late parents, who instilled in me the right values'. He closed by thanking Dorking for making him feel that 'my constituency is my home, and my constituents are my family'. He then added, 'But my wife is, of course, Ann ...'

Mr and Mrs Thomas are at present purchasing a house in the constituency. He says that by doing so he hopes 'to put Dorking on the map.' See also picture page 15.

From *My Way: Memoirs of a Former Minister,* by Sir John Thomas

In the first few weeks of my parliamentary career, I had the immense good fortune to be proposed for membership of the Albemarle Club by a very dear old friend. The club was then, as now, something of a bastion of Tory stalwarts, and a highly civilised watering-hole to boot. I have always found it a highly convivial forum for the discussion of ideas – and perhaps the odd bit of gossip! – over traditional English 'grub'. I might also add that our cellar is the envy of many of our more celebrated rivals ...

Letter from John Thomas MP to Bertram Slingsby, 27 July 1945

⤳ HOUSE OF COMMONS ✝⤲

Dear Slingsby,

I am just writing to say how *awfully* sorry I was to hear that you have not yet found a parliamentary seat to fight. I heard about what everyone is now calling the 'lilac' incident. Between the two of us, let me make it absolutely clear that I consider it most dreadfully unfair. Incidentally, I am told that some of the Conservative Associations in the Welsh mining constituencies are very much on the lookout for a young, active fellow who is willing to spend a reasonable amount of time cultivating the miners' vote in the run-up of five years or so to the next election. Might one of them not be worth a stab? I wish I could offer you more advice on how to swing it, but, alas, my own constituency of Dorking, though it spreads as far west as Abinger Hammer, provides refuge to precious few miners!

Coincidentally, in my first few days at the Commons, I have become decidedly friendly with Eskdaill Laughton, who is, as you know, the Deputy Chief Whip of the Party, and obviously wields considerable influence. I feel sure that, by hook or by crook, I could arrange a quiet luncheon for the three of us, to chew the cud, as it were, on 'placing you' with a suitable constituency – perhaps even in an area a little more civilised than darkest Wales! I would imagine a pleasant Gentleman's Club would be the most suitable venue for such a meeting, *n'est-ce-pas?*

Yours ever,
John

PS. Oddly enough, I have been thinking of joining a club myself. Do I remember somebody once telling me you were a member of the Albemarle? This would be just the sort of place, I would have thought, for a pleasant lunch, though I insist that you come as my guest. Might one be proposed, do you think? J.

From the main noticeboard, the Albemarle Club, 14 August 1945

The election of the following Gentleman to Membership of this Club has been approved by the Secretary of the Membership Committee:

John Thomas MP

From John Thomas MP to Bertram Slingsby, 19 August 1945

THE ALBEMARLE CLUB SW1

Dear Bertie,
Just a short note to thank you for so successfully proposing me for membership of this delightful watering-hole, and to offer you a drink here *à deux* – at my expense! – in the not-too-distant future. At the moment, I am up to my neck in paperwork, but after Christmas things should start easing off. Alas, my constituents keep me working flat out, or otherwise I would be able to socialise more!

With many thanks and best wishes,
Yours ever,
John

From John Thomas MP to Bertram Slingsby, 25 August 1945

Dear Bertram,

Thank you for your letter. No, I have not forgotten my suggestion ('firm promise' is putting it a little strongly, I think!) to introduce you to our Deputy Chairman. As you may imagine, he is desperately busy at the moment, as am I, but I hope to be in touch before the end of the year.

Yours faithfully
Floella Lacloche
pp John Thomas MP

Letter from Ann Thomas to Judy Cholmondley, 24 January 1946

Johnny is leading a positively hectic routine, here one minute and gone the next, absolutely up to his neck in constituency and parliamentary matters! He is away for the second weekend running with some parliamentary delegation or other! Sometimes I think if only he were a little less conscientious in his public duties we might have a little more private life. Thankfully, he has the most marvellous secretary who labours under the name of Floella to help him through the mountain of work, not very pretty (piano legs!!), poor thing but terribly nice, very hard-working and awfully *well-meaning*, which is the main thing.

Receipt from the Royal Hotel, Droitwich, 16–18 January 1946

Mr and Mrs J. Thomas
Two nights dinner bed breakfast
2 bots Champagne – room service
Gin and Tonic
1 bot Claret
1 bot Chablis

£19 15s. 6d. PAID

Receipt from the Hotel Splendide, Brighton, 23–25 July 1946

Mr and Mrs J. Thomas
Two nights dinner bed breakfast

2 bots Champagne – room service

2 bots Sancerre

4 Gin plus Tonic

£17 19s. 6d.
Received with thanks

Postcard from Ann Thomas to Judy Cholmondley, 27 July 1946

Dying to see you for the weekend of August 8th –
will try to arrive around 5-ish, if that's all right by
you, so as to avoid rush hour. J *so* sorry he can't make
it – says August parliamentary schedule busiest ever!

From the Parliamentary Timetable,
House of Commons Yearbook, 1946

Summer Recess: 15 July – 30 September

From a letter from Hattie Litherland to Judy Cholmondley,
23 June 1950

... Though I'll say in his defence he's not all hot air – Ann let slip that
ever since April he's *insisted* that it's only right and proper for them
both to give a little bit back to society, so he's taken out a standing
order with his bank to pay £20 each month – quite a sum when you
think of it – to a special charity account. I call that pretty good, don't
you? Obviously, for tax reasons, it suits them best if the sum comes
from Ann's family account, but it all stems from John's initiative.
Perhaps he's not so bad after all and we should all be saying our
penances for ever thinking he was!!

Certificate of Birth

Name and Surname:	*Daniella Laclache*
Date of Birth:	*Twenty-first April 1950*
Sex:	*Female*
Name of Mother:	*Floella Rose Laclache*
Name of Father:	*Unknown*
Place of Birth { Registration District:	SURREY SOUTH-EASTERN
Sub-district:	HORLEY

From the *Surrey Advertiser*, 17 September 1950

Local MP Makes his Mark

NEW DORKING MP Mr John Stewart Thomas made his mark at the Conservative Conference in Blackpool yesterday, bringing the Conference Hall to its feet with his appeal to 'wind back the clock to a time when common decency among the young and respect for the old was nothing to be ashamed of. Let us get back to basic family values.'

Scuffles

His speech came after scuffles between police and unemployed youths at Great Yarmouth last weekend. Mr Thomas made his plea during a debate on the importance of family, for which there were no opposers.

On the map

'I think I have voiced what a great many people in my constituency are thinking,' Mr Thomas told the Surrey Advertiser last night, 'and I hope I have put Dorking on the map once more.'

Letter from the office of John Thomas MP to Mr Oliver Thomas, 21 January 1951

Mr Thomas thanks you for your recent communication and/or good wishes. He has read your views with considerable interest. He regrets he is unable to answer letters individually.

Letter from the office of John Thomas MP to Mr Oliver Thomas, 24 January 1951

Mr Thomas thanks you for your recent communication and/or good wishes. He has read your views with considerable interest. He regrets he is unable to answer letters individually.

Letter from the office of John Thomas MP to Mr Oliver Thomas, 28 January 1951

Mr Thomas thanks you for your recent communication and/or good wishes. He has read your views with considerable interest. He regrets he is unable to answer letters individually.

Letter from the office of John Thomas MP to Mr Oliver Thomas, 30 January 1951

Mr Thomas thanks you for your recent communication and/or good wishes. He has read your views with considerable interest. He regrets he is unable to answer letters individually.

From the *Surrey Advertiser*, 18 February 1951

Local MP set to defy Party Whips over Playgrounds Bill

DORKING MP Mr John Thomas yesterday revealed to a Surrey Advertiser reporter that he was prepared to defy Conservative whips in order to vote with Mr Attlee's Labour Government for a bill to provide more free playgrounds in poor areas of the country's cities.

Sticks neck out

'Some things transcend party politics,' said Mr Thomas. 'Frankly, I think the people of Dorking are an independent lot. The last thing they want is a 'yes-man' – so I'm prepared to stick my neck out on this one. In my view, while food rationing is still going on, and a great many members of the working class, after many loyal years service in the war, are struggling to find jobs – well, it's only fair that their little ones should be afforded some diversion through the provision of playgrounds.

Matter of principle

Asked whether he might be penalised by the Party whips for such an act of defiance, Mr Thomas retorted, 'I see this very much as a matter of principle. I have every confidence that the powers-that-be will respect me for it. By this act, I intend to put Dorking on the map.'

Memo to John Thomas MP from Eskdaill Laughton MP, Conservative Deputy Chief Whip, House of Commons, 19 February 1951

Dear John,

I would hate to see a particularly promising parliamentary career blighted by an early act of political recklessness. These are hard times for the Party, and we really must pull together. Incidentally, I hear on the grapevine that the Spokesman for Clean Air is on the lookout for an able PPS, a post requiring, I need hardly add, the utmost loyalty.

Yours ever, Eskdaill.

From *Hansard,* 25 February 1951

Mr John Thomas (Cons): Mr Speaker, is it not the case that a great many of the facilities provided at present in so-called playgrounds are potential death-traps? Every day, children fall from slides, topple from see-saws and hurtle headlong from swings – yet this Socialist Government wants to see this ghastly spectacle repeated on a daily basis the length and breadth of this once great nation of ours! Personally, I would prefer that no slide were erected by this Government, or by any other, if it meant saving the life of just one small, defenceless child. But in its forward march towards the shibboleth (cries of 'Ooooh' from the Government benches) towards the *shibboleth* of 'progress', this Government seems dedicated to marching over anything standing in its way – even the broken corpse of a poor little child! (cries of 'Shame, shame' from the Opposition benches.)

Local MP swings votes

DORKING MP Mr John Thomas admitted yesterday that his impassioned speech against the Playground (Provision) Bill in the House of Commons yesterday 'may have swung a few votes'. Nevertheless, the sizeable Labour Government majority ensured the Bill was voted through.

Brave

Mr Thomas, previously associated with a move among Tory backbenchers to defy the Party whip, stated yesterday that 'it took quite a bit of courage to change my mind. But I've never been afraid to stick my neck out and in the end I decided that the safety of little children is infinitely more important than the Labour Party's pursuit of "progress at all costs".'

Tribute

Mr Thomas then paid tribute to the people of Dorking. 'The people of Dorking are an independent lot who like to think for themselves. They have told me they thank goodness their Member of Parliament is man enough to change his mind on matters of such grave importance to the daily lives of the young folk of this country – and I salute them for it.'

Promotion for Local MP

DORKING MP Mr John Stewart Thomas has been appointed Parliamentary Private Secretary to the Opposition Spokesman for Clean Air, Sir Cedric Scott. This promotion comes less than six years after Mr Thomas was first elected to the House of Commons.

Thrilled

'I'm utterly thrilled and also very grateful to the Minister for showing such confidence in me,' said Mr Thomas yesterday, 'and to the people of Dorking for giving me such encouragement.'

Fête

On Saturday, Mr Thomas will be opening the Holmbury St Mary Village Fête. Starting time: 2.30. Admission free.

Letter to Bertram Slingsby from John Thomas MP, 10 April 1951

Dear Bertram,

How good of you to bother to write. It does indeed seem ages since we last met – and believe me I haven't forgotten that promise of a good chat over a nice cup of coffee when I get half a mo. But you may have heard that I have reached the giddy heights of PPS so I am quite literally rushed off my feet. Incidentally, I sometimes catch sight of your name on the 'subscriptions overdue' (!) noticeboard of the Albemarle Club. I also happen to be a member – so perhaps we will bump into one another there before too long. I do hope so.

Glad to hear that sales of bathroom suites are picking up!

Yours ever,
Araminta Plunkett
(Dictated by John Thomas MP and signed in his absence.)

From *My Way: Memoirs of a Former Minister* by Sir John Thomas

Within the space of six years, I had gained not only my seat in Parliament but also promotion to Parliamentary Private Secretary to an outstanding Spokesman for Clean Air, Sir Cedric Scott. I had been rewarded with the trust and devotion of my constituency and the admiration of MPs on both sides of the House. I had reason to be content. Yet I felt there remained areas in which whatever talents others may have felt I possessed were still not being stretched to their full advantage.

I had long been of the belief – and it is a belief I hold to this day – that Members of Parliament can benefit immensely from having interests beyond the confining world of politics. For instance, a continuing experience of the world outside can provide an excellent resource for getting to grips with the very real problems facing the commercial sector. I therefore decided, in June 1951, to accept the offer from one of our leading business enterprises – Jesse James Toys Ltd, manufacturers of small-scale roundabouts for public playgrounds – of a role as Executive Director and Parliamentary Adviser. I need hardly add that throughout my parliamentary career, this directorship has in no way interfered with or influenced my political decisions, other than to equip me, in the most practical sense, with a fuller understanding of the wider world.

From *Hansard,* Questions to the Minister for Parks, 27 June 1951

John Thomas (Cons): Has the Rt. Hon. Gentleman any understanding whatsoever of our crying need for more roundabouts in our public playgrounds, and of the immeasurable benefits to health, satisfaction and high morale that would accrue to any community in possession of one?

From *Hansard,* Questions to the Prime Minister, 7 July 1951

John Thomas (Cons): While the Prime Minister busies himself over preparing for his various – ahem – research trips this summer to luxurious foreign climes (Opposition laughter), might it not occur to him to take a close look at a problem rather closer to home, namely the provision in our public playgrounds of wholly safe and reliable roundabouts, which experts and scientists the world over acknowledge to be a contributory factor to a healthy childhood?

From *Hansard,* Questions to the Secretary of State for Health, 17 July 1951

John Thomas (Cons): While the Rt. Hon. Gentleman busies himself with his plans for spending the nation's money on setting up a so-called 'National Health Service' (Opposition jeers) will he allocate time to consider the crying need for more roundabouts in our national playgrounds as a supreme method of ensuring that our grandchildren and our grandchildren's grandchildren have proper access to well-ventilated sporting facilities?

From *Hansard,* Debate on the Economy, 21 July 1951

John Thomas (Cons): Many of us on this side of the House have some sympathy with those on the benches opposite who are concerning themselves with the revival of our economy after the devastation wrought by a long and bitter World War. But is it not the case that one way of breathing fresh life into rundown areas is by embarking upon a fresh approach to children's roundabouts? Our counterparts in the United States have spent millions of dollars in recent years on children's roundabouts of every shape and variety. If we wish to keep up with their flourishing economy, is it not high time we followed suit?

From the Albemarle Club Annual Chairman's Report, 1950

INTRODUCTION BY THE CHAIRMAN

These are days of social change. One class simply has no means of knowing what the other class is up to, or within which class they might find themselves if and when they wake up tomorrow. My fellow committee members and I have therefore drawn up the following 'guidelines'. They are to assist members new and old in knowing exactly 'where they stand'.

I should emphasise that this guidebook is designed not to intimidate, but to reassure. New members may draw comfort from the knowledge that there are still some institutions in Great Britain where traditional values still apply, even if their maintenance requires constant vigilance from one and all.

John Thomas MP
Chairman
October 1950

Staff

Our club servants are one of our most precious assets, and should be treated as such. On no account should they be 'tipped': they do not expect it and it would only make them feel awkward. Please remember that each one of them is an individual, and should be treated as such. For their convenience and that of members, all club servants answer to the name of 'George'.

Deaths

From time to time, it is inevitable that the club will be inconvenienced by the death of a servant. In such cases, the committee replaces the servant or servants with one similar, without prior reference to the various members' committees. In this manner, we ensure a smooth turnover, with a minimum of upset.

Funerals

Club members are advised not to attend the funerals of servants. This arrangement is of course reciprocal.

The library

Members must ensure that the books in the library remain on the shelves at all times. An open book can prove an intolerable source of irritation for fellow-members. Those members wishing to read books are requested to do so away from the premises.

Language in the dining-room

To its regret, the committee reports a sharp increase in the use of offensive words, expressions and phrases within the club. Many consider such language highly divisive. Members should therefore avoid direct use of the following:

'*Spoon*': This implement, used widely for the consumption of soups and certain puddings (though of course jelly should always be eaten with a conventional fork) should be referred to at all times by its generic title 'fork'. If a rounded fork and a pronged fork are to be used at the same time, for instance when eating apple crumble and custard, they should be referred to as 'fork and fork', as in the expression, 'I think this tempting dish is best eaten with a fork and fork, Angus.'

'*Whoops*': The expression 'whoops', often employed when a member or a member's guest has dropped an item or items, is an Americanism of recent import, and therefore best avoided.

'*A drink*': as in the expression 'Would you like a drink?' should be avoided at all costs. The drink in question should either be referred to by its specific title (e.g., 'Would you like a gin-and-tonic-water?" or as a verb (e.g., 'Would you like something *to drink*?').

'*Table*': The word 'table' should never be formally spoken. The Head Waiter will volunteer to 'show you to your er', hesitating rather than employing the word in question. Members and members' guests should follow suit. Like most words with the letters 'b' and 'l' together ('blanket', 'enable', 'comfortable', 'blancmange') and also – in reverse 'elbow') the word 'table' is best avoided within what one might call 'gentlemanly society'...

Human contact

Touch between members or members' guests is best avoided, though a brisk handshake between strangers is permitted in the hall area.

Umbrellas

Gentlemen are reminded that they should carry an umbrella in the Upper Morning Room between the hours of 6.00 and 6.30 p.m.

Families

Families are not permitted in the club other than by prior arrangement with the Secretary, and then only on the occasion of memorial receptions for elder sons.

Conversation

Gentlemen will need no reminding of the innumerable topics of conversation that are on offer, though conversations on matters of personal importance and conversations appertaining, however loosely, to topics of gender, religion, 'different points of view' or current affairs should be avoided. The Upper Morning Room between the hours of 6.00 and 6.30 is reserved for conversations concerning the weather.

Ambulances

Gentlemen who find cause to either:
(a) summon an ambulance or
(b) have an ambulance summoned for them
are reminded that non-members, including ambulance drivers, medical officers, nurses, etc., are not permitted to use the main entrance without prior permission in handwriting from the Secretary, countersigned by the Chairman. They should instead enter and exit from the club employing the back (basement) entrance in Gill Street.

Disability entitlements

Gentlemen suffering from physical disabilities are entitled to a 20 per cent additional surcharge on their annual subscription, to cover the cost of wear and tear on carpeting, staff resources, hindrance to active members, etc.

Club Anniversary Ball

Next year sees the 125th Anniversary of the foundation of the club by Viscount Albemarle. We plan to celebrate this occasion with a Grand Ball. For this night only, members will be permitted to bring their wives, who may be placed in either the Club Garden or the Lower Scullery, where dancing will be available. Alternatively, on arrival wives may be deposited in the cloakroom for collection on departure.

Recent deaths

We regret to announce the recent death of George Simpson, who gave valiant service in the second-floor bar for over twenty-five years. His tremendous contribution to the welfare of the club will not be forgotten. He will be replaced by George Koe.

Resignations

The resignation of the following member has been accepted owing to unavoidable delays in the delivery of overdue subscription fees:

B. Slingsby esq.

Election

I am pleased to announce the election of the following new member to the Albemarle Club:

Eskdaill Laughton MP

⌒⌒⌒

Letter from John Thomas MP to Eskdaill Laughton, Conservative Chief Whip, 25 July 1951

FROM THE OFFICE OF THE RT. HON. SIR CEDRIC SCOTT

My dear Eskdaill,

Many thanks for your letter addressed to the Opposition Spokesman for Clean Air. As you may or may not know, Sir Cedric is off 'on the open road', as it were – all in the interests of 'research', he assures me! I must say, it is tremendously stimulating to be working as a junior to Sir Cedric: he generously allows one an enormous sense of responsibility, leaving piles of unanswered letters, unformulated Bills, unwritten speeches, solemn undertakings etcetera, etcetera, for one to make of what one will. Few in his elevated position would be so diligent in leaving so much for a mere PPS to 'clear up', and I pay tribute to him for so doing.

As you mentioned in your letter, Sir Cedric has promised Mr Churchill a full and comprehensive copy of his ten-year plan for cleaner air in our cities in time for the next General Election, which most people now seem to think is at very most a few months away. This makes for a situation of some urgency. I agree with Mr Churchill that cleaner air for all our people should be a major part of our election platform. I only wish I could give you a more precise idea of what plans Sir Cedric had himself formulated for this important new initiative. Alas, for all my innumerable searches through the genial clutter of Sir Cedric's desk, the closest I can find to a 10-year plan is a scribble in Sir Cedric's hand on a crumpled piece of notepaper saying:

Clean Air Nicer Than Dirty Air – (good election slogan?)

and, beneath it, the scribbled inscription:

but how do we clean it? Some sort of v. large vacuum cleaner?
You've got me there: oh, well!

Is this sufficient? If it is not, I will, of course, do my level best to come up personally with something more detailed as a matter of urgency – though there are, of course, limits to what someone occupying the comparatively humble role of PPS can achieve! Nevertheless, I suspect there is some very hard work to do – and, as I hope you know, that is something of which I have never been frightened!

On a personal note – I do hope to see you in the Albemarle soon – do let's share a drink in celebration of my masterminding of your recent election!

Yours ever,
John

Letter from John Thomas MP to The Rt. Hon. Sir Cedric Scott MP, 25 July 1951

Dear Sir Cedric,
Just a short note to let you know that everything is going very smoothly in the office, with no major panics or setbacks. If I were you, I would extend my leave for an extra day or two, as things are so very quiet.

I have placed your voluminous ten-year plan for Cleaner Air in the back of the filing system for safe-keeping; it will then be ready if and when Mr Churchill asks to see it. But as most people seem to think that the election won't be called for at least six months, there is little urgency.

I will probably not see you until after the Long Recess – in which case may I take this opportunity to wish you a very happy and contented summer holiday.

With very best wishes,
Yours ever,
John

From Dorking Conservative October 1951 General Election Pamphlet

AN ELECTION MESSAGE
FROM YOUR MEMBER FOR PARLIAMENT, JOHN THOMAS MP

Everywhere I go, I find that I am met on the doorsteps by ordinary men and women.

They say to me, 'Isn't it about time ordinary folk such as ourselves joined forces to oust this terrible Socialistic government? In our opinion, when common sense and patriotism combine, there will be nothing the Socialists can do to stay in power!'

And to this I reply, 'Yes! How right you are! All fair-minded people wishing to stand up for proper family values will use their vote to secure a significant Conservative majority under Mr Churchill! On the other hand, those who wish to see the destruction of all that we hold dear will place their 'X' against the ugly face of Socialism.'

About your MP
John Thomas was born in the Midlands and educated at Oxford University.

His youthful years were blighted by the early deaths of both his parents, but he never allowed this tragedy to dispirit him in his fight for a better tomorrow. 'My respect fror the memory of my parents is boundless,' he comments, 'and I feel them looking at me from their place in Heaven, cheering me on to do my best for Britain.'

He became first Secretary and later President of the Oxford Union. Even at this early age, he was arguing for a return to positive family values, an increased awareness of the dangers of subversive literature, a respect for tradition and the benefits of 'standing on one's own two feet.'

He married his devoted wife, Ann, in 1945. Since entering Parliament that same year, he has championed many causes, including more playgrounds for the disabled. Since March 1951, he has been the Parliamentary Private Secretary to the Opposition Spokesman for Clean Air. His diligence and loyalty have ensured that he is widely tipped for high office. 'In six brief years,' he says, 'I think I have succeeded, in all humility, in putting Dorking on the map.'

His hobbies include the family, walking, helping others and outdoor sports.

VOTE CONSERVATIVE X

VOTE JOHN THOMAS X

From the *Surrey Advertiser*, 28 October 1951

Major promotion for Thomas after Tory election triumph

LOCAL DORKING MP Mr John Thomas, 31, has been promoted by Mr Churchill to the post of Minister for Clean Air, following the veteran Sir Cedric Scott's surprise retirement to the backbenches on the grounds of ill-health.

Stout refusal
In recent months, Mr Thomas has served as Sir Cedric's Junior Spokesman and so, in his own words, 'knows the ropes'. Yesterday, he paid generous tribute to his predecessor, praising Sir Cedric for 'his relaxed and affable style' and his 'stout refusal to become bogged down in detail'. Mr Thomas said that he hoped to bring to the job 'a combination of dynamism, energy and big ideas' along with 'meticulous attention to detail'.

Demanding post
In an exclusive statement to the Surrey Advertiser, Mr Thomas announced, 'My appointment to this demanding post helps put Dorking on the map. I am delighted not only for my own sake but for the sake of all the people of Dorking and surrounding areas.'

From the *Evening Standard,* 28 October 1951

Man arrested in pub brawl

Mr Bertram Slingsby, 32, un-employed, was arrested by police in Clapham late last night following a disturbance in the King and Crown public house, Clapham.

Mr Slingsby will be appearing before Clapham magistrates today on charges of being drunk and disorderly.

Private Memo from Sir Cedric Scott MP to John Thomas MP

TRAITOR! TRAITOR! TRAITOR! I'll see you rot in hell!

From *My Way: Memoirs of a Former Minister,* by Sir John Thomas

Let no-one kid you that being a Member of Parliament is an easy task, or some sort of 'soft option'. Far from it. The Member of Parliament – from whichever party – has to work the most ungodly hours, often spending days, even weeks, away from home. Combine this with the combined stresses of public speaking, dealing with constituents' problems, helping to shape party policy, opening fêtes, gymkhanas and what-have-you, entertaining foreign delegations and much valuable committee work, and you have quite a job on your hands.

But helping others brings its own satisfactions.

Letter from John Thomas MP to Miss Becky Bean, 19 March 1952

FROM THE OFFICE OF THE SECRETARY OF STATE FOR CLEAN AIR

Dear Miss Bean,
It was delightful to meet you and have the pleasure of making your charming acquaintance at last night's presentation and reception for final year students at the Royal Academy for Dramatic Arts. As I mentioned last night, I was highly impressed by your sensitive and powerful performance as the French Maid in the Molière, and I honestly believe that, with help – and a little luck! – you could have a glittering future on the international stage.

As a Member of Parliament, and one widely known for his lifelong interest in giving a 'leg up' to the young, I have developed a number of fruitful contacts in the Arts world. I was wondering if you thought there might be any point in my putting your name forward for any future projects they may or may not be undertaking?

If you would care to discuss this and other matters further on a more informal basis, I would be delighted to offer you a spot of dinner in the Members' Dining-Room at the House of Commons, and then we could 'take it from there'. How about next Tuesday 21st? 7.30-ish? St Stephen's Entrance? Do be a poppet and let me know.

Until then – with very best wishes and, once again, warmest congratulations,
from your friend and admirer,
John

Letter from Ann Thomas to Judy Cholmondley, 21 March 1952

... and the delphiniums are, as always, simply super. Poor old Johnny, it literally never stops – dinner tonight with some dreadful little Captain of Industry and his minions, and Westcott is simply too far to drive after a long day and up early in the morning so he's having to stay overnight in the flat all on his own-i-o, poor love. By the way, I forgot to remark on what a simply *beautiful* flower arrangement you had in the kitchen last weekend – all those blues and greens and reds – quite staggering. You *are* clever. How's Richard and the children? Well, I hope ...

From the Diary of Becky Bean, 21 March 1952

... so we went to dinner in this huge grate dining-room and the funny thing was I saw two other RADA students their too Lottie Toppling from the 2nd year and Dee-Dee Jones who played Juliet last year and both dinning with MPs small world really anyway Johnny was lovly he said he really likd my French Maid and he'd really lik to see it again, so I said actuly that was the last perf and he seemd dissap disapoyn dissapon upset and said what a shame the costum really suted you and I said actuly Ive still got the costum I mad it myself and he said o yes and I said if you realy want you can see it agan but I live in Swiss

Cottage and he said well thats not too far off the beetn track I think we can manidge that ...

From the Headmistress's Introduction in the annual school magazine, St Catherine's College for Girls, Box Hill, 14 November 1952

... and we are sorry to be saying goodbye to Mrs Bridge, who will be enjoying her richly deserved retirement at Peacehaven, on the Sussex coast.

The Autumn term was rounded off to a splendid finish when our local MP, Mr John Thomas, gave up a few hours of his precious time to judge our annual Public Speaking competition on the subject of 'The Pleasures of the Country Versus the Pleasures of the Town'. In summing up, Mr John Thomas declared that the overall standard of entrants had been very high indeed, and that he had found it almost impossible to reach a final decision! Nevertheless, he felt that Blossom, J. S. (Apsley's) gave a 'strapping, rounded and vastly appealing' performance, 'full of bounce' which he found 'well-suited to a splendid cup'. He accordingly awarded Joanna the Sir Arnold Strutt-Parker Memorial Cup, and further informed her, as a special prize, that he would be delighted to take her on a tour of the Palace of Westminster as his personal guest at some stage during the Christmas Holidays. We are all very grateful to Mr John Thomas for the time and effort he put into his skilful adjudication – and we trust we did not distract him for too long from his many more important affairs.

On the sporting front, the school continued to excel at lacrosse, with only two away losses recorded over the course of the whole year and a 'full house' of home victories, though recent results on the hockey pitch have proved slightly disappointing ...

Letter from Miss Becky Bean to John Thomas, 27 November 1952

THE IMPERIAL THEATRE, BRIDPORT

Johnny Darling,

Panto rehursuls are brill and Derek says I can understudie the Good Fary which is grate becus you dont get much recernision as the frunt halve of Dozy Dobbin even tho its a trific turific trrifi very demanding roll reqiring insit and xpereuns as to your reqest vesa-ve the costum Im sur I cood sneek it away afta the dress rehursul on nite of Sat 23 and into my logings so meet me outside stage door 9.40 Sat and well have a bit of fun. XXXXX BECKS

Letter from John Thomas MP to Miss Joanna Blossom, 14 December 1952

FROM THE OFFICE OF THE SECRETARY OF STATE FOR CLEAN AIR

My dear Joanna,

It was delightful to meet you once more and have the pleasure of renewing your charming acquaintance yesterday. As I mentioned over luncheon, I was highly impressed by your sensitive and powerful speech at your little school competition, and I honestly believe that, with help – and a little luck! – you could have a glittering future as an orator, a councillor or – who knows? – as a fully-fledged MP.

As a Member of Parliament, and one widely known for his lifelong interest in giving a 'leg up' to the young, I have developed a number of fruitful contacts in the world of the constituency organisations. I was wondering if you thought there might be any point in my putting your name forward for any future projects they may or may not be undertaking.

If you would care to discuss this and other matters further on a more informal basis, I would be delighted to give you a little personal tuition in voice projection, general deportment and so forth. To be frank, I often find that novices in this area sometimes find their clothes, jewellery and so forth to be an unnecessary restriction, both on the vocal chords and on one's self-image, being all too easy to hide behind, so it may be as well to conduct these informal training sessions in my private flat, if you are amenable.

I would be delighted to offer you a spot of dinner in the Members' Dining-Room at the House of Commons, and then we could 'take it from there'. How about next Thursday 19th? 7.30ish? St Stephen's Entrance? Do be a poppet and let me know.

Until then – with very best wishes and, once again, warmest congratulations,
From your friend and admirer,
John

From the *Bridport Examiner*, page 5, 8 January 1953

Just fancy that!

POLICE were summoned to Chantry Lane, Bridport on Tuesday after neighbours had reported seeing a wild horse at an upstairs window. 'It was bucking and rearing like anything' says pensioner Mrs Sylvia Threlfall, 73, 'We were worried it would do damage.'

But after thorough investigations of the premises, police confirmed that it was in fact only a pantomime horse from the Imperial Theatre's forthcoming production of Cinderella.

A man and a woman were released after questioning.

From 'Old Girls' News', *The Boxonian*, journal of past pupils of St Catherine's School for Girls, Box Hill, November 1953

Bacon, Daphne (*Campbell's*) has recently given birth to a baby girl, Penelope Amanda – 'better known as Penny!' – a little sister for Prudence, Geoffrey, Simon and Amelia.

Bannerman, Elizabeth (*Carstairs'*) is reported missing in Peru.

Baxter, Pamela (*Jordan's*) married someone unsuitable and is now living in a purpose-built maisonette near Chipping Norton.

Beard, Abigail (*Sutton's*) is reading Chemistry at St Andrew's University and hopes to become a secondary teacher.

Blossom, Joanna (*Apsley's*) is a political researcher for local Dorking MP John Thomas.

Brannigan, Caroline (*Sutton's*) is studying flower arrangement with a view to marriage.

Bunn, Rachel (*Jordan's*) is wanted by police in five countries for her part in a highly successful international drugs ring.

Bumfrey, Alison (*Apsley's*) is unhappily married to an insurance broker who is 90 per cent homosexual.

Letter from Ann Thomas to Judy Cholmondley, 4 December 1953

... and anyway who says geraniums go well with nasturtiums? Not me! Yesterday, I was flicking through a mag from one of the schools in the constituency which we get sent for some unfathomable reason and under 'Blossom, Joanna' it said, 'is a political researcher for John

Thomas MP'. Well, I never, I thought, so I said to Johnny over drinks, 'I never knew you had a researcher'. 'Didn't you?' he said, 'Oh, we all do.' 'Well, tell me all about her, then!' I said. 'Nothing much to tell really,' he replied, 'she's the wrong side of fifty and suffers from corns.' 'Says here she only left school last year,' I said. 'Really?' he said, 'There's no telling these days what age they are.' Honestly, sometimes he's so vague, I really think he's not interested in people at all, just politics, politics, politics! Incidentally, the tulips I told you about are looking simply super, I've put them near the tallboy in the drawing-room which could probably do with a jolly good polish, if only one could find the time...

Postcard postmarked 'Palace of Westminster 23 May 1954', addressed to Miss Joanna Blossom, signed 'J'

Of course I will leave her, of course I will, you have my word on it, but these things take time and what with one thing and another I don't want to hurt her any more than is absolutely necessary and it'll look bad in the constituency which at this stage in my career won't help one bit, but of course I love you – dammit – division bell – must go – *believe* me, J.

Letter from John Thomas MP to Miss Francesca Lamour, 3 April, 1955

FROM THE SECRETARY OF STATE FOR COMMUNICATIONS

Dear Miss Lamour,
It was delightful to meet you and have the pleasure of making your charming acquaintance after bumping into you so opportunely while you were queuing for the Public Gallery at the House of Commons, and I am only too pleased that I was able to 'sneak you in' as my personal guest. As I may have mentioned over our little drink afterwards, I am highly impressed by your command of the English Language, and I honestly believe that, with help – and a little luck – you could have a glittering future as an interpreter specialising in politics and world affairs.

As a Member of Parliament, and one widely known for the many links he has forged with political leaders of very many European countries, I was wondering if you thought there might be any point in my putting your name forward for any future projects that may require your undoubted talents. If you would care to discuss this and other matters further on a more informal basis, I would be delighted to offer you a spot of dinner in the Members' Dining-Room at the House of Commons, and then we could 'take it from there'. How about next Tuesday 7th? 7.30-ish? St Stephen's Entrance? Do be a poppet and let me know.

Until then — with very best wishes and, once again, warmest congratulations on your command of the English language.

John Thomas

From 'Old Girls' News', *The Boxonian,* Journal of Past Pupils of St Catherine's School for Girls, Box Hill, 1956

Bacon, Daphne (*Campbell's*) has recently given birth to twins, Clarissa Mary and Margaret Elizabeth, sisters for Gordon, Penny, Prudence, Geoffrey, Simon and Amelia.

Bannerman, Elizabeth (*Carstairs'*) remains missing in Peru.

Baxter, Pamela (*Jordan's*) is still bitterly unhappy, perhaps even more so now that her husband has left her for a qualified chiropodist.

Beard, Abigail (*Sutton's*) teaches at St Michael's, Carshalton, where she is mercilessly teased about her nervous twitch.

Blossom, Joanna (*Apsley's*) is working on behalf of the Labour Party in the field of Women's Rights. She is at present on her third course of particularly powerful anti-depressants.

Brannigan, Caroline (*Sutton's*) is completing her fourth year of study in flower arrangement. She is still unmarried.

Bunn, Rachel (*Jordan's*) now lives in Ohio, in the State Penitentiary.

Bumfrey, Alison (*Apsley's*) has moved in with a woman friend and is much happier.

Letter from Ann Thomas to Judy Cholmondley, 9 November 1956

... not that irises have ever been my favourites, particularly yellows. 'I see that the Blossom girl now works for the Labour Party,' I said to

Johnny at drinks the other day. 'Quite a leap, isn't it!? I wonder what on earth made her change her mind?' 'Blossom? Blossom? Oh, *her* – poor old Labour Party is all I can say!' he joked, 'By the way, how are those new rose bushes coming along?' I sometimes think he's more interested in the garden than in people! Any chance of you and Alan staying the weekend after next? It would be *simply super* if you could. How are the children?...

From the *Sunday Times*, 25 November 1957

Profile: rising star John Thomas

SINCE his elevation at the age of only 37 to the post of Home Secretary, Sir John Thomas has been widely tipped by fellow MPs as a possible future leader of the Conservative Party.

He is a man of many qualities, both gregarious and conscientious. 'There's no one who likes a pleasant chat more than John,' says his friend and colleague Sir Alan Telfont, 'but at the same time, he always keeps a diligent eye on the time, being ever-mindful of his wider parliamentary obligations.'

Others praise his ability to relax, and the enjoyment he finds in simple pleasures. 'He loves a healthy walk,' adds Telfont, 'and I have often watched in admiration as he set off on a walk by himself for up to four miles in London, even after he had been offered a lift in a chauffeur-driven car. He is the most completely relaxed and rounded man I know, very social, but at the same time quite content with just himself for company.'

Further evidence of this easygoing approach combined with tremendous powers of concentration has been widely praised. 'I have watched him in committee, under quite tough conditions, delightfully twiddling his thumbs, as if he hadn't a care in the world,' says Harry Whittingham MP, 'yet at the same time he can master a brief in a matter of seconds. To my mind, his thumb-twiddling is proof of a man at ease with the world, the master of any situation, no matter how overwhelming it may appear to others.'

From the Minutes of the Albemarle Club General Management Committee, 27 November 1958

Junior staff member George Koe, second-floor barman, was called before the committee to answer complaints of ill-mannered and abusive behaviour towards various members.

In his defence, he claimed that the aforesaid members were 'a stuck-up bunch of – ,' employing a word grossly unsuitable for repetition in the minutes of the Club.

Asked by the Chairman, Sir John Thomas MP, whether he had anything more prudent to say in his defence, Koe replied that he thought that the members should start trying to live in the modern world. Asked to expound on this advice by the Chairman, Koe ventured that there was 'no place for kow-towing' in the modern world, and that the future would be based on 'a classless society, where all men are equal, and everyone is entitled to a little luxury'.

After a brief conference, Koe was dismissed on grounds of general attitude.

From a transcript of *Desert Island Discs*, first broadcast on the Home service in November 1959

Roy Plomley: And my castaway today is John Thomas MP, who, I think I am right in saying, is our youngest-ever Home Secretary.

John Thomas: Absolutely right, Roy.

RP: John, if we could deal with your childhood. You were brought up in the Midlands?

JT: That's quite correct. I still have a very warm spot in my heart for the people of the Midlands.

RP: And your parents died when you were comparatively young?

JT: Yes, yes indeed, Roy. I can barely remember them. I was four or five when they died.

RP: Not an easy start, then?

JT: Not at all, Roy. But I think their death taught me one very important lesson, which is this. No matter what your circumstances, it is always possible to conquer adversity, to put one's problems behind one, and make a go of it. I'll always be immensely grateful to them for that.

RP: And what did your father do, John? What sort of man was he?

JT: He was what would nowadays be called, I suppose, a Gentleman Farmer. He was a thoroughly decent chap, by all accounts: dependable, trustworthy, popular, a stickler for tradition and a keen churchgoer – as I say, a thoroughly decent chap.

RP: And your mother?

JT: Oh, ditto, ditto. Very much so.

RP: Let's hear your first record, shall we?

JT: It's 'Surrey with the Fringe on Top', Roy, to remind me of my constitutents in Dorking, which, as you know, is situated in the very heart of Surrey...

❖

RP: ...The delightful 'Surrey with the Fringe on Top'. Now, Sir John, you enjoyed a successful university career, ending up, I believe, in the immensely distinguished position of President of the Oxford Union?

JT: Yes, Roy. From the very start of my Oxford career, I had been shocked by what I called the slackers and wasters among my fellow undergraduates – fellows who seemed keener on lounging around reading foreign books, often of an unpleasant nature, rather than thinking of what they could do for their country. So I like to think I made my mark in the Union by arguing for a return to decent family values – and it's a point I've continued to hammer home ever since.

RP: And you then worked briefly as a PPS to the late Sir Cedric Scott. Quite a character, I should think.

JT: Oh, yes, Roy, very much so. Much as I loved the old boy, he never did a stroke of work. I often dine out, Roy, on the tale of the time Mr Churchill asked for Cedric's ten-year plan for cleaner air, and the poor chap hadn't even written the first, so I had to make all sorts of excuses so as to save his bacon! But what a marvellous character he was, as you rightly say, Roy.

RP: And after the 1952 General Election, you found yourself appointed to his old job ...

JT: Yes, Roy, a terrific thrill.

RP:	And how did he take that?
JT:	To be honest, Roy, he was absolutely thrilled on my behalf, giving me all sorts of helpful tips to 'smooth my path' as it were. In many ways, I suppose you could say, Roy *(chokes)* that – that – that he was like the – the – the father I never had ...
RP:	Your next record ...
JT:	I have always found solace in the seaside, and cliffs in particular, so I think, Roy, I will plump for 'The White Cliffs of Dover' sung here by the great Vera Lynn...

❖

RP:	... Alas, you lost your wife Ann earlier this year. That must have been a tragic loss.
JT:	Tragic indeed, Roy. But happily the coroner exonerated me from all responsibility. Behind every cloud, as they say, Roy.
RP:	How would you cope on a desert island, Sir John? Would you grow lonely, do you think?
JT:	Well, Roy, I'm very much what I believe is called these days 'a people person'. I have made many, many close friends on all sides of the House, of course, but I also count myself lucky to have kept up with a tremendous number of old friends from my Oxford days. As you might imagine, we often get together to mull over old times, and to indulge in a little gentle leg-pulling ...

Letter from Bertram Slingsby to The Rt. Hon. Sir John Thomas MP, 30 November 1959

John, old man –

Remember how I gave you that vital chance arguing with the Treasurer and the Secretary to 'give the poor chap a chance' in that crucial Oxford Union debate all those donkey's yonks ago? And how you and I trounced the Opposition – mainly owing to your famous 'Lady Chatterley' oration? Happy days, eh?

And then I somehow or other fixed it for you to get elected to my club, the good old Albemarle, putting your name forward and making sure that as many of my fellow members as possible knew what a swell chap you were, and we were always planning that celebration drink, but somehow or another, what with one thing and another, and you so busy and so very very important, other fish to fry etcetera ... so now we haven't seen each other for – what? Could it really be twenty years?!

Ah, well – what I always say is that these youthful friendships count for the most in life, don't you agree, John? However much water passes under the bridge, the bridge stands firm, and people can walk over you as much as they like, and yet the friendship never collapses, eh? If you and I were to meet now, we'd be exactly the same as we always were, swapping jokes and anecdotes, arguing the toss over matters political, engaging in waspish banter and heaven knows what else.

You'll probably be wondering what the hell I've been up to. Well, the honest answer is 'a bit of this' and 'a bit of that' – though not much of 'the other', to tell you the truth!!!! To be honest, I got into a spot of bother a few years back – a drop too many meant a trip to clinky, if I'm to be utterly frank – but that's all behind me now, and I have a number of very interesting projects on the go which to be frank I'd welcome your advice on re. garnering plentiful investment from the city, Parliament, etcetera, etcetera.

'The Right Honourable Sir John' indeed! You've done so well for yourself since the days when you were just plain John Thomas, eh? Brilliantly well. Hear you on the wireless virtually every bloody day, putting the case for I don't know what, high time this and high time that, and one further point, if I may Mr Chairman, etcetera etcetera and I must say I feel bloody proud to be able to tell the other fellows in the bar of The York that I gave you your leg-up, and that without me you'd be nowhere, absolutely nowhere, nothing, nothing at all and they're greatly amused when I tell them of how in the old days you used to hang around with the aesthetes with their weak handshakes, and to be so full of fancy talk of poems and verdant hues and mortality and all the rest of it, my deaaaah! And they simply roar their heads off, because they can't believe this is the same bloke who now gets so red in the face and hot under the collar about the preservation of traditional values, maintaining the moral backbone of the nation, the supremacy of common sense, dah-di-dah. You should hear their laughter, Johnny! Happy days, eh?! All good clean fun, what?

Marvellous set of fellows down at The York, incidentally. True Blue to a man, and full to the gills with robust good humour – never dirty, mind, or vicious, nothing nasty. Laugh with you, not at you, if you know what I mean. And, my word, they know how to keep a secret! Roger, the Colonel, Harry, Monty, Robinson, Sparks, George and

Splodger? Why, I'd trust them with my life – or a fiver, whichever they valued most!!! Only pulling your proverbial, Johnny!

But – and this really brings me (at long last, I hear you yell!) to the point of what one might call this light-hearted loiter down memory lane! – there is one secret I would never share with 'em, not in a million years, not over my dead body, or even yours, come to that, Johnny, only kidding. Absolutely not. Never betray a confidence. No, no, no, no, no. I've told them, I've said, 'There's one secret I am absolutely not going to share with you. Absolutely not. No, no, no, no, no, no, no. Not now or ever.' And then I continue, and they are agog. 'It concerns our dear old friend the Minister, but I will not, I repeat *not* be repeating it before the assembled company – it's far too *rude!*'

Suffice it to say, by this time the gang of 'em – absolute sweeties, by the way – are dribbling to hear more about your mummy and daddy, John Thomas, simply *drib-bur-ling* Whoops! Did I say your mummy and daddy? Silly me! But then, of course, you know all about them already, don't you, John Thomas *Mellors* – whoops!!? so there's no need for little me to keep them a secret from you, is there?!! Eh? Eh? EH*?*

By the by, John Thomas, how is your dear darling mother keeping? Still going strong? I hope so. I must admit to being just a little put out when I heard you describe her on Uncle Roy's wireless programme as no longer with us, particularly as I still remember her so vividly from the night of our Great Debate, the occasion of our joint triumph. Do you remember that splendid evening, John Thomas? You had finished your speech to a veritable flood of applause – approximately one hundred times louder than the sprinkling that had greeted my own, no hard feelings – when suddenly a woman, somewhat colourfully painted, had rushed out of the debating chamber in a flood of tears.

Seconds later, you went after her, leaving me all alone to parry the points from the floor. At first, I imagined you must have departed from the chamber to spend the proverbial penny, but you remained outside for such an unconscionably long period that I soon became worried.

The floor-speakers all seemed to be attacking our libertarian opponents, so I judged the time right to creep from my seat at the front and come looking for you. Alerted by the sound of sobby-sob-sobs, I tippy-toed into the courtyard outside, there to see the highly-painted woman in tears and my little friend John Thomas casting the most extreme admonishments upon her, relating the most extraordinary tale of debauchery and deceit.

To be honest, I didn't like to 'barge right in' at this most sensitive of moments, so I stayed discreetly by the door, not wishing for a moment to get in anyone's way, or almost as important! – to stem the flow of tip-top revelations. But after a while you must have sensed my presence in the archway, for you turned round in my direction. 'Er, John Thomas,' I said, as if I had just entered, 'the contributions from the floor are drawing to a close – the vote is about to be taken! Come quickly!'

Of course, I never ever *ever* mentioned the incident to you. One doesn't, does one? what a pickle you might have found yourself in, dear Johnny, if I had been what I call the *blurting* type. We might almost have had the dearest little Greek Tragedy on our hands, give or take a few of the more uncouth Midland trowels and vowels(!). But no – I was good old solid dependable stuttering Slingsby, and I was very much in the habit of keeping secrets, for I always find that secrets *mature* if kept, don't *you* John Thomas?

As I was saying before I so rudely interrupted myself with that little hop-skip-and-jump down dear old Memory Lane, I rather think it might be worth our while getting together for a nice little drinkie or two to chat about this and that, and to exchange ideas – and who knows what else! – on the future and the past. One would so hate for our little secret to get out, and we must surely sift through all available strategies to ensure that it does not.

How say you the Albemarle Club? Though no longer a member myself, I am more than happy to be entertained as the guest of the Chairman.

12.30. This Wednesday. Prompt.

Toodle-pip, old man – and mum's the word!

Your old friend, Bertie

From the *Evening Standard*, 3 December 1959

Man falls from train

THE BODY of a tramp believed to have fallen from a mainline train was found 100 yards from Clapham Junction last night. He had been dead for several hours, said police experts.

The man has been identified as Mr Bert Slingsby, 40, of no fixed address. He had a history of alcoholism, which police believe may have contributed to his fatal accident. A broken bottle was all that was found on his person.

From *Desert Island Discs,* November 1959

Roy Plomley: And how do you think you would fend on this desert island? Are you a practical man, Sir John?

John Thomas: I think, Roy, that I have always been very adept at coping in adverse conditions, and so I would probably make a pretty good job of it. I am perfectly capable of chopping and pushing and shoving, and cutting down on my own problems, so I wouldn't let anything stand in my way, and I think I probably wouldn't do too badly.

RP: Your next record?

JT: I am greatly amused by a record that has recently been in the 'Hit Parade'. It's by Louis Armstrong, and it's called 'Mack the Knife'.

Letter from Bertram Slingsby to Joy Greenley, postmarked 2 December 1959

Dear Miss Greenley,

I believe we were contemporaries at Oxford in the late thirties, and that we share an interest in another 'Notable Contemporary' of ours. I read somewhere that you are now planning a biography of D. H. Lawrence. Being a great admirer of your works on Conrad, Beatrice Webb and Hardy, I feel you would be just the person to whom to offer my sacred information regarding the connection between Mr Lawrence and our 'Notable Contemporary'.

May we commune, Miss Greenley? I feel sure such a meeting would prove of *inestimable* benefit to us both. I write as a matter of some urgency.

Yours sincerely
Bertram Slingsby MA

INQUEST ON TRAIN VICTIM RECORDS ACCIDENTAL DEATH.

Letter from Joy Greenley to Bertram Slingsby, 4 December 1959

Dear Mr Slingsby,
Thank you for your letter. I am indeed most interested in your information re DHL. I would be most happy to meet you at your earliest convenience.

Sincerely
Joy Greenley

(Letter returned marked 'DECEASED'.)

From *In For the Quill: My Life in Letters,* by Sir Harvey Marlowe (1967)

I shall always remember the day I first heard the news that Joy was within the proverbial whisker of discovering the true Lady Chatterley, not to mention the identity of her son.

It was in late October or early November 1959, and we were meeting either in my office, or in the restaurant at Claridges, I forget which. I had rarely seen her so excited; I think she may even have smiled. So desperate was the poor woman to 'tell me all about it' that she began to expatiate on the subject – Lawrence this, Lawrence that – even before I had plumped for my first course. 'A word in your ear, my dear Joy,' I quipped. 'It is the primary rule of publishing that a fellow may be permitted to peruse his "Menu du Jour" at his leisure before getting down to brass tacks!' I then roared with warm-hearted laughter, chose the onion soup followed by the Beef Wellington with sauté potatoes and green beans, plus a halfway decent claret, before announcing, 'And now, my dear Joy, you have become the beneficiary of my *undivided* attention.'

Letter from Joy Greenley to The Rt. Hon. Sir John Thomas MP, 15 December 1959

Dear Sir John Thomas,
I am at present engaged in writing a biography of the novelist

D. H. Lawrence. I believe you may be able to help me in my researches.

I would be most grateful if you could manage to spare me a moment to discuss the matter with you.

Yours sincerely,
Joy Greenley

From *In for The Quill: My Life in Letters,* by Sir Harvey Marlowe (1967)

Joy then told me she had 'firm proof' – always something of a shaky phrase in the Greenley vocabulary, I fear! – that a senior Conservative politician was in fact the illegitimate son of Mellors, the notoriously uppity gamekeeper in D. H. Lawrence's *Lady Chatterley's Lover.*

'Good Lord,' I said, signalling for a top-up of wine from a passing waiter, 'And who might that be?'

And that was the very first time that I ever heard the name John Thomas mentioned in connection with Lady Chatterley.

Letter from the office of The Rt. Hon. Sir John Thomas MP, 17 December 1959

Dear Miss Greenley,
Sir John has asked me to thank you for your letter dated December 15th and to thank you for your good wishes. He regrets he is unable to help you on the matter to which you refer.

Yours sincerely,
P. Bellamie (Miss)
Secretary to the Rt. Hon. Sir John Thomas

Letter from Joy Greenley to The Rt. Hon. Sir John Thomas MP, 18 December 1959

Dear Sir John Thomas,
Thank you for your letter of the 17th December. I cannot stress

sufficiently the importance to your own reputation of a meeting between us at the earliest opportunity.

Yours sincerely,
Joy Greenley

From *My Way: Memoirs of a Former Minister*, by Sir John Thomas

Even my worst enemies would never accuse me of being less than total in my support for the Arts in this country. There is nothing I enjoy more than a night out at the theatre with close friends or a good read by a swimming-pool in the height of summer. So when a young woman biographer wrote to my office requesting a tip or two, I felt it incumbent upon myself to meet her.

The diary of a Cabinet Minister is always packed. As it was coming up to Christmas, I found it hard to grab a moment from my duties as Secretary of State. Nevertheless, moving hell and high water, I managed to squeeze in an hour or two on New Year's Day, 1960, and thus arranged to liaise with her that morning at Beachy Head, a convenient meeting-place between her lodgings in Brighton and my own home in London. Little did I realise then that my 'helping hand' would soon be bitten – and bitten very sorely indeed!

Undated postcard to Joy Greenley, signed J T

BEACHY HEAD. 1 Jan. 10.00 a.m. Come alone. J T.

From 'Note on the Author' in *Hollow Goblet: The Life and Times of F. Scott Fitzgerald* by Joy Greenley (566pp., Yale University Press, 1959)

Joy Greenley was born in Westhampton East, New Jersey, in 1919, and graduated from Girton College, Oxford, England, with a First Degree in English Literature. Her numerous biographies include *City Slicker: The Life of Thomas Hardy* (1950), *Beatrice Webb: A Life on the Razzle* (1952) and *Dry Land: The Myth of Joseph Conrad* (1956), her famous exposé of Joseph Conrad's sea-faring claims. Miss Greenley is a visiting Professor of Cultural Revisionism at Sussex University. She lives in Brighton, England, where she is currently working on a literary biography of

D. H. Lawrence. In 1958, she was elected a Fellow of the Royal Society for Literature. She shares her Brighton home with her three cats, 'Josie', 'Tom-Tom' and 'Hen-Pen', each named after the subject of one of her biographies.

From an interview with Joy Greenley in the *Paris Review*, 'Biography and Biographers' Special Issue, Spring 1959

The writer occupies a first-floor flat in a Regency house on the Brighton sea-front. Her writing desk – the same desk at which she wrote Hollow Goblet: The Life and Times F. Scott Fitzgerald, *to be published by Yale University Press later this year – overlooks the rough English ocean. The desk is clear but for an Osmiroid fountain-pen and two bottles of fast-drying black ink, manufactured by the British company Quink.*

The room is sparsely decorated, but there are papers, books and manuscripts – many relating to her current subject, the novelist D. H. Lawrence – strewn over tables, chairs and the floor. To the left of her desk hangs a skilful line-drawing of a middle-aged man. It is, Miss Greenley states, a specially commissioned artist's depiction of what Joseph Conrad looked like without his clip-on beard. This is a direct allusion to Greenley's allegation that Conrad's beard was artificially created for him by a Wolverhampton firm, sparking the explosive academic controversy that surrounded the publication of her book, Dry Land: The Myth of Joseph Conrad *in 1956.*

Miss Greenley herself is a small, almost bird-like creature, more frail-looking than one might expect from her fierce rebuttals of the abuse that has so often rained down upon her from critics and academics.

Her long hair is swept off her tiny face in a large bun. Though she is ready to answer questions on the nature and practice of biography, she refuses to answer any questions of a more personal nature: her private life, she says, has no bearing on her work.

Q. You were born in Westhampton East in 1922. Did your upbringing in New Jersey in any way affect your future career as a biographer?

A. No.

Q. Could you expand on that?

A. No.

Q. Do you have any particular personal memory of your childhood which might illuminate themes that run through your adult *oeuvre*?

A. No.

From the Daily Telegraph, 5 October 1950

New biography stirs controversy

Hardy aficionados 'up in arms'

A NEW BIOGRAPHY of the novelist and poet Thomas Hardy, who died in 1928, has provoked fierce opposition from many leading Hardy experts.

The biography, *City Slicker: The Life of Thomas Hardy*, alleges that, far from being the great rural chronicler of West Country life, Hardy spent most of his life 'living it up' in London. He penned sombre tales of rural tragedies, contends his biographer, Miss Joy Greenley, 31, because his first efforts – waspish tales of metropolitan life – could not find a publisher.

'He wrote *Far From the Madding Crowd* standing at the cocktail bar of the Cafe Royal with a map of the Dorchester area and a copy of *Farming Times* at his side,' insists Miss Greenley, an American. 'He visited the Wessex region as little as possible, and then only for promotional purposes. He would agree to his publishers' demands to wear mud-spattered country tweeds only if he could wear them over his beloved lime-green silk pyjamas, hand-fitted by Turnbull & Asser.'

The 600-strong Hardy Society is up in arms at the allegations contained in *City Slicker: The Life of Thomas Hardy* (Marlowe Press, 12s. 6d.) 'The woman doesn't know what she's on about,' says Martin Skeff, Secretary of the Society.

Skeff raises particular objections to Miss Greenley's claim that Hardy had originally intended his masterpiece T*ess of the D'Urbervilles* to end happily with the heroine Tess joining the D'Oyly Carte Opera Company to play the role of 'Buttercup' in *HMS Pinafore* before, in the closing scenes of the book, marrying the veteran actor who played Sir Joseph Porter.

From a letter from Joy Greenley to the *Times Literary Supplement*, 15 September 1952

Sir,
In his characteristically intemperate response to my recent biography,

Beatrice Webb: A Life on the Razzle, (Sept 8th) Professor J. T. Schweele claims there is 'no evidence whatsoever, written, spoken or photographic, for my "repeated assertion" that Beatrice Webb had a passion for drinking pink champagne out of high-heeled shoes. He further claims that 'Mrs Webb was never to be seen in high-heels; she always favoured the sensible walking-shoe.'

Rarely have the limitations of the academic approach to biography been so clearly demonstrated. May I take this opportunity to enlighten Professor Schweele that it was Beatty Webb's inner confusion at her predilection – one might almost term it her obsession – for drinking pink champagne from whatever high-heeled shoes were to hand that forced her to devote her considerable intellectual resources to its concealment. This is confirmed rather than contradicted by Professor Schweele's assurance that 'Mrs Webb was never to be seen in high-heels.' It seems perfectly obvious that whenever she found herself in any danger of being observed, Beatty Webb would wear only sensible walking-shoes.

Yours faithfully,
Joy Greenley

From *In for the Quill: My Life in Letters,* by Sir Harvey Marlowe (1967)

Joy's instinct was not always as sound as she imagined. I spent a fair measure of time as her publisher dissuading Joy from embarking upon some of her more hare-brained schemes. It was only by indulging in the fanciest of footwork, for instance, that I managed to discourage her from a new biography of Marcel Proust. Far from being the sadistic homosexual of popular imagination, he was, she maintained, a happily married man, though this was hushed up at the time, lest it adversely affected his sales figures among the affluent Bohemian set. Only my suggestion that a brand new Joseph Conrad was long overdue managed to divert her from that unwise trail.

From an interview with Joy Greenley in the *Paris Review,* 'Biography and Biographers' Special Issue, Spring 1959

Q.   Following the success of your Beatrice Webb, you decided to tackle Joseph Conrad. This was indeed a revolutionary biography, altering the face of Conrad studies for all time. May I ask you why you yourself believe this particular work became so, for want of a better word, *notorious* in Conradian circles?

A.   They were, I believe, wedded to Conrad's own claims that he had been a great seafarer and adventurer. It now goes without saying that he was not; absolutely the opposite, in fact.

Q.   But you claimed …

A.   I claimed nothing. I proved a substantial amount. Joseph Conrad had long maintained that, between the years 1878 and 1894, he had been a merchant seaman aboard ships journeying between Singapore and Borneo. My investigations proved this bogus. During that period he worked in a profitable Estate Agency in Cheltenham Spa, with branches in Malvern and Worcester. His knowledge of the exotic jungle region of Borneo was extracted largely from the 1886 first edition of Joan Wynford-Davies's neglected children's work, *The Great Big Book of Borneo*. I also set out to prove that his self-proclaimed expert knowledge of sea-lore and the mechanics of seafaring is in fact very scant: paltry, you might say. The greater part of it could well have been picked up on a brief round-trip of the Serpentine pond in London's Hyde Park as early as 1883, for which he had plenty of opportunity, as he was often in London during this period. But I am used to the critics, and people who begin their questions, 'But you claimed −'. It was just the same when I wrote my piece in *Scrutiny* on 'Lytton Strachey and the Lure of Rugby Football'. They simply couldn't grasp the fact that Strachey might have sacrificed the whole of the winter of '28 to following the Welsh Rugby Team on its international tour, often sharing a pint of beer with them afterwards. I was upset at the strength of this academic reaction at the time; but now I take it for granted.

Q.   I read somewhere that you write every morning from 8.30 to 1.00, revising what you have written in the afternoon, writing for another hour between 6.30 and 7.30 in the evening.

A.   Where did you read that?

Q.   I can't quite remember, but −

A.   You can't remember? You can't remember?

Q.   No, but I −

A.   It's grossly unprofessional to state a transparent inaccuracy on the merest supposition and then, challenged as to your source, to claim you 'can't remember'. It's absurd, quite absurd. I was led to believe this was to be a question-and-answer interview, not some form of inquisition, with false accusations about my private life.

From *My Way: Memoirs of a Former Minister,* by Sir John Thomas

Politicians on all sides of the political spectrum must expect their actions and speeches to be wilfully misinterpreted by those with a vested interest in the propagation of untruths. This is all part and parcel of the political process, the price we pay for living in a democracy. But the incident that came to haunt me as 'The John Thomas Affair' must surely take the biscuit. Never in the colourful field of post-war politics has an action so innocent been more grotesquely or cruelly misrepresented by the foes of free speech. In retrospect, it was just my luck that I presented such a perfect target for the sworn enemies of the British way of doing things.

From the Logbook of Lighthouse Keeper Ronnie Firbank, Beachy Head, 1 Jan 1960

7.30: Blustery day. Winds at 93 m.p.h., sleet coming in at an angle of 30°. 'What Do You Want to Make Those Eyes at Me For' is playing on the wireless. Can't see a thing through the weather. Still, what I always say is 'all right if you're a duck'!

8.00: Just finished breakfast. Rice Krispies followed by boiled egg and soldiers – the usual! Washed up. Placed '1 bottle washing-up liquid' on order ledger.

8.15: Remembered to put 'bread' on order ledger.

8.17: Also 'Rich Tea Biscuits (one pkt)'.

8.30: Waves rising higher. Slightly foggy. All right if you're a duck – that's what I always say! No one on cliffs – probably everyone (except yours truly!) sleeping it off after last night's festivities! Counted sixty-three seagulls – two down on before breakfast, three up on last night, even accounting for duplication. Probably means nothing, though, or, if it does mean something, I don't know what it is as I don't have the expertise.

8.34: Seems to be turning into a boring day. Have got that tune in my head: 'If they don't mean what they saaaay!' etc.

8.46: Had an itch on my back. Itched it. Seems to have stopped itching. Hopefully!

8.55: Things still quiet.

9.02: A bit bored. Look out of window. Thank golly I'm not out there on a day like today! Brrrr! All right if you're a duck!

9.15: Pencil needs sharpening. Sharpen pencil. Write this with it!

9.17: Make sure the pencil sharpenings are tidied away nicely.

9.18: Still got that song on my brain. No rest for the wicked!

9.28: Only just over half-an-hour until my next authorised check on the lantern. On a whim, I cross 'Rich Tea Biscuits' off the ledger. Change it to 'Standard Digestive'.

9.32: Change it back again. Standard digestives can get a bit dull. Sea still choppy. All right if you're a duck! Try to remember who the song's by.

9.35: Emile Ford and the Detectives! Emile Ford and the *Defectives*, more like! Laugh at own joke.

9.36: Slight drop in spirits, then for no particular reason they rise again to where they were before.

9.45: Spirits still not quite as high as they were during breakfast. Decide to have a nice cup of tea after checking the lantern at 10.00. Still got song on brain.

From *My Way: Memoirs of a Former Minister,* by Sir John Thomas

It was on the fateful morning of January 1st 1960 at approximately 9.45 a.m. that I found myself driving from the Royal Plaza Hotel in Eastbourne on the Sussex Coast to meet Miss Joy Greenley at Beachy Head, the popular local beauty spot. I had never met her before in my life, of course, though this was disputed at the trial.

From the Logbook of Lighthouse Keeper Ronnie Firbank, Beachy Head

9.49: Looking forward to my nice cup of tea. Postpone the choice between the blue mug and the china cup and saucer until later. Fill in time before 10 by counting seagulls once more. Get up to thirty-two then lose track. Hey ho. Start again.

9.52: A car has drawn up on the cliff! Through my binos, I see it is a Jag. Middle-aged man in a dark suit sitting in it, looking out to sea. Will he drive it over? Offer myself good odds of 5–1. Accept them. Fingers crossed.

9.55: A second car joins it – Hillman Hunter, by the look of things, with woman inside. Man gets out of Jag and walks towards Hillman. Oy! Oy!

From *My Way: Memoirs of a Former Minister,* by Sir John Thomas

But the fact that I had never met Miss Greenley before should not be construed, as the smear-mongers would have it, as anything remotely 'sinister' or 'unusual'. I had arranged to meet her at a suitable location, at a mutually convenient time, in order to discuss a new biography upon which she was, she claimed, planning to embark. It is in the nature of things that a Member of Parliament will engage in many meetings with total strangers, if only for the purpose of giving a 'leg-up' to those in need. Following the hoo-ha, is one to regard all such meetings as reprehensible, or suggestive of malpractice? Surely not! Miss Greenley was a biographer and a critic. She had asked to meet me on a purely academic matter. It was a morning meeting, conducted in the clear light of day in a very public place. I cannot make it sufficiently clear that I had no prior intention – absolutely not – of pushing the poor, misguided creature to her death.

From the Logbook of Lighthouse Keeper Ronnie Firbank, Beachy Head

10.02: Lantern duly operative.

10.05: Man and the woman have been in Hillman Hunter for ten minutes now. Talking – not snogging, worst luck!! I decide to plump for the mug.

10.08: Man exits from passenger seat of Hillman Hunter. Slams door, no cheery-byes. Woman runs after him, forty or so, dressed in red coat, not exactly pretty. Catches him halfway to the Jag. Waves a sheet of paper in his face, trying to make him look at it. He is wearing black gloves. Tries to brush her piece of paper away. Then seems to change mind and tries to snatch it. She's shouting at him. Take good long sip. Tea excellent – warm and wet!

From *My Way: Memoirs of a Former Minister*, by Sir John Thomas

Any person or persons who has reached the top of their chosen profession will know that healthy disagreement, based on fruitful argument, lies at the very nub of a productive organisation. Thus I welcomed the frank discussion in which I engaged Miss Greenley as to the ownership and contents of the document she had produced for my examination. Far from seeking its suppression, I was anxious only that it should be viewed in a manner that best served the complex nature of its frame of reference. For this reason, and this reason alone, I sought to remove it from her safekeeping. I need hardly add how dismayed I was by the barrage of insults – many couched in language unsuitable for repetition – with which she greeted my attempted manoeuvre.

From the Logbook of Lighthouse Keeper Ronnie Firbank, Beachy Head

10.12: They've been screaming blue murder at each other for four minutes now. Every time he grabs at her papers, she nips them away, then waggles a finger at him. They must be soaked through! Talk about all right if you're a duck!

10.14: She's running away from him, towards the cliff, still with the paper in her hand. He's after her. What a carry on! Still, makes a pleasant change.

From *My Way: Memoirs of a Former Minister*, by Sir John Thomas

I have long been an advocate of the inestimable value of human touch, especially in negotiations which may or may not be proving difficult. over the course of a crowded life in politics, I have found that a handshake here, a pat on the back there, can prove infinitely more beneficial than mere words. For this reason, I attempted to calm Miss Greenley down on the occasion in question by the sheer force of human contact. Following my instincts as a statesman, I placed my right hand upon her back, while with my left hand I attempted to steady her shoulder. Unfortunately, and to my lasting regret, for reasons of her own Miss Greenley failed to maintain her balance. Much against my wishes, she proceeded to plummet in a forwardly direction headlong over the cliff.

From the Logbook of Lighthouse Keeper Ronnie Firbank, Beachy Head

10.14: She's just gone over! But the man's still standing at the top – so bang goes my bet! She tried to run – he chased her a good fifty yards – but he caught her and marched her to the cliff edge – and over she went. All right if she was a seagull – but she wasn't, she was a woman!

He's running back to his car without a backward glance. Uh-oh! Something's gone wrong. It's not starting! He looks proper cheesed off, I'll say!

From *My Way: Memoirs of a Former Minister*, by Sir John Thomas

When Miss Greenley met with her tragic accident, my first thought was to get help. Therefore, I returned with great speed to my car, parked beside hers on the cliff-top. During my brief period at the Ministry of Transport, a period within which the *Daily Telegraph* was kind enough to describe me as 'one of the most forward-looking of all the junior ministers, with a ready sense of humour and a special interest in the future of the indigenous motor-car industry', I had learnt of the difficulties imposed on manufacturers of British motor cars by the haphazard nature of our good (and sometimes not-so-good!) old British weather. Sadly, a mixture of sleet, high winds and hail, together with an incoming fog, saw to it that my own Jaguar failed to start at this most crucial of times. For this reason, I transferred to Miss Greenley's car, and drove away.

From the Logbook of Lighthouse Keeper Ronnie Firbank, Beachy Head

10.17: He's got behind his Jaguar and he's pushing it, really pushing it, over the cliff-edge!

It's gone over, hit the sea, and smashed to smithereens! With the evidence destroyed, he's got into the Hillman and he's driving it away. Fancy! Award myself another bickie. Yum-yum!

From *My Way: Memoirs of a Former Minister*, by Sir John Thomas

I was later to learn, to my undoubted distress, that my own car, a dearly loved Jaguar, just three and a half years old and a most agreeable shade of green, had also met with a tragic cliff top accident. It seems probable that in the crisis of the moment duty overcame caution, and I forgot to pull the handbrake on. But what is a car compared with a human life?

From the Logbook of Lighthouse Keeper Ronnie Firbank, Beachy Head

10.23: I'm looking at the sea with my binos, trying to spot some trace of wreckage.

10.26: There's someone on the cliff, on a ledge about twenty foot from the top!

10.28: It's her! It's the woman! On a ledge, with about three hundred foot below her! Golly Gumdrops, Ronnie, I say to myself – better ring the coastguards!

10.35: What a morning! I've rung the coastguards, so I sit back looking at the woman, wondering if she's dead or alive. Give myself 2-1 on she's alive. Have another bickie. After all that, the blessed tune's still in my head!

10.38: Uh-oh! Pencil needs another good sharpen!

10.39: Sharpen it. Write this.

From the *Daily Telegraph*, 2 January 1960

Cabinet Minister in Police Inquiry

SIR JOHN THOMAS IN 'WOMAN ON CLIFF' MYSTERY

Thomas Missing say Police

From the *Sunday Times*, 3 January 1960

Profile: Missing Minister John Thomas

SINCE the disappearance of Sir John Thomas following an incident at Beachy Head, Sussex, on the morning of January 1st, his true character has become the subject of heated speculation in the corridors of Westminster.

Close colleagues say that, though gregarious, he exhibited what they call 'a darker side'. 'Sometimes when you were talking to him, John would look down at his watch, his face riddled with a look of pure anxiety,' his friend and colleague Sir Alan Telfont revealed last night. 'Behind all the mask of affability, I always sensed that there was a darker, more desperate side to his extraordinarily complex character.'

Others mentioned his obsessive solitariness. 'I have known him walk entirely alone for up to four miles in London, even after he had been offered a lift in a chauffeur-driven car. And I often thought at the time that it was as if he were attempting to exorcise some ghost, some darker demon within himself,' said close Cabinet colleague Sir Alan Telfont yesterday. His strange habit of what some have spoken of as 'manic' thumb-twiddling has also provoked widespread comment. 'I have watched him in committee at times when he was entirely unaware that he was being observed,' says Sir Alan, 'And I have watched those thumbs of his twiddling in a mad, frenetic way. He is a man driven by very pent-up emotions – heaven knows what he would end up doing were he to find himself trapped in a situation not to his liking.'

From *My Way: Memoirs of a Former Minister,* by Sir John Thomas

At this point in my story, one finds oneself struggling against a veritable barrage of hints, half-baked gossip, deliberate misinformation and plain, honest-to-goodness untruths.

I am only too well aware that rumours have circulated over the years to the effect that I was in some measure to blame for the predicament in which Miss Greenley found herself. Yet nothing could be further from the truth. Having witnessed her unfortunate accident, I departed with due haste in her car to summon the immediate help of the emergency services. However, as I was later to explain to the police and the judiciary – who, I may say, all behaved impeccably throughout this distressing episode – to my great regret I happened to lose my way. Sadly, by the time I had managed to locate a telephone box, I was forced to conclude that there was no point whatsoever in interrupting a rescue operation which, at that late stage, would undoubtedly be well under way. As a Cabinet Minister, I knew only too well the strain placed on the emergency services by what one might term 'nuisance' telephone calls from members of the public. Above all, I was anxious not to add to the burden of their demanding task by creating a further diversion from the job in hand. This was a decision for which I was later to be privately commended by a very senior member of the police force, a fine body of men for whom I retain a very great deal of respect.

From the *Daily Mail,* 4 January 1960

Thomas: search widens

PORTS PLACED ON RED ALERT

Greenley out of hospital: 'Back to work'

From *My Way: Memoirs of a Former Minister,* by Sir John Thomas

As I was only too happy to explain at the time, I decided on impulse that, with a few days well-earned rest on my hands, I would go on a brief motoring tour of the British Isles, to pursue, to employ the old adage, 'a trip down memory lane', sleeping under bush and twig in the great outdoors. Inevitably, there have been one or two politically motivated critics who have found it expedient to suggest that I had in some way 'stolen' Miss Greenley's vehicle. Nothing could be further from the truth: from the outset, I was clear in my own mind that I was keeping an eye on the vehicle until such time as Miss Greenley should have recovered fully from her tragic accident. How such pernicious gossip got about, heaven only knows. As I once found cause to remark to my old friend and mentor Anthony Eden as we strolled through Central Lobby, the little people will always purloin the ideas of others, and use them for their own ends. He emitted a rueful laugh, and agreed with me wholeheartedly.

From *The Memoirs of Anthony Eden,* Vol III

'The little people will always purloin the ideas of others, and use them for their own ends,' I remarked to Winston as we strolled through

Central Lobby in the winter of '48. He emitted a rueful laugh, and agreed with me wholeheartedly.

From *The Times,* 5 January 1960

Sir John Thomas arrested at Harwich

'WHOLLY INNOCENT' OF ATTEMPTED MURDER

Letter from Sir John Thomas to the Prime Minister, 6 January 1960

Wandsworth Prison
London SW18

Dear Prime Minister,

It is with great personal sadness that I have decided, perhaps against my better judgement, to offer you my resignation from Cabinet office.

I have no doubt whatsoever that my forthcoming trial will fully vindicate whatever actions I may or may not have taken in the service of this Party I love so much. But for the moment the various biases, lies and misrepresentations from some sectors of the Press are making my position as one of your most trusted Ministers untenable. To save you, the Party and the country as a whole any further embarrassment, I am taking the only course open to me.

I have greatly enjoyed my time serving the country, first as a PPS, then as a Junior Opposition spokesman, then as an Opposition Spokesman and, most recently, as Secretary of State for Communications.

During this time, I have been able to help draft much valuable legislation. One of my proudest achievements as a backbencher was the success of my private member's bill, The Sticky Tape (Reclassification) Bill, in which I sought to reclassify Sticky Tape as a material rather than a fabric. After prolonged debate, in which I was glad to have played a vigorous role, we carried the day, and the success of the Sticky Tape Act 1953 is to be seen all around us today.

Serving with Sir Cedric Scott as first his PPS and then his Junior Opposition Spokesman for Clean Air, I was able to mastermind the formulation of our Party's highly successful ten-year plan for cleaner air, to which many people credited the massive support we received from the country as a whole in the subsequent General Election. In my penultimate post, as Secretary of State for Communications, I took significant steps in tackling the number of 'pips' to signify that a telephone line is engaged, successfully reducing the amount from seventy per minute to under fifty four. These are all notable achievements, of which I am rightly proud.

During my period in office, I have been the grateful beneficiary of your many acts of personal kindness. I have been happy to play a significant role in the success of this Conservative Government, and I feel sure that, under your strong leadership, we are set to retain the support of the electorate throughout the coming decade. As you know, I am now determined to pursue plans outside political office, including preparing for my appearance in the High Courts. Nevertheless, I look forward to supporting both you and your Government with utmost vigour from the backbenches, up until such time as I am asked to return to my position in your Cabinet.

Yours ever,
John

From a letter from the Prime Minister to Sir John Thomas, 6 January 1960

Dear Thomas,
It was considerate of you to put your office at my disposal.
For your convenience, I make haste in offering my acceptance.

Yours faithfully,
H. Macmillan

From *The Neophiliacs: The Revolution in English Life in the Fifties and Sixties* by Christopher Booker (1969)

The trial of Sir John Thomas in April 1960 represented a watershed between the presumptions and fantasies of two chronologically linked yet philosophically opposing eras, a notion for which I have coined the useful term *oppodecadophilosequentialism*. Even the central characters – the thin-lipped American biographer Joy Greenley, the disgraced ex-Minister John Thomas, the pitiful, shuffling figures of Lady Chatterley and the supermarket tycoon Thomas/Mellors, both elderly and defeated, staring down mournfully from the visitors' gallery – seemed to herald a Wagnerian clash between hope and disintegration, a polarisation of illusion versus stark reality. At some stages, it even seemed as though the chief witness for the prosecution, the lighthouse keeper Firbank, was, in his mesmerising vacuity, an unconscious symbol of a nation's disillusion with itself, a human signal of incompetence and incoherence placed upon its outer rocks by a foundering Imperial power, as if to warn others of perils ahead.

Many important aspects of the case were agreed by both counsels: that John Thomas and Joy Greenley had met at Beachy Head on the morning of January 1st 1960; that there had been some form of argument over documents; that Greenley had been pushed by John Thomas; that she had ended up on a precarious ledge, hundreds of yards above the sea; and that John Thomas had then vanished from the scene.

But there were disagreements, too: Thomas's defence counsel argued that Greenley was blackmailing John Thomas, threatening to make public that his parents were alive (he had often spoken of his sadness at being an orphan) and (a potential source of grave embarrassment for any righteous Tory) that they were the original Lady Chatterley and her gamekeeper Mellors. Against the charge of attempted murder, he was to maintain that Thomas had known of the existence of the precarious ledge, and that he had arranged Greenley's fall so that she would end up on it. 'He wanted to give her a jolt, but no more than a jolt. He wished only to bring her to her senses.'

To many observers, the defence case seemed doomed: Sir John Thomas, electing not to give evidence in his own defence, sat pin-striped and port-faced in the dock, the personification of a ruling class living a fraudulent double life, a life of unwieldy self-delusion: simultaneously domineering and weak, bossy and frightened, the master of circumstance yet also its victim. In his public life, Thomas had argued the Conservative case that a human being is far more than the sum of these external forces, that everyone is capable of overcoming misfortunes of birth to act in a responsible and profitable manner; yet in his private life, this man was obsessively secret, so oppressed by the truth of his parentage that to conceal it he was prepared to descend even to murder. In this act of violence he stood revealed not as a man of action, triumphing over his birthright, but – to use a phrase the politician within him would have abhorred – as another of life's little victims.

But in its second week the trial took an unexpected turn. In the witness-box, Dr Joy Greenley made an unsympathetic impression: solipsistic, vengeful, humourless and destructive, a woman resenting in others the privacy she sought for herself. John Thomas's Defence Counsel took advantage of this, and with devastating results:

Prosecution Counsel: Miss Greenley, I must ask you this: was it your intention at any time to ruin Sir John?

Greenley: No. I only wanted to tell him the truth.

Prosecution Council: And what was the truth?

Greenley: It involved his relationship to Lady Chatterley and Mellors –

(*Sob from Lady Chatterley in the public gallery.*)

Defence Counsel: My Lord, I object! The court must not collude in the blackmail of broadcasting personal tittle-tattle!

Judge: I agree. I do not wish to hear anything about the defendant's relationship to Lady, er, Lady, er, Lady –

Prosecution Counsel: Chatterley, My Lord.

Judge: I thought I had made it quite clear that I do not wish to hear that name in my court. As the court may be aware, the publishers of a book with that woman's name in the title are shortly to appear before the High Courts on a charge of criminal obscenity. It would be quite wrong to pre-empt their findings, quite wrong.

Greenley: But –

Judge: But nothing, Miss Greenley. But nothing.

Prosecution Counsel: You had documents in your hand. You wished to show them to Sir John?

Greenley: Correct.

Prosecution Counsel: And Sir John wished to see them?

Greenley: Correct.

Prosecution Counsel: So what was the problem?

Greenley: I sensed that he wished to destroy them. It was my job as a biographer to keep hold of them. Only then would the whole connection with Lady Chatter –

Defence Counsel: Your Honour!

Judge: I repeat, I will not have that person's name mentioned again in this court. Do I make myself clear?

(*Further sob from the public gallery.*)

On the second day of the trial, the divide grew ever wider between what the ordinary British jury saw as the role of the biographer and Greenley's understanding of it, and the Defence sought to play up this gulf:

Defence Counsel: Miss Greenley, could you describe to the court the type of biography you write?

Greenley: I tend to write about famous figures, often writers.

Defence Counsel: Men and women who appear as giants in the public mind.

Greenley (*smirking*): I guess you could say that.

Defence Counsel: And you see it as your job to cut them down to size? The great Thomas Hardy, the great Beatrice Webb, the great Joseph Conrad – all cut down to size by little Miss Greenley and her great big scissors, eh? EH?

Greenley: I –

Defence Counsel: But your destructive lust is never satiated, is it, Miss Greenley, and you simply could not *resist* taking on another hero, another great figure, another great *British* figure. Only this time you wanted a *living* victim, a man in the prime of his life, a public servant of the highest repute, a Member of Parliament, a Privy Councillor, a Secretary of State, a Parliamentarian of unblemished reputation! And you just couldn't stop yourself, could you, Miss Greenley?

Greenley: I –

Defence Councel: And so you arranged to meet the poor man at Beachy Head on a cold, damp, foggy January morning! And you waited for your moment, and when the time came you struck him, again and again, with the blunt end of your crude hypothesis ...

Greenley: I –

Defence Counsel: Again and again and again, so that he was forced to raise an arm in supplication! Again and again and again – until his only option was to defend himself from your mortal blows to his reputation!

Greenley: I – no – I

Defence Counsel: But instead he took the truly Christian course, Miss Greenley – he placed you on that ledge and walked away, turning the other cheek!

Greenley: But I –

Defence Counsel: I suspect, Miss Greenley, that members of the jury have already heard quite sufficient.

In his speech to the jury, the Defence Counsel seemed to admit that this was the end of the ministerial career of Sir John Thomas. 'You may think he has paid a very high price', he said, 'for generously agreeing to assist an American woman with her so-called "literary biography".' He further acknowledged the sensitivity that John Thomas had long felt on the subject of his parental roots. 'This is in many ways a Greek tragedy. John Thomas was blessed with many virtues – courage, honesty, intelligence, conviction, charm, decency, a heightened sense of duty – but he was never, alas, blessed in one department in which his blessings were sorely deficient; the *parental* department.'

At this point, another loud sob was heard from the public gallery. Lady Chatterley, sitting in a fur coat and heavy make-up, tears streaming down her face, was a broken woman. Next to her, immobile and strangely detached, as if unaware of his companion's distress, sat Oliver Mellors, a stout, thick-set figure in a sharp pin-striped suit, probably better known to most of the jury as the beaming figure holding the string of sausages in the 'YOU'LL NEVER DO BETTER THAN TO SHOP AT THOMAS'S' poster advertising campaign.

'Ladies and Gentlemen of the jury,' continued the Defence Counsel, 'the more he struggled to overcome – through sheer British pluck – the influence of this *infamous* couple, the further he knew he might fall when set upon by an unscrupulous gossip. And fall, Ladies and Gentlemen of the jury, fall John Thomas most certainly did.

'Would you cast the first stone, Ladies and Gentlemen of the jury? If you had grown up calling Lady Chatterley 'Mummy', if you had grown up calling Mellors 'Daddy' – would you not have been tempted to do as John Thomas did? Before you cast that stone, please ask yourselves those simple questions – and, once you have done so, I beseech you to return the only possible verdict, Ladies and Gentlemen – the verdict of Not Guilty.'

By now, four members of the jury were crying quite openly. Everyone in that court knew that a conviction was now out of the question. After a perfunctory summing-up by the Judge, the jury retired. Five minutes later, they were to return, and Sir John Thomas, MP, PC, was to walk out of the court a free man. In many ways, this was a victory for Britain over America, for manners over logic, for the private over the public, of decorum over reality. But this was the world in 1960; by 1969, such values would have changed, and changed forever.

From the *Daily Telegraph,* 3 May 1960

Thomas verdict: 'not guilty'

'JUSTICE SEEN TO BE DONE' DECLARES DELIGHTED FORMER MINISTER

THE former Home Secretary, Sir John Thomas, cleared of a charge of attempted murder and related charges of stealing a car at the end of a four-day trial at the Old Bailey yesterday, declared, 'I am delighted with the result. I am glad justice was done.'

Later in the day, he posed for photographers on the steps of his Chelsea home. 'I have nothing to add to my statement after the hearing,' he said, 'not even what I had for breakfast. eriod.'

From *My Way: Memoirs of a Former Minister,* by Sir John Thomas

Following the long ordeal of my trial and subsequent acquittal, I was touched by how many of my parliamentary colleagues on all sides of the House offered me their loyalty and encouragement. I also received countless thousands of letters from ordinary, decent members of the public, pledging their support.

Letter from Sir John Thomas to the Prime Minister, 4 May 1960

My dear Harold,
Just a short note to inform you, if you have not already heard, that

yesterday, much to my relief, I was acquitted at the old Bailey of all the charges against me. Needless to say, it is a tremendous weight off my shoulders. I delight in the fact that British justice, under your doughty leadership, may still count itself the finest in the world.

May I also take this opportunity to lay my services and whatever abilities I may possess once more at your disposal? I believe I still have much to offer the country; I further believe when the time comes that the trial of an innocent man is seen to jeopardise his future career in politics, then that will be the day when the enemies of freedom will have triumphed.

With my very best regards to Dorothy.
Yours ever,
John

PS. On a more personal note, I can't tell you how much I look forward to more evenings at No. 10 indulging in our customarily forthright exchanges of news and views! J.

Letter from Downing Street to Sir John Thomas MP, 6 May 1960

PRIVATE AND CONFIDENTIAL

Dear Sir John,
The Prime Minister has asked me to thank you for your kind letter. He acknowledges with due approval that your name has been cleared. He is glad to note that he can count on your continued and loyal support from the back benches.

Yours sincerely,
Tufnell Park
Private Secretary to the Prime Minister

Letter from Sir John Thomas MP
to Alfred Absted, Editor of the *Daily Courier*, 5 May 1960

My dear Alf,
Thank you very much indeed for your letter, and for your kind remarks.

In answer to your request, I regret that my answer must be a resounding 'no'. I have decided to put the affairs of the past six months behind me. I have also always believed that a man's private life should be his own, and that 'the sins of the father should not be visited upon the son'. For these reasons, I must firmly decline your generous offer of an exclusive piece entitled either:

'MY COURT ORDEAL BY CLIFF-TOP MP'

or

'MY CHATTERLEY SHAME – MP SPEAKS HIS MIND'

However, I would be most happy to contribute to your editorial pages in some capacity other than autobiographical. May I therefore take this opportunity to propose the following suggestions for no-holds-barred opinion pieces:

a) Five Good Reasons Why Lord Stansgate Should Remain a Peer
b) Let's Stamp Out This 'Teddy Boy' Menace
c) Satellites in Space: The Great Red Herrings
d) Princess Margaret and Armstrong-Jones: A Marriage Built to Last
e) A Bright Future for the British Motor Car

I greatly look forward to hearing from you. What about luncheon soon – on me!!

With best wishes,
Yours ever,
John

Letter from Alfred Apsted, Editor of the *Daily Courier* to Sir John Thomas, 7 May 1960

Dear John,

I was disappointed to learn of your decision re. the two articles we discussed. Would the offer of an extra £2,500 be sufficient to sway you?

I will bear in mind your proposals for other articles, but since space in the *Courier* is at a premium, I suggest you might be better advised to try to find a home for them elsewhere.

As you know, I am always happy to hear from you, but sadly my lunch diary is booked up for some weeks ahead.

With best wishes,
Yours sincerely,
Alfred

From *My Way: Memoirs of a Former Minister,* by Sir John Thomas

Often complete strangers would come up to me in the street, demand to shake me by the hand, and tell me how utterly delighted they were that justice had been done. Everywhere I went, I felt among friends. There is, I concluded, something truly marvellous about the British. What other band of men would stand shoulder to shoulder with a fellow citizen in his time of greatest need?

Letter from the Chairman of the Albemarle Club to Sir John Thomas, 10 May 1960

Dear John,
Thank you for your letter of the 8th May.

First, allow me to congratulate you on behalf of all members of the club on your recent acquittal, no doubt richly deserved.

Second, in response to the comments in your letter, I can only express the profuse apologies of all of us at the Albemarle that on your visit here last Monday you were received in such an inappropriate manner by various members of the staff of the club.

It was inexcusable that they should have shown you the door in such an aggressive fashion, particularly as they had been expressly instructed to ask you to leave in a discreet manner, more suited to your former standing.

To avoid any such embarrassment in future, I would strongly advise you to steer well clear of the club for the time being. Were you to choose, in the light of this, to resign on a more formal basis, we would, of course, fully understand. Pursuant to this, I enclose the appropriate form.

May I add that it has been a pleasure to have had you as such a long-standing member of the Albemarle, and to assure you that the good wishes of the club go with you.

Yours ever,
Hon. Harry Whittingham
Chairman of the Albemarle Club

From *My Way: Memoirs of a Former Minister,* by Sir John Thomas

Such was the sympathy shown to me by all sections of society during my trial and subsequent acquittal that I felt as though I had carved myself a very special place in the heart of the great British Public. And once again people wanted to hear what I had to say on national and international affairs. Requests from the radio and television media for me to express my views on any number of important topics had, most gratifyingly, never been more plentiful.

Letter from Sir John Thomas to Mr Al Sharply, Executive Producer of *What's My Line,* 12 May 1960

Dear Mr Sharply,
Thank you for your letter of the 10th.
I regret to say that your request for me to appear on your television programme performing a mime of 'pushing someone over a cliff' for what you term 'the warm-hearted amusement' of your audience appears to me frankly distasteful, as does your suggestion that 'they would be laughing with you, not at you'.

Yours sincerely,
Sir John Thomas

Letter from Sir John Thomas to Mr Al Sharply, Executive Producer of *What's My Line,* 13 May 1960

Dear Mr Sharply,
Further to my perhaps somewhat brusque letter of the 12th, I should

add that if you would wish that I should appear as a special guest or regular panellist on your excellent *What's My Line* programme, this would be quite another matter, and I would be more than happy to discuss it. As you probably know, I am a seasoned performer on television programmes, and I have many interests outside the immediate field of politics, including horse-racing, trains, reading, walking, the family, wine and good food. And even my political enemies have never denied I have what they are good enough to call a 'ready wit'!

Do get in touch.
With best wishes, JST.

Letter from Mr Dickie Dormann, Manager, the Gaumont Theatre, Southport to Sir John Thomas, 17 May 1960

Dear Sir John,
Pray allow me to introduce myself: Dickie Dormann, late of the Astoria, Beckenham, where I succeeded in raising 'bums-on-seats' (pardon my French!) to a record-breaking 89 per cent in my final season, now most comfortably ensconced at the thriving Gaumont, Southport where we continue to 'pack 'em in', six nights a week plus two matinées, come rain or shine as such.

I need hardly say that you have a great many fans in Southport – Southporters love a fighter, as my old mum used to say! – and as such we are all very keen indeed to tempt you to 'tread the boards' down Southport way. Any chance?

To one not 'in the profession' as such, it may seem to you ridiculously early to start planning for Christmas – but that's the way the cookie crumbleth 'au Theatre'!! What I wished to suggest was that you take 'star billing' in our seasonal pantomime, Dec. 18th–January 21st, with a three-week rehearsal period, which this year promises to be that extra special family favourite, *Cinderella*.

We had in mind for you the hilarious role of 'Widow Twankey', the ever-so-slightly scatter-brained (!) – old dear with a heart as big as her monstrous hats! I think you would be excellently suited to the part, which would afford you, believe me, a lot of fun.

There is as such a veritable galaxy of talent among your fellow stars, with definite acceptances so far from:

• Roger Trehearne and his Cheeky Chipmunk;

- Mr Tubby and Mr Shorty, Renowned Comedy Duo (who will appear – as always! – as the Ugly Sisters!);

- Arthur Smythe and his Performing Hedgehogs.

We are also currently in negotiation for recording artiste Miss Sally Carmichael ('I Never Saw a Guy Walk that Way Before', 'I Love a Man with a Fringe', 'What's in Your Sponge-Bag, Terry' etc, etc) to appear in the title role, and we have high hopes of persuading the tremendously versatile Frank Damone from television's 'Fun with Cardboard' to take on the demanding role of 'Buttons'. Needless to say, your name would add additional lustre to what is already, by any standards, a real cracker of an international bill as such.

   Please give me a bell soonest to arrange fees, terms of contract, etc.
– I can guarantee you a laugh a minute with a thoroughly crazy crew!

Yours in entertainment,
Dickie Dormann

From Hansard, Questions to the Prime Minister, 23 May 1960

Sir John Thomas (Cons): Is the Prime Minister aware of the widespread support –
Mr Dennis Mitchell (Lab): It's The Beachy Head Kid!
(*Opposition laughter*)
Sir John Thomas (Cons): Is the Prime Minister aware of the widespread support he has garnered from ordinary, decent men and women up and down this great country of ours for –
Mr Jim Scutcher (Lab): Is Mummy tucked up warm with the Gamekeeper, then?
(*Opposition laughter*)
Sir John Thomas (Cons): ... ordinary, decent men and women up and down this great country of ours for his major initiatives to curtail the dubious activities of gangs of –
Mr Dennis Mitchell (Lab): Hark who's talkin'!
(*Opposition cheers*)
Mr Speaker: Order! Order! I would remind the House that every Member has a right to speak without being interrupted by this continuous ribaldry! Sir John –
Sir John Thomas (cons): ... dubious activities of gangs of Teddy Boys, terrorising our seaside towns and villages with their often aggressive

behaviour and foul language, and will he assure the House that he will not hesitate –

Mr Jim Scutcher (Lab): Was he a Pheasant Plucker, then?

(*Opposition laughter*)

Sir John Thomas (Cons): ... to crack down even harder, should their behaviour fail to improve?

Prime Minister: I thank the Right Honourable Gentleman for his kind remarks and his unswerving loyalty, and I can assure him that, in a manner of speaking, if these unruly fellows reach the edge of the cliff, as it were, I will not hesitate to push them all the way over!

(*Laughter and cheers from all sides of the House*)

From the Index of *The Memoirs of Lord Telfont* (1969)

firm against Housing Bill 355; sticks neck out on Housing Bill in major off-the-record briefing 366; friendly words from Chief Whip 367; prefers loyalty to irresponsibility 368; votes with party 369; appointed Junior Minister 370; attitude to inner city poverty (*see* Resources, drain on) 371; rising reputation in Commons 372-91; appointed Sec. of State for Employment 395; new strategy for unemployed (*see* crackdown on workshy) 347; tours Bermuda for in-depth study solutions to unemployment 400; appointed Home Secretary 403; major success in new post.403-93; Leadership election 493-506; Peerage 507; major contribution to ongoing political debate 508-63; elected Chancellor of Oxford University 534; attends funeral of wife 559; heads Parliamentary tour of Kenya 560; overall achievements 564-572 (and footnotes); WORKS: *A Future from the Past* 301; *A New Outlook for the Present* 434; *Facing Up to the Future* 501; *A Life of Contrasts (Autobiography Vol. 1)* 550; *Time and Tide (Autobiography, Vol. 2)* 562; *A Sense of Accomplishment (Autobiography Vol. 3)* 570

From *The Memoirs of Lord Telfont,* page 404 (1969)

A further blow to the fortunes of the Party came at the beginning of 1960 with the John Thomas Affair. I barely knew Thomas, and so was able to take a more even-handed approach to his disgrace than some of my colleagues. Whilst fighting for his individual rights as a sitting MP, I was not in a position to prevent the Boundary Commission advising upon the eventual confluence of his constituency of Dorking into the neighbouring constituency of Guildford, thus depriving him of his Parliamentary foothold.

Of somewhat greater consequence for Britain were the Colorado Trade Talks, scheduled to begin in the September of that year ...

From the index of *My Way: Memoirs of a Former Minister,* by Sir John Thomas

From the private diary of Sir Alan Telfont MP, 1960

25 May: Bumped into poor old John Thomas in Central Lobby. Greeted me like long-lost friend – How are you old boy, How's the wife, Must have lunch etc., etc. Pathetic, absolutely *pathetic*. Hated to disillusion him. Forced me to accept large scotch in Members' Bar. Downed it at the double in hope of getting away before Messrs Park, Henley-Phipps and Soames spotted me with him. Just about succeeded, but as I was taking last gulp and saying 'Must keep in touch', old Park spies us and yells, 'Hold on to the bar pretty tight, Telfers, if you don't want to be pushed over it!' Highly embarrassing, but JT pretended not to hear and I shuffled off pronto with a half-hearted wave.

Poor old JT. What is to become of him? He's fallen so low but still seems to think there's a chance that he'll be able to pick himself up and carry on as if nothing had happened. There but for the grace of God, etc. I only wish there were something one could do for the fellow.

26 May: John Thomas telephones me in the Ministry. 'I'll come to the point, Alan,' he says. 'I was wondering if you could do something for me.'

I tell him that at the moment I am up to my neck, but I'll call back as soon as poss.

27 May: John Thomas comes up to me in Annie's Bar. 'You never called back,' he says. My God, I wish there weren't so many guilt-mongerers mewling their way around the back-benches. He really must learn to stand on his own two feet. 'Ring me in the morning,' I replied. 'Must rush.'

28 May: What a start to the day! John Thomas rings at precisely 9.00 a.m. 'I thought you might care for a bite of lunch,' he says. I want to reply, 'I might indeed, but not with you', but judge it best to get it over with and suggest 'a quick bite' tomorrow at 1.00 p.m. at Wheeler's, to be back in Westminster on the dot of 2.00 p.m. One doesn't like to ditch old friends. Or so one keeps telling oneself.

29 May: 'Fancy a spot of lunch today, Alan?' says the Secretary of State at noon. Sticking to the rules, I try to ring John Thomas to cancel, but he is nowhere to be found. I could just duck out but instead, I do the decent thing and go to the trouble of leaving a message at the front desk of Wheeler's, blaming pressure of work, the new French contracts, etc., etc.

Over lunch, the Secretary of State mentions that the PM says his advisers are saying that backbench opinion is saying that John Thomas is in danger of becoming an embarrassment to one and all, 'prowling around the corridors of Westminster like Banquo's ghost, making a complete and utter arse of himself in the Chamber.'

I stick up for John Thomas, arguing that, even before the scandal, he was hardly a figure of much substance, and that he could prove a most valuable asset, for the longer the opposition spend poking fun at him, the less time they have to make absolute idiots of the rest of us. 'Point taken,' he says, but without much conviction.

Memo from Conservative Chief Whip to Sir Alan Telfont MP, 4 June 1960

Al – As the B'dry Comm. is yr dept, cd you xamine the posbty of mkng J.Thos' constit. disparu in tim. for nxt G.Elec?

PM rqsts urgnt – Grge.

Letter from Sir John Thomas to Sir Alan Telfont MP, 7 June 1960

My dear Alan,
So sorry we missed each other for lunch on the 29th May. But not to worry – I arrived at Wheeler's in good time, and they were able to give me a solo table, where I drank your health, and recalled many of the

happy moments we have shared together: in the Oxford Union, as young whippersnappers on the backbenches, as PPSs, in the Whips Office, at your stag night(!), at country weekends and so forth. Happy days, eh? The benefits of nostalgia are vouchsafed to those who dine alone, as I have been happy to discover recently.

But let us to the future, old boy! I'd be most grateful if you could find space in your hectic ministerial diary for the incorporation of a bite to eat with your 'old mucker'. As well as chewing the cud, there are a number of issues I'd like to pick your brains on – for instance, the possibility of my re-establishing a foothold in Govt. by 'working my way up from the bottom', as it were, perhaps with a job as your PPS.

Keep in touch.
Yours ever,
John

Memo from Sir Alan Telfont MP to Sir John Thomas MP, 10 June 1960

Thanks for letter. Sorry about lunch! I feel sure there is every possibility of re-establishing a foothold, etc. Have you considered offering your undoubted talents to British Industry or one of the banks?

Yours ever,
Alan

Letter from Sir John Thomas to Sir Alan Telfont MP, 15 September 1960

Imperial Hotel,
Brighton

My dear Alan,
Heartiest congratulations on your platform speech yesterday afternoon. The audience was, as you could no doubt see for yourself, quite flabbergasted by the sparkle (and punch!) of your oratory. Your call for a 'return to basic moral values' will undoubtedly have an immense effect, and echoes what I have been saying for a very long time.

Don't you think it's about time for that lunch we keep promising ourselves? I would be delighted to buy you a slap-up dinner on Thursday or Friday ...

Incidentally, I saw you over the room at Lord Camomile's get-together in the Ballroom on Sunday – I waved in your direction, but as you were surrounded, needless to say, by all the 'people who matter', you obviously didn't see me or else you would have waved. Hope for a bite with you tomorrow or the next day.

Again, hearty congrats!
Yours, John

PS. I enclose a leaflet advertising a 'fringe' meeting I am addressing in the Lower Community Hall at 221 Bassett Street (off the Macclesfield Road – just ten-fifteen minutes drive from the Imperial) on the subject of 'Let's Get Tough on Crime' at 4.15 p.m., tomorrow night (Tuesday). I'd be *delighted* to see you there. A great deal of interest has been expressed, so do let me know if you'd like me to reserve you a seat. J.

From the *Bassett Road Examiner*, Motto: 'Free to All Households in Bassett Road and Intersecting Streets'

John Thomas comes to Bassett Road

INFAMOUS 'Lady Chatterley's son' MP Sir John Thomas paid a visit to the Lower Community Hall in Bassett Road last week to address a Conservative Party Conference fringe meeting on the subject of 'Let's Get Tough on Crime'. Between fifteen and twenty people turned up to hear the famous 'Cliff-top Scandal' MP speak. No other Members of Parliament were present. 'Many of them were listening to the Transport Secretary's keynote address, and quite right too,' Sir John explained.

His speech was well received. It was followed by a question-and-answer session, in which two members of the public put questions to him. A choice of coffee or tea was served, with biscuits. £1 25s. 6d. was raised for church roof repairs.

Afterwards, in an exclusive interview with the Bassett Road Examiner, Sir John told us he was 'delighted' by the response to the meeting. 'People are beginning to accept that a tougher response is needed to the vandals and bully-boys in our society,' he said.

Asked whether this meeting heralded a 'political comeback' for him after his resignation last year, Sir John commented 'That's for others to decide. I am content to serve my country in whatever capacity I can. It is too early to announce anything absolutely definite quite yet.'

Sir John was full of admiration for Bassett Road. 'It is a splendid road,' he told the *Examiner*, 'Full of houses and people.'

Memo from Sir Alan Telfont to Conservative Chief Whip, Blackpool, 17 September 1960

Grge – Hd another wrd. with Bdry Commissr. Drkng Constit. to be mrgd with G'ford soonst – Yrs Aln.

Postcard from Sir Alan Telfont to Sir John Thomas, 17 September 1960

Sorry not to have replied sooner to your kind invitation(s).

So little time, so much to do, etc. Hope to bump into you back in Westminster in new session. Feel sure your career will revive over coming year & will do my utmost to make sure it does.

Alan.

From the *Daily Telegraph*, 26 October 1960

John Thomas set to lose seat in boundary changes

'LADY CHATTERLEY' MP TO GO

Dorking to Merge with Guildford

Letter from the Prime Minister to Sir John Thomas, 4 November 1960

My dear John,

Thank you for your letter. I am sorry you feel as you do. I can assure you that no member of my Government has had what you refer to as 'a hand in this'.

As you know, the Boundary Commissioner must remain independent from the Government of the day. For this reason, I am unable to 'bring to bear my influence' upon him.

On a personal note, let me add how sorry I am to see you go. You may look back on your career as one of outstanding promise.

With very best wishes for the future,
Yours ever,
Harold

Memo from the Prime Minister to Sir Alan Telfont, 26 October 1960

Excellent work.

From the Index of the *Authorised History of the Conservative and Unionist Party, 1959–64,* by Sir Eskdaill Laughton

From *My Way: Memoirs of a Former Minister,* by Sir John Thomas

Towards the end of 1960, I was to learn that my own constituency of Dorking was to be merged with the neighbouring constituency of Guildford. As a consequence, I was to lose my seat in the House of Commons, a seat I had held for over fourteen years. A further blow came when I was informed that this change would take place not at the next General Election, as is traditional, but from the outset of the New Year, affording me just two months to 'clear my desk', as it were, and create a new life for myself.

I cannot deny that it was a shock, but I took it philosophically. Such are the ups and downs of the political life. It is impossible to appreciate the peaks if one has never ventured into the valleys. As in all things, one must take the rough with the smooth. I would leave behind me in the Commons a great many hopes and dreams, yes, but I would also be leaving with a great many delightful memories intact: memories of happy times with colleagues who had offered me their friendship and support throughout my career there. Outside commentators often make the mistake of portraying Westminster as a hotbed of intrigue and disloyalty. Nothing could be further from the truth. There are, of course, occasional differences in attitude to policy and its presentation. In a democracy, that is not only inevitable but desirable. But there is also a great sense of camaraderie, of good humour and of shared beliefs, of a shared community of bastards bastards bastards. 'Bastards bastards' bastards. Bastards bastards bastards (bastards bastards bastards) bastards bastards bastards. Bastards bastards bastards bastards bastards – bastards! BASTARDS! BASTARDS! BASTARDS! BASTARDS! BASTARDS! BASTARDS! Bastards, bastards, bastards, bastards, bastards. BASTARDS. B*ST*RDS, Bastards bastards; bastards. Bastards bastards bastards bastards bastards bastards bastards bastards bastards bastards. BaStArDs. Ba-st-ar-ds! Bastards bastards bastards BASTARDS bastards bastards bastards. Bastards bastards bastards bastards & bastards bastards bastards bastards. BASTARDS. BASTARDS. BASTARDS. BASTARDS. Bastards bastards bastards. (bastards) bastards bastards *bastards* bastards

From the *Surrey Advertiser*, 1 January 1961

Dorking gains new MP!

'I'll put Dorking on the map' vows Guildford man

On the stroke of midnight last night, Dorking gained itself a brand new MP – and without any of the usual fuss and bother of a General Election!

Luncheon

The overnight switch came about as a result of changes implemented by the Boundary

Commission. And Dorking is definitely 'going up in the world', as the new Dorking MP is the high-ranking Conservative Cabinet Minister Sir Alan Telfont. Sir Alan, who was already the Member of Parliament for Guildford, told the Surrey Advertiser last night, 'May I say at once how delighted I am to be representing the people of Dorking in the House of Commons. Dorking is a town that has always been very close to my heart, ever since I attended a formal luncheon there seven years ago.

Slings and arrows

In what many believed to be a reference to the outgoing MP, Sir John Thomas, Sir Alan added, 'I hope that Dorking will be able to put the 'slings and arrows' of recent years behind it, and, with their new Member of Parliament, look ahead with renewed hope and vigour. Certainly, it is my intention to help put Dorking on the map once more.'

Capable hands

Dorking's outgoing 'Lady Chatterley' MP Sir John Thomas was not available for comment last night. On December 30th he issued the following statement: 'I am delighted to be leaving Dorking in the capable hands of Sir Alan Telfont. I will be answering no further questions on this or any other matter.'

(*A New Broom for Dorking: Profile of Sir Alan Telfont, page 14*.)

From *My Way: Memoirs of a Former Minister*, by Sir John Thomas

If I had been at all nervous about how to fill my time after losing my seat in the House of Commons, such worries were to prove groundless. In early January 1961, I was to embark upon a new career as a newspaper columnist and opinion-former of no little distinction. I like to think that my hallmark was plain old-fashioned common sense. One week, I might review an important new book, the next week, I might pen an observation culled from personal experience, and the following week a closely argued critique of a controverisal new proposal from government.

It was with a strong measure of delight that I accepted this new challenge. Here would be a chance to speak out on all the major issues, but in a much more open and detached manner than ever I could muster in the party-political atmosphere of the House of Commons.

From the *Daily Express,* 15 February 1961

Elizabeth Taylor takes poodle to the Ritz!

'I GO EVERYWHERE WITH MY POOCH' SAYS STAR

From an article by Sir John Thomas, dated 17 February 1961

⌐ OVERPAID AND OVER HERE ⌐

That overpaid but scarcely overworked motion-picture actress Miss Elizabeth Taylor has reportedly treated her pet poodle to a night of luxury at the gaudy Ritz Hotel.

No doubt she will wish to give the wretched dog a slap-up five-course dinner there as well.

Is there not something positively foul about the way the British pamper and cosset these yapping, salivating tail-waggers?

Don't get me wrong. I have great admiration for Miss Taylor. She is a first-class actress who has pushed herself to the limits and deserves every penny she gets.

And if she wants to spend the money she earns on treating her delightful pet poodle to a superb night out at one of the world's finest hotels, who can honestly blame her?

The British are world-beaters when it comes to caring for our four-legged friends.

And, once again, Elizabeth Taylor leads the way when it comes to good, old-fashioned, star-quality loveliness.

From *The Times,* 6 May 1961

US puts man in space

ALAN B. SHEPARD JR ORBITS 115 MILES ABOVE EARTH

From an article by Sir John Thomas, dated 9 May 1961

↜ SPACE BETWEEN THE EARS ↝

Has it never occured to the Yanks – never the most intelligent of species – that there is nothing to space but ... space?

Over the last decade they have spent many millions of pounds – or 'dollars' as they call them – in trying to get some poor nutcase in a singularly unattractive vehicle as far away from terra firma as is humanly possible.

And why? All for the sake of 'international prestige'! What baloney!
 But don't get me wrong.

I have long considered the Americans the most adventurous and inventive people on this earth. In recent years, they have conquered so many other horizons that it is quite logical for them to regard space as 'the last frontier'.

And those who pooh-pooh the immense cost of this pioneering expedition to send a brave human being into space are the type of people who would have wagged a disapproving finger at Columbus, Newton and Alexander Graham Bell for 'wasting time and money'.

Man never got anywhere without great application and resources.

In recognising this, the United states of America once more gained the respect and admiration of the international community.

I salute them!

From *My Way: Memoirs of a Former Minister*, by Sir John Thomas

My articles were often forthright, always well-argued and – I like to think! – read with delight and annoyance in roughly equal measure. Even if my own career had enjoyed its fair share of ups and downs, my opinions had undoubtedly lost none of that tremendous force and direction for which I was so well known. A clear head and a strong sense of priorities are essential in a columnist, and I was blessed with both. When Sir John Thomas spoke, the world was forced to listen.

From a letter from the Editor, *The Chippenham Herald*, to Sir John Thomas, 3 September 1961

Dear Sir or Madam,
As you may have already guessed, our newspaper receives literally

thousands of unsolicited manuscripts every year.

We take care to read each and every one, and we are delighted to be given the opportunity. Sadly though, your article(s) have proved unsuitable for publication in the *Chippenham Herald*.

We wish you luck with them elsewhere. Once again, thank you for thinking of us.

Yours sincerely,
Mr M. Booth, Editor.

encs. unpublished manuscripts:
    'A Breath of Fresh Air'
    'Overpaid and Over Here'
    'Space Between the Ears'
    'A Breath of Fresh Air' (2)
    'Standing on Our Own Two Feet'
    'Time for a Change'
    'Never the Same Again'

Official slip inserted into the Sussex University English Faculty Student prospectus, 1961

ADDENDUM

On page 3, under the complete list of Faculty Staff,
OMIT: *Dr Joy Greenley MA*
ADD: *The announcement of an appointee to this post is imminent.*

On page 15,
OMIT: *Dr Joy Greenley conducts a course of 10 lectures on The Uses of Comedy in the Later Plays of Strindberg*
ADD: *Visiting Professor Norman V. Sedgeforth (University of Adelaide) conducts a course of 10 lectures on 'The Dangers Inherent in a Biographical Reading of the Fictional Text'*

On page 19,
OMIT: *Dr J. Greenley: 'Shakespeare Unclothed'.*
ADD: *J. B. Spillers: 'Shakespeare As Others Saw Him'*

On page 28,

OMIT: ... *and under Dr Greenley's forceful and imaginative chairmanship, the English Faculty Modern Cinema Encounter Group continues to flourish.*

On page 32,
OMIT: *Dr Greenley*

Letter from the Headmistress, Westhampton High School, 8 September 1962

My Dear Joy,

This is an exceptionally difficult letter to write, and I do hope you will forgive me if it emerges a little blunt.

There has been a number of rather strongly-worded objections from parents at your inclusion as the Chairman of the Judges in this year's High School Drama competition. I hope I do not need to 'spell out' the nature of their objections, as I would hate to hurt your feelings, but the words 'vicious, corrupt and deceitful blackmailer' have been recurring regularly.

In view of this, I hope you would understand if we now chose to postpone your Chairmanship for at least a year? I feel sure that before the decade is out we would wish to extend an invitation to you to partipate in this major event in the school's calendar, if not as Chairman, at least as a highly skilled observer.

I hope all is well.
Yours ever,
Dorothy Ableman xxxx

Letter from the Vice-Chancellor, Newnham College, Oxford to Dr Joy Greenley, 19 May 1963

Dear Dr Greenley,
I regret to inform you that, in a busy year, your application for the post of:
TEMPORARY LECTURESHIP, MODERN ENGLISH NOVEL
has been unsuccessful.

May I take this opportunity to wish you the best of luck elsewhere.

Yours sincerely
Deirdre Skiff
Secretary to the Vice-Chancellor

Notice of Intention to Remove Goods from a Rented Premises in Lieu of Monies Owed. From B. Smithers and Daughter Ltd, Registered Bailiffs, addressed to Dr. J. Greenley, 8 Regency Square, Brighton, 9 January 1964

Dear _J. Greenley_
Further to the accordings due on behalf of and owing to our client(s)

>   *Messrs Brighton Deluxe and Deteriorating Property*
>   *Holdings and Lettings and Sons Ltd*

we are beholden to inform you this ___9th___ day of ___January___ 19**63** of our intention to inquire upon the underformentioned premises:

>   *8 Regency Square*

and with purpose and foresight to remove thereof and to our pleasure item(s) convenient and not unadjacent to the sum of:

>   *£950/19s/6d*

representing the monies assumed by and debts owing to our client(s) in their services applying to and with application towards:

>   *Due rental of above (unfurnished) premises*

and we furthermore hasten to beg your attention towards notice of legal proceedings appertaining to said removals if our access to the property is in any way, manner or form restricted, hampered or impeded on the abovementioned date.

Yours sincerely
B. Smithers & Daughter
Registered Bailiffs

——— HAVE YOU JOINED OUR CHRISTMAS CLUB? ———

From the *Daily Express*, 17 August 1966

Whatever Happened to ... ? (No. 67)

DR JOY GREENLEY

DR JOY GREENLEY was the literary biographer who rose to prominence in the spring of 1960 following her part in the notorious John Thomas scandal.

Researching a biography of the novelist D. H. Lawrence, she uncovered proof that the leading Conservative MP was in fact the son of the real Lady Chatterley. After the acquittal of Thomas on a charge of attempted murder, Greenley herself faced charges of blackmail with menaces, for which she received a two-year suspended sentence.

These days, Joy has put the world of letters and academia behind her. 'It just wasn't for me,' she says. 'Now that I am living in the real world I am getting much more out of life!' For the past two years, Joy has found part-time employment as a cleaner at a supermarket in Birmingham.

From the *Sunday Express*, page 32. Cryptic Crossword 9 May 1967

ACROSS:
1 Lady Chatterley's Lecturer? (3, 8)

Letter from Joy Greenley to Mr Clive Marlowe, 16 June 1967

16g Balls Pond Rise
Birmingham

Dear Mr Marlowe,

I trust there is no need for me to introduce myself. I was the celebrated author of a number of bestselling literary biographies in the late 1950s. They helped make your late father's name as a 'Great Editor' (!), though he never expressed a single word of gratitude to me, not one word. But then perhaps he was 'too busy'. That was his usual story.

Since then, I have been taking time off from my academic and biographical duties to consider the direction in which my writing career should flow. I have now compiled a shortlist of possible ideas for literary biographies. Owing to my previous association with your firm, I will permit you to see this list before anyone else. I am sure you will agree that the promise of 'the first new Greenley biography in twelve years' would be an extremely powerful advertisement for any book.

I look forward to hearing from you.

Yours sincerely,
Joy Greenley

From Marlowe Publishers to Joy Greenley, 25 July 1967

Dear Reader/Writer
Thank you for your recent letter. We are always interested to hear from writers and readers.

Regrettably, at present we are unable to find a place in our busy publishing schedule for your idea/manuscript.

Wishing you all the very best in placing it elsewhere.

Yours sincerely,
D. M. Nokes
Editorial Consultant

From Joy Greenley to Clive Marlowe, 26 July 1967

Dear Mr Marlowe,
In reply to my recent (or not-so-recent) letter to you I have received a circular notation of refusal from a Mr Nokes, whom I have never met. I have no doubt that it was sent in error, for no reputable publishing house would send so curt a dismissal to one of its most prestigious biographers.

Nevertheless, perhaps I should be more specific in listing the biographies and literary compilations I have in mind. They are:

◆ 'The Wit of John Bunyan' (3 Vols)

- "Pearl One, Old Goat': The Place of Knitwear in the Works of Ernest Hemingway'
- 'William Shakespeare: Playwright, Poet, Maori'

I trust you will join in the bidding for at least one of these titles. I look forward to hearing from you at your earliest opportunity so that I can put the writing into immediate operation.

Yours sincerely,
Joy Greenley

From the Diary of Clive Marlowe

28th July 1967 Delivered direct from the Department of Forgotten Names – a letter from Joy Greenley! Obviously very desperate, mad to get published again, though it seems the years have not staled her infinite self-confidence. Not to be touched with the proverbial barge-pole, I fear.

From Marlowe Publishers to Joy Greenley, 3 September 1967

Dear Reader/Writer
Thank you for your recent letter. We are always interested to hear from writers and readers.

Regrettably, at present we are unable to find a place in our busy publishing schedule for your idea/manuscript.

Wishing you all the very best in placing it elsewhere,

Yours sincerely,
Miss H. Kimbell
pp D. M. Nokes
Editorial Consultant

Bankruptcy Writ served on Ex-MP

Ex-MP Sir John Thomas, who rose to prominence five years ago in the 1960 'Son of Lady Chatterley' court case, has been declared bankrupt.

Sir John has tried his hand at a variety of jobs since losing his Dorking seat in the boundary changes of 1961, but with little success. After losing a number of lucrative directorships in the wake of his trial for attempted murder, he attempted to find work as a newspaper columnist, but with little success. Subsequently, he has been reported at different times working as a financial adviser, a croupier, a telephonist and a part-time postman.

'I am flourishing,' he said yesterday, as he left the Lewisham bed-and-breakfast at which he is being lodged by the council. 'I am still in close touch with my Cabinet colleagues, though any influence I may have is strictly "hush-hush".'

Letter from the office of The Rt. Hon. Colliers Pinkney MP to Sir John Thomas, 6 September 1965

Dear Sir John,

Mr Pinkney has asked me to thank you for your letter and the kind comments contained therein.

He regrets that owing to pressure of work he is unable to deal with your problem on a personal basis, but has passed a copy of your letter to the Rehabilitation Officer at your local Council Headquarters.

He is anxious to add that he is delighted to hear you are well. However, he regrets that his appointment book is too full to accept your kind invitation to luncheon at a restaurant of his choosing.

Yours sincerely,
P. B. Jessop (Mrs)
Secretary to The Rt. Hon. Colliers Pinkney MP, PC

Letter from Archibald Saunders-Parker to Sir John Thomas, 15 September 1965

Dear Sir John,

Having read of your 'case', as it were, within the well-thumbed pages of my local library's *Daily Telegraph*, my memory was jogged sufficiently to pen you this noble missive in order to invite you to join a rather illustrious little Association, The Third Tuesday Club, of which I am honoured to be President.

Our lofty membership is gathered from the ranks of ex-MPs of the Conservative persuasion, the only stipulation being that they must have 'fallen from favour', through what the gentlemen of the Press so brutally term a 'scandal'. Our 30-odd members meet regularly in the upstairs room of the Old Turnpike Inn in Maida Vale, generally on the third Tuesday of every month – hence the nomenclature!

May I introduce myself? I left the House back in 1947, having become known to the popular Press as the 'Hit and Run MP', after a civilian – a known alcoholic, by the way, who was wearing no necktie – fetched up on my fender, causing, I might add, no little damage to the paintwork!!! As I explained later in the most copious detail to the good gents of the local constabulary, I was absolutely determined to report his demise at the earliest possible opportunity, having taken a couple of weeks off to 'get over' the trauma – but as rotten luck would have it this admission was pre-empted by my arrest at London Airport on my return to these fair shores.

Ergo, the end of a highly promising parliamentary career, and the start of a lifetime devoted to the heartfelt care of those with careers similarly smashed to the proverbial smithereens. But I have been lucky enough to retain close friends and contacts in both Houses, receiving regular Christmas cards from Angus Miffin, MP for Derbyshire North, and Lord 'Toothy' Hickle, ex-frontbench spokesman on Youth Affairs in the Upper Chamber (until the recent hoo-haa).

But that's enough of me! Our present management committee is composed of:

- *Clarence Squinter*, formerly Conservative MP for Newbury, resigned 1959 following famous 'Murdered Prostitute in MP's Bedroom' upset.

- *Albion Hartley*, formerly Conservative MP for Brighton and Hove, resigned 1944 after discovered holidaying over a long weekend in the South Ruhr as personal guest of Field Marshal Goering.

- *Arthur Robinson*, formerly Conservative MP for Edinburgh South and Secretary of State for Health, resigned 1932 following allegations of drunkenly consuming elderly constituent's pet dachsund as a forfeit in a party game.

- *Sir Juniper Smedley*, formerly Conservative MP for Norfolk North East, resigned 1958 following arrest after attempting to sell range of Constituency Association silverware in jumble sale.

- *Frank Rowbotham* OBE, formerly Conservative MP for Old Chelsea and Minister for Rationing, resigned 1942 following regrettable 'Ladies Knickers for Petrol Coupons' incident.

- *Sir Hal Godley*, formerly Conservative MP for Croydon, resigned last year in wake of disclosures concerning a Scot's Guard, a cat-o'-nine tails and a steel comb after complaints from neighbours of yelping noises emerging from his discreet Mayfair mews.

- *Everett Stone-Belchamp*, formerly Conservative MP for Eastbourne, resigned 1933 after mistakenly attempting to solicit sexual favours in the Westminster twilight from the bewigged Lord Chief Justice Hawtrey.

Needless to say, we all look forward to warmly welcoming you to our burgeoning ranks. Our meetings are friendly, informal affairs, with many an enjoyable hour devoted to imbibing and reminiscing.

But we also have a more serious purpose, letting current Members of Parliament know exactly where we stand on all the major issues at home and abroad, sending letters of advice to world figures and forming a sort of advisory service to current Members with what one might describe as 'little local difficulties'.

We also have a sister association, 'The Stand-Bys', formed of wives who have agreed to stand by us. This latter association meets only occasionally, for memorial services, inquests, funerals, photographic 'shoots' and so forth. Do join us if you can!

Yours etc.,
Archibald Saunders-Parker
President, Third Tuesday Club

Postcard in window of Anderson's Newsagent and Retail Outlet, 33
Kennington Rise, London SE1, 19 March–24 July 1966

CASUAL FISH FILLETER REQUIRED
NIGHTS ONLY BILLINGSGATE

- 7/6 an hour
- Must provide own knife and plasters
- No qualifications preferred
- Own transport a necessity
- 24-hour Casualty Hospital within easy walking

From *My Way: Memoirs of a Former Minister,* by Sir John Thomas

At the end of July 1966, I had the great good fortune to make contact
with senior executives in the steadily expanding market of fresh fish.
After careful consideration, I decided upon the acceptance of a non-
executive post. This would allow me free rein to exercise my proven
ability in the market place as well as affording me plenty of travel. It
was fascinating for me to learn first-hand about life at the sharp end of
the fish trade, supplementing the considerable theoretical and economic
knowledge I had accrued through my two valuable years as on the
Conservative Backbench Committee of Fresh Water Fish.

After six very full and active months of mutually beneficial
employment in this rapidly developing sector, I decided to move to
pastures new. However, I retain warm memories of the fresh-fish
industry, and all who work in and prosper by it.

From *Fortnightly Fish Trader* magazine, issue 17.003, page 19, 17 February 1967

Fish filleter fired following reading incident at Billingsgate

An unskilled casual fish filleter, Mr J. Thomas, of no fixed address, was fired from night duties at Billingsgate on Thursday after refusing to wrap the innards of an octopus in a copy of that day's *Daily Telegraph*.

'We've had trouble with him in the past,' explained Mr D. Frederick, owner of Frederick's Fish Filleters. 'Instead of using the newspapers to wrap the innards, he would spend his time reading them. I'm very sorry, but when he said he wished to finish the Parliamentary Page last Thursday, I saw red. There's no room for shirkers in this business, so he was OUT.'

Frederick's Fish Filleters continue to supply ready filleted fresh fish to many leading restaurants and nightclubs, including Wiltons in London's famous West End.

Thomas was unavailable for comment last night.

From *My Way: Memoirs of a Former Minister*, by Sir John Thomas

Wishing to further my knowledge of the opportunities facing British industry in the 1960s, and to prepare myself and my country for the challenges of the 1970s, I looked around for a post in the fast-growing catering industry. As luck would have it, I did not have to look very far. If this country is to thrive in the years ahead, it is up to all of us to make sure our tourism is second to none. For this reason I was particularly pleased to offer whatever abilities I may have to the worldwide KoesyInns Oganisation. Sir George Koe was, of course, an old friend of mine from my days as a Minister, and his immense knowledge and wisdom have long proved invaluable not only for his own business empire but for tourism as a whole.

From *Hotel and Caterer* magazine, 23 May 1967

KOESYINNS LTD
Cleaner Required
(LARGELY TOILETS)
Folkestone area
Unattractive hours
No holiday payment
Might suit partially sighted
or otherwise handicapped
Unpleasant atmosphere
Definitely no whistlers
APPLY H&C BOX 1091

From the noticeboard of the Old Ratting House, Koesylnn Folkestone By-pass, 9 July 1967

ᴄ SUMMER CLEANING ROSTER ᴐ

Andrews: 5.00 a.m. – 10.30 a.m.
10.30 am – 1.00 p.m.
Hartley: 1.00 p.m. – 6.30 p.m.
6.35 p.m. – 9.00 p.m.
Thomas: 9.00 p.m. – 2.30 a.m.
2.35 a.m. – 5.00 a.m.

Remember:
No whistling or singing
NEVER clean a toilet before first checking
that the guest in question has exited from the cubicle
No fraternising with guests
No talking to self or others

From *My Way: Memoirs of a Former Minister,* by Sir John Thomas

The catering industry, I was to discover, affords one splendid opportunity to make contact with all sides of the community – customer, management and workforce alike. I worked long and hard 'sounding out' all the various sides of the catering equation. I like to think I made it absolutely clear to one and all that only by pulling together could we hope to achieve the targets we had set ourselves. In this, I rather think, my ministerial experience – which, perforce, involves a very great deal of listening and talking – was an invaluable asset, both to my own needs and to the needs of the wider community.

From the noticeboard of the Old Ratting House, Koesylnn Folkestone By-pass, 19 September 1967

IMPORTANT

To be read and inwardly digested by ALL STAFF
Staff should be aware that information received on a strictly secret basis

suggests that Sir George Koe may be touring Kent and surrounding areas on a spot-check basis during the coming weeks.

I need hardly overstate the importance of ALL STAFF remaining alert AT ALL TIMES. KoesyInns Ltd has achieved its worldwide success in the catering and tourism markets by attention to detail, respect for the guest and a sound cost-paring operation ensuring minimum wastage. Sir George has an eagle eye for discrepancies re these company maxims. It is up to each one of us to present the Old Ratting House as a flagship for the famous '3 Ks', or Koesy Kwality Konditions of:

1) Know-How
2) Kustomer Kare
3) Kash Kontrol

I must remind you that Sir George makes it his sworn practice to visit the units in his chain entirely unannounced. It is thus essential that ALL staff, from senior management down to cleaning staff, execute their duties with utter thoroughness, being mindful of Sir George's reputation for the immediate closure of operations which fail to meet his own exacting standards.

G. B. Hazzard,
Executive Manager

From *My Way: Memoirs of a Former Minister,* by Sir John Thomas

While working for and on behalf of the KoesyInn operation, I always found it a great pleasure to bump into the great Sir (now Lord) Koe. Old friends from 'way back when' and − years ago! − fellow clubmen, on such occasions we would greet each other most warmly, swapping banter and jokes, though never, of course, forgetting our shared and overriding purpose: the advancement of KoesyInns, nationally and internationally.

Employee Dismissal Report, Koesylnn Organisation, dated 3 October 1967

Branch: _Old Ratting House, Folkestone By-Pass_

Date: _October 3rd 1967_

Employee (surname only): _Thomas_

Initial(s): _J. S._

Job description: _Night cleaner_

Brief description of offence: _During spot-check visit by Sir George, employee approached Sir George in offensive and familiar manner calling Sir George by 1st name, failing to employ his proper title, stretching out rt. arm, with possible view to physical abuse._

Action taken: _Employee wrestled to the ground by Asst. Man. Rob Smythe. Taken immedtly to store-rm for questioning following conclusion of visit. Dismissed with five (5) days pay._

Legal defence: _Possible mental instability considered unsafe for guests._

Letter from Sir George Koe to G. B. Hazzard, Executive Manager, Old Ratting House, Koesylnn Folkestone By-Pass, 6 October 1967

Dear Hazzard,

A short note in appreciation of your hospitality on my visit to The Old Ratting House last week.

I found it excellently run and above all spotlessly clean. Your staff have good cause to feel proud of themselves.

As you noted at the time, and again in your kind letter of the 4th, there was a regrettable incident involving an employee since dismissed. But let me again stress that this in no way affected my enjoyment. As all Captains of Industry are aware, a variety of odd fish can occasionally swim through the net of any organisation. Your response to this upheaval was admirably swift.

Yours sincerely,
E. R. Hitchen
pp Sir George Koe

Memo from Sir George Koe to Staff Relations Officer (Management), Koesylnns Organisation, 6 October 1967

Pse check suitability of Hazzard, Folkestone by-pass brnch.
INCOMPETENT??

From *Koesylnns Kronicle*, the journal of the Koesylnns Organisation, issue 304, Spring 1968, Page 37:

New Manager Rob Smythe has BIG plans for The Old Ratting House KoesyInn, just off the Folkestone by-pass!

Enthuses Rob, 34: 'I'm hoping to introduce a lot of new, bright young ideas to ensure a great stay for all our guests.'

First change, reveals Rob, is the name itself! 'The Old Ratting House' is to be changed in March to 'The Traveller's Rest'.

'It's a very much more 'today' name!' explains Rob, married to brunette receptionist Marilyn, 25, 'and we've got to stay 'in tune' if KoesyInns are to remain the Number One destination for the business and leisure traveller in the 1970s!'

From *My Way: Memoirs of a Former Minister,* by Sir John Thomas

My thirst for knowledge in other fields proved even greater than my devotion to the catering industry. Not for the first time, I decided to 'move on'. The time had come, I thought, to secure myself a first-class London base in a central location within easy reach of my old stamping-ground, the Houses of Parliament and the City. By a stroke of luck, I came across an excellently-located little corner, just west of The Savoy Hotel, scene of many of my most enjoyable luncheons with Parliamentary colleagues, civil-service advisers and senior foreign dignitaries.

Press Release from Conservative Central Office, 19 November 1968

Conservative MPs draw attention to plight of homeless under Labour Government

A top-flight delegation of Conservative MPs is to pay a special visit to the destitute living under the famous 'Arches' at Charing Cross.

'After four long years of Labour government, the situation for the homeless and destitute has never been worse,' reports The Rt. Hon. Colliers Pinkney, the leader of the delegation. 'We aim to draw attention to the plight of these poor victims of socialist policy by staying with them, offering them our sympathy, talking to them and hearing what they have to say for anything up to three-quarters of an hour.

'It is a national disgrace that in this day and age, only a short taxi-ride from the Palace of Westminster, people should be forced to live in these conditions. I truly believe that their only hope of proper housing and decent living conditions lies with a truly Conservative Government – a Government for ALL the people, and not just for the vociferous minority.'

Photocall: 10.45 a.m. prompt
Concludes: 11.30 a.m.
Press Conference followed by finger buffet, River Room, Savoy Hotel: 12 noon.

From *My Way: Memoirs of a Former Minister,* by Sir John Thomas

Around this time I was happy to entertain 'At Home' a spirited delegation of Conservative MPs. Some were new to me – eager-beavers from the two elections that had occurred since my departure from the House – but there was also a fair smattering of familiar old faces with whom I was delighted to pass the time of day. I was pleased to note, with a certain wry amusement, that, for all their cocksure ways, even the youngest in the delegation proved mustard-keen to ascertain my views on such important issues facing our society as housing, poverty, nutrition and heating.

From a strictly confidential report to the Conservative Chief Whip from The Rt. Hon. Colliers Pinkney MP, 19 November 1968

Frank – our morning visit to destitute went swimmingly, oodles of press interest, nice bright day for decent pictures, red faces all round for Labour Govt, convivial finger-buffet afterwards at Savoy. First-class manoeuvre, brilliantly executed.

Nota Bene: As I was speeding along the line of the Great Unwashed, vigorously shaking my (strategically gloved!) hand with theirs, passing round the hat (cameras at the ready!) for any complaints against the Government, offering them each a sausage-roll and a cup of soup, I came to a sinister-looking cove in a moth-eaten pin-striped suit with some sort of dead weed in his buttonhole, beard sprouting from his every orifice, gruesomely familiar in a funny sort of way, yet devilishly hard to place.

'Colliers!' he barked as I thrust my hand in his general direction, 'It's been yonks!'

Lordy be, I thought to myself, what have we here? I summoned my research assistant, hoping he'd palm the weirdo off with a few leaflets and a friendly smile, but the fellow grabbed my hand and said, 'It must be – what? – six, seven years! How's Natalie and the kids? And what about...?'

He then mentioned a piece of extremely sensitive information of a personal nature, known only to myself and a bare handful of others. I don't mind telling you, I was *astonished.*

'Who *are* you?' I said, but before he could answer I had glanced down at the fat and grubby old pad of foolscap in his other hand. The title on its cover, neatly written in large capital letters with a pencil and underlined in red biro, read as plain as day:

'MY WAY: MEMOIRS OF A FORMER MINISTER'
BY
SIR JOHN THOMAS

From *My Way: Memoirs of a Former Minister,* by Sir John Thomas

'It must be – what?' I said, ' – six or seven years! How's Natalie and the kids. And what about that secretary of yours? What was her name? Miriam? Marilyn? Martha? No that's it – *Martin.* I see you're going a finer shade of red, Colliers, you old rascal, you!!!'

You can imagine my horror, for it was *him*, John Thomas, standing there before me as though nothing had happened, a man who once rejoiced in the title of Secretary of State for Communications now begging in rags beneath the arches at Charing Cross! It was just too bad, it really was – and I was absolutely determined that his presence should on no account prove a source of embarrassment. The little rats of the Press and television would have a field day if they realised that standing before them, unshaven, unclean and dressed like a tramp, was a man who had once been tipped to lead the Conservative Party!

'I don't think I know you,' I said, 'Have a sausage roll.' And without further ado, I stuffed one of Mr Wall's finest straight into his mouth.

'Nnnn-nnn,' he said through the sausage roll, but by then I had turned smartly on my heels. I marched over to the Press, looked at my watch and bellowed, 'Gentlemen, I think we might adjourn for a little light refreshment – the good burghers of the Savoy await us with an impressive array of their finest sweetmeats and *viandes*!' Within seconds they had downed tools, scattering headlong into the warm bosom of the River Room, leaving the homeless and destitute to stand on their own two feet for once.

From *My Way: Memoirs of a Former Minister,* by Sir John Thomas

Over a pleasant sausage roll, we reminisced of old times, swapping banter and opinions, vowing to keep in touch. In my experience, senior Ministers greatly value the opportunity to 'sound out' those in the outside world. They realise we will speak without fear or favour, affording the Government a fresh perspective on the vital questions of the day, untainted by the need to bolster morale or score 'party points'.

From a Strictly Confidential Report to the Conservative Chief Whip from the Rt. Hon. Colliers Pinkney, 19 November 1968

I consider it *vital* that this potential embarrassment to the Party be removed from under the arches at Charing Cross as early as possible. If the press get wind of his presence, it would greatly damage our reputation as a go-ahead, *caring* party in the country as a whole.

Could you sort this one out – sharpish?

Yours ever,
CP

Memo from Jack Smythe MP, Labour Assistant Deputy Chief Whip, to Harry Cronin MP, Under-Secretary of State at the Home Office, 20 November 1968

URGENT AND STRICTLY CONFIDENTIAL

Harry – A little birdie in the Beeb who sings our tunes most sweetly tells me he's discovered our old friend John Thomas (our once and future PM – remember?!!) lodging beneath the arches at Charing Cross, I kid you not, living the life of a tramp.

My little birdie is anxious the story gets the coverage it so richly deserves, but feels constrained by the cries of 'sensationalism' and 'anti-Tory bias' that will rain down upon Aunty Beeb's blessed head. He's sure he can confirm identification by today noon. A plant at today's Questions to the Home Secretary at 2.30 should set the plates spinning, followed by a detailed response from the Home Sec, so he can give it max. coverage on the evening news – over to you!

Jack

From *Hansard*, Questions to the Home Secretary, 20 November 1968

Home Secretary: Her Majesty's Government has no intention whatsoever of treating Mr John Lennon and his foreign lady friend Miss Ono any differently from others suspected of possessing the drug 'cannabis resin'. They will be dealt with in the normal manner, and the deportation or otherwise of Miss Ono is a matter that will not arise until or unless she is found guilty of that possession, in which case it will be a matter to be reviewed in the normal manner by the appropriate regulatory bodies.

Mr Archibald Munro (Lab): Can my Right Honourable Friend confirm that the former Conservative Cabinet Minister Sir John Thomas is today to be found penniless, lonely and in rags just a few minutes from this House beneath the arches of Charing Cross –

Mr Speaker: Order! Order! Mr Munro –

Mr Archibald Munro (Lab): and does he not think that this reflects disgracefully on those members of the Opposition who were proud to call themselves his colleagues –

Mr Speaker: Order! Order!

Mr Archibald Munro (Lab): and does he not also agree that if this is how the Opposition treats its own kind, this bodes ill for the many millions of Britons of other political persuasions should they ever again gain power!?

Mr Speaker: Order! Order!

Mr Jonathan Skews (Cons): On a point of order, Mr Speaker!

Mr Speaker: Mr Jonathan Skews!

Mr Jonathan Skews (Cons): The Honourable Gentleman has no right to introduce unsubstantiated rumour amounting to malicious *gossip* –

Mr Speaker: Order! Order!

Mr Jonathan Skews (Cons): – into this Chamber, and I feel it would be only right, Mr Speaker, were you to ask him to withdraw these disgraceful allegations against an ex-Member of this House.

Mr Speaker: The Home Secretary!

Home Secretary: Regrettably, I can indeed confirm that Sir John Thomas has this morning been detained by the Metropolitan Police, who are considering obtaining charges of vagrancy against him. I do not wish to comment further lest I interfere with the due processes of the courts, but let me add that I heartily agree with the Honourable Gentleman that it reflects ill on the Opposition, and sends out a message about their claims to compassion and caring that the country at large might be well advised to heed.

Mr Speaker: Order! Order!

From the *Daily Telegraph*, Page 1, 21 November 1968

Son of Lady Chatterley faces charges of vagrancy

JOHN THOMAS DETAINED BY POLICE

From the *Daily Mirror*, Page 1, 21 November 1968

Lady Chatterley's Loafer!

SCANDAL TORY FOUND BEGGING UNDER ARCHES

From *My Way: Memoirs of a Former Minister*, by Sir John Thomas

Following my genial meeting with Colliers, I was approached by senior figures in the Metropolitan Police. They wished to sound me out on a wide range of important issues concerning life in Great Britain in the latter half of the twentieth century. After full and detailed discussions, I was royally entertained for a number of days in their Bow Street headquarters, very much the elder statesman offering a few choice crumbs of his hard-earned experience to the oh mummy mummy mummy why did you do this to me mummy mummy mummy mummy mummy mummy mummy mummy mummy mummy mummy where are you mummy mummy mummy what did i do to deserve it mummy come home mummy mummy mummy mummy mummy mummy mummy mummy mummy mummy come home mummy come home come home

From the diary of Sir Clifford Chatterley, 28 March 1969

Grim days indeed, and grimmer ahead. Snap in *The Times* this morning of the 'Beatle' J. Lennon, looking like something one might brush against in a ghost train, sitting in a bed in the Amsterdam Hilton of all places with his nip wife, described somewhat improbably as 'an artist', but looking rather more like a wine gum left in one's pocket a good three years. The lovely couple – ahem – are on honeymoon, and are now performing what is known as 'a bed-in' for peace. No better argument for all-out nuclear war has ever come my way.

Bank sends *shitty* letter. Won't even dignify it with reply.

From The Manager, Barclays Bank, Tevershall, 27 March 1969

Dear Sir Clifford,
I regret to inform you that despite my repeated requests, your account with us is now overdrawn to the tune of £156,567.96.

After consultation with our Head Office in London, I am bound to inform you that if the situation fails to improve we shall henceforth be applying to the High Court to free your assets. In this event, possession of your house and land and contents therein will revert immediately to Barclays Bank Ltd.

Yours sincerely,
Mr O. C. Stephens
Manager

From the diary of Sir Clifford Chatterley, 30 March 1969

'Bed-In' continues, and the spastically 'relevant' *Times* has to tell us all about it. Lennon plus Wine Gum are urging world leaders to hold peace talks around a table inside a giant bag. They say all soldiers should be forced to remove their trousers before going into battle.

Talk about the rot setting in. When did Britain begin its spiralling descent down the bloody plug-hole? The beginning of the Sixties? The Fifties? The Thirties? No: much, much earlier. I date it to when Connie felt she had to invite infernal DH – i.e. Damned Hateful – Lawrence to stay that beastly weekend. If he had never set foot in Wragby, none of this – our divorce, my forty-odd years of total mis., the ghastly publicity in '60, the worldwide scorn poured down on my cuckolded head, the Labour Government, Loss of Empire, Angry Young Men, Pot, The Beatles and all the shower – need ever have happened.

From The Manager, Barclays Bank, Tevershall, 2 April 1969

Dear Sir Clifford,

As I have had no reply to my last letter, I have decide with the greatest regret to apply for transference of all your assets to Barclays Bank. This step will be operative from Tuesday, April 5th. Nevertheless, it is possible even at this late date that a convincing business plan drawn up by you and your financial advisers might save the day; I urge you most earnestly to take whatever action is open to you.

Yours sincerely,
Mr O.C. Stephens
Manager

From the diary of Sir Clifford Chatterley, 3 April 1969

On the other hand, perhaps we'd all be better off living in a bag. Life at Wragby has never been happy, save for those few, fleeting years with Connie, before her great deception. Why did you do it, Connie? Why, oh, why? Life without you has been pretty shitty, but life without Wragby is inconceivable. Think of suicide. Total bore. Wretched nuisance. Decide to put it off at least until tomorrow or the next day.

Letter from Trulee Grate Gigs Ltd to Sir Clifford Chatterley, 4 April 1969

Dear Sir Chatterley

I suspect I don't need no – na na na na na na – introDUCTION (as Mickie J. might say!) but anyway 'ere we go!!!

I am the guy – the *numero uno*, you might say, behind Contrax Inc., incorporating Firecracker Records (Tinned Peaches, Steve Naylor, Strawberry Sinners, Rik Aitch, In Your Face, Excessive Melange, etc., etc., etc.). We also operate Trulee Grate Gigs Ltd and the Stoned Hedz management company, which numbers among its clients Suzi Small, Aking Donut and Plimsoll. We also control over half the world's tinned pear market, and we are developing substantial holdings in the construction and travel arenas.

Last year the annual turnover of Contrax Inc. was estimated by

Forbes magazine at $250 million worldwide. May I suggest a business meeting soonest? My helicopter surveillance crew has given the grounds of Wragby a definite thumbs-up for a 5-day rock festival, probably on an annual basis, with catering, recording, filming and subsidiary rights negotiable.

Obviously we are talking about substantial remuneration to you as owner of Wragby, coupled with guarantees as to security, damage to property, etc. We are talking in the region of £55,000 p.a. for starters, no kidding.

Please give me a tinkle soonest if interested.

Yours in music,
Dicky 'Dodo' Dixon
Chairman and Founder, Contrax Inc.

From Sir Clifford Chatterley to The Manager, Barclays Bank, Tevershall, 5 April 1969

Dear Mr Stephens,
It may interest you to know that your Mr Dixon has been threatening me with pop-groups, drugs, hot dogs, helicopters and general nudity if I don't pay you all £55,000 a year. This is blackmail, pure and simple – the business methods of the protection rackets in 'down-town' Chicago sponsored by a once-great British bank.

Unless I hear from you by return of post, I shall have no hestitation in reporting the matter to the local constabulary.

Yours faithfully,
Sir Clifford Chatterley

From The Manager, Barclays Bank, Tevershall, 6 April 1969

Dear Sir Clifford,
In reply to your letter of the 5th inst. and the very serious allegations it contains, we know nothing of this letter. I would be grateful if you

forward a copy of said letter at your earliest convenience for our fullest investigations.

Yours sincerely,
Mr O. C. Stephens

From The Manager, Barclays Bank, Tevershall, 9 April 1969

Dear Sir Clifford,
Thank you for forwarding the letter written to you by a Mr 'Dodo' Dixon. First, I must assure you that Mr Dixon is not, and never has been, an employee of Barclays Bank. Second, I must urge you to consider his offer most seriously: from what I can gather, he is an impresario and entrepreneur of considerable commercial acumen. His proposition, if accepted, may well offer Wragby Hall its only chance of survival under the present ownership. I have no wish to pressurise you into taking a decision contrary to your instincts; nevertheless, the monies owed by you to my bank are now at such a level that, in the long run, such a decision may be taken out of your hands.

Yours sincerely,
O. C. Stephens

From Sir Clifford Chatterley to the Manager, Barclays Bank, Tevershall, 10 April 1969

Dear Mr Stephens,

Over my dead body.

Yours sincerely,
Sir Clifford Chatterley

From *New Musical Express*, 15 May 1969

WRAGBY WROCKS
Aking Donut, Rik Aitch, Plimsoll, Frijid Pink, Roy Harper, Steve Naylor Confirmed For Festival – Dylan, Who, Zappa Rumoured

feelfreefeelfreefeelfreefeelfreefeelfreefeelfreefeel

♥ love ♥ peace ♥ good vibes ♥
and
ROCK ROCK ROCK ROCK

Trulee Great Gigs present

PIDGIN ENGLISH • TINNED PEACHES • FRANK ZAPPA
PLIMSOLL • BLIND FAITH • AKING DONUT • FRIJID PINK
ROY HARPER • STEVE NAYLOR • EXCESSIVE MELANGE

and many many more

at Wragby Hall
five days of tuning in freaking out and turning on

19 – 24 July 1969

feelfreefeelfreefeelfreefeelfreefeelfreefeelfreefeel

5-DAY TICKET £12.50
SINGLE DAY £3.00
CARPARK 50 pence
Camping space £2.00 per night ♥ Sleeping Bag Hire 25p per night
Tents 75p per night ♥ Polythene Groundsheets 20p ♥
T-Shirts 50p ♥ Joss Sticks 25p a set ♥ Burgers ♥
Fortune Tellers ♥ Soul Food ♥ Hot Dogs ♥ Posters All Available

feelfreefeelfreefeelfreefeelfreefeel

From the taped diary of Dodo Dixon, 18 July 1969

Wragby: Weeeeeee-haaaah! Yeah – it's a tie-up and tomorrow should be a freak-out, right? You got it. Talk about GAS-GAS-GAS! Yeah – maaaan!

If I can get my head round this tape recorder … right. OK. Cool…

Everything's set for tomorrow – stage up, electrics cool, bands all present and correct, Major, la-di-da-di-da. Even the odd hundred rock freaks have arrived, camping out beyond the gates. Looks all set to be a smackerooni – yeee-haah! Stand to make, hmmmmm, lemme see, 50, 90, plus 25, 70, take away nananana – yeah, upwards of 100 grand – or 200 grand if the live album's a triple.

I'm resting my boots in Wragby Hall itself – as specified in contract, tee hee. Not a bad old place, s'pose, if you don't mind cobwebs and scratchy baths. Also here is – or should I say are, if we're being AWFULLY POSH, DON'T YER KNOW, also here *are:*

Sir Clifford Chatterley – grumpy old grandad who owns the shithole and is about as unturned on as you can be, wheelchair and all.

Sir Asquith Harcourt – in-house lawyer I pay a load of bread every year to make me an even bigger load of bread – too right.

Rik Aitch – the only superbloodystar big enough to deserve a comfy bed in a statelybloodyhome. He may be a superstar, but his albums aren't selling a bundle, mind – there's been no chart activity on the *The Crimson Virgin Takes Breakfast in Sierra Leone* album for six weeks, and the single did zilch. Remarketing, repackaging, reselling – that's what Rik needs, but whenever did Rik know what Rik needed, I ask my bloody self!?

Rik's chick, Dandelion – cool.

Vernon Huff – legendary mind-expanding Canadian poet and free spirit, 'The Voice of the Sixties', you can say that again, who might just appear with Plimsoll in an improvisational sound-poem he's specially written for Saturday.

And here's the great news – John and Yoko, that's right, JOHN AND YOKO have said they might drop by – talk about far out. Sir Cliff's vacating the master bedroom just for them. Looks like being some kind of groovy scene – yeaah!

From the diary of Sir Clifford Chatterley, 18 July 1969

Frightful shower here, courtesy Barclays Bank. The dread Dixon told me with his mouth full during dinner that he had some quite *great* news. 'John and Yoko might just be joining us,' he said.

'What?' I snapped.

'John and Yoko. I'll be putting them in your room, Cliff, the Pink Room, if that's OK by you. And I'll be getting one of the roadies to repaint it white. They're very *into* white are John and Yoko.'

'Well they can get *out of* white pretty damn sharpish,' I barked, 'and they're *not* having my room – the cost of fumigation would prove astronomic.'

At this point, the shitty noov solicitor Asquith Harcourt motioned over, all slimey and toad-like. 'A word, if I may, Sir Clifford,' he said. He thrust me into a corner and pulled out the contract. 'May I draw your particular attention to clause 235(b),' he slimed.

From page 33, Contract between Sir Clifford Chatterley and Contrax Inc., dated 7 May 1969

... event of the sudden deaths of any of the artistes the lower ground floor of the PROPERTY may be employed as a makeshift hospital and/or mortuary. Clearance of vomit, and/or blood and/or OTHER shall be the SOLE AND EXCLUSIVE responsibility of the LEASEE.

235(b): OCCUPIER shall be PERMITTED TO remain in residence for the duration ON CONDITION THAT he be prepared to SURRENDER all rooms, facilities and operations at the request of and to THE LEASEE without PRIOR NOTICE.

235(c): All NOISE within the PROPERTY including SHOUTING, INFORMAL DISAGREEMENT AND EXTRANEOUS BODILY SOUNDS issued between the ABOVE NAMED dates is the sole and rightful property of the LEASEE and shall not be RECORDED for commercial or private use without WRITTEN AUTHORITY.

From the diary of Sir Clifford Chatterley, 18 July 1969

'Very well then,' I muttered with all the dignity I could muster, 'but there'll be a complete change of sheets once they've pissed off, bag or no bloody bag.'

So I packed up my stuff and wheeled myself down the corridor to the Yellow Room. Just as I was about to push open the door out popped a half-naked young lady, clad in some sort of Arabian head-dress. Behind her I could make out the silhouette of a body lying prostrate upon the floor, off-putting, vaguely pig-like sounds – grunt, groan, grunt, groan, oink, oink, oink – emerging from its every orifice.

'It's Rik,' she said.

'Is it indeed?' I commented drily.

''E's bloody chokin' on 'is own vomit – bloody fetch Dodo!'

'Dodo ... Dodo ... remind me?' I said.

'Quick!' she said, 'Dodo Dixon!'

'Ah!' I said, 'The Delectable Mr Dixon!'

'Fetch 'im!' she said.

Dixon himself then appeared from nowhere, perhaps alerted by the piggy-noises still emerging from the Yellow (now alas even more Yellow) Room.

''Ello, 'ello, 'ello – what goin' on 'ere then?' he said in a dreadfully unjocular voice, imitating, I shouldn't wonder, his oiky namesake from the gogglebox.

'Oh my God!' said the Arabian lady.

'Speaking,' said Dixon.

'It's Rik – it's Rik – I think he's drowning in his own vomit!'

'Ho hum,' said Dixon, 'ho hum.'

From the taped diary of Dodo Dixon, 18 July 1969

'Ho hum,' says I, 'ho hum.'

To be straight-up, I was playing for time. When I heard all those splurges and gurgles coming from upstairs, I thought to myself 'Rik up to his old tricks again', only this time it sounded for real. And then it struck me.

Don't get me wrong. No way did I want Rik to peg it. No, man – no way, José. It's just that, well, put it this way, if the two of us together and totally in unison, Rik and Dodo, Dodo and Rik, were to figure out an effective marketing strategy – that's a strategy incorporating a thorough rethink, repackage, redesign and relaunch – then for the whole international sales thing it would be more effective if Rik was in a basic Dead Karma/On His Way to Nirvana situation. You only have to look at the soar in the sales chart of Bryan Shinn's album after he wrapped himself around that tree to see that a tragic death can be highly beneficial to the career structure of the artist involved, are you with me?

So 'Ho hum,' I said, and again, 'Ho hum, ho hum.'

From the diary of Sir Clifford Chatterley, 18 July 1969

Even to my own jaundiced ears, the expression 'ho hum' is too casual a response to the sound of a 'pop' star choking on his own vomit, though Dixon at least took the trouble to enunciate it in multiples of three. As his gurgles seemed to be dribbling to an end I found myself speaking up for the poor chap on the floor. 'Shouldn't we do something?' I asked.

From the taped diary of Dodo Dixon, 18 July 1969

'"Shouldn't We Do Something" – hey, what a fantastic title for a rock song – or even a Concept Album!' I said, trying to lighten the atmosphere. At that moment, the whole truth of the situation came to me in a totally far-out flash – 'Shouldn't We *Do* Something: A Memorial Tribute Album to Rik Aitch by His Rock 'n' Roll Family', recorded live at a Benefit Concert, maybe at the Albert Hall.

'I think Rik may be dead,' I said, playing for time. Then I delivered a few sincere, heartfelt words I thought up out the top of my head, like they were *inspired* by some higher being, some Godhead. 'Oh my God, he was like a brother to me – a real brother – a brother.' Then I paused tastefully before saying, 'Anyone here got the number of an undertaker? Might be worth giving 'em a bell – bound to be too busy in the morning.'

From the diary of Sir Clifford Chatterley, 18 July 1969

Pitter-patter on the stairs and up pops the little shit Asquith Harcourt, glass in hand, to find out what all the commotion is about.

'Dead? *dead*?' he says. 'The moment I set eyes on that young man I knew he'd be trouble.'

'How dare you?!' said the dolly-bird, her bountiful globes swinging to and fro beneath her flimsy dressing-gown. 'He was voted third fastest guitarist in the world by a panel of *New Musical Express* experts the year before last! Rik was a bloody GENIUS!' The dolly was visibly distraught, the odd tear tastily gathering on the protuberances of her dressing-gown, lending it a delicious moist translucency.

'Rik came THIRD, he did – behind Alvin Lee of Ten Years After

who was first and ... and ... ooh, I could kill myself sometimes –
memory like a sieve – now who the hell was second? It wasn't Clapton,
no, and it wasn' ... ooh, it'll irritate me all day if I don't get it, you
know how these things *do*.'

'George Formby?' I ventured, 'Or is he banjo? Old hat, no doubt.' I
wheeled over to the poor thing, placing my hand on her lower back
purely by way of comfort.

'I think it was that one in King Crimson – erm, erm – is it Dave
something?' she replied.

At this point Dixon, who had been affecting an interest in the body
on the floor, chipped in with a frantic yell.

'Nah!' he said, 'Nah waaay! Dave thingy couldn't even brush his
teeth with a guitar, let alone play the crappy thing!!!'

'Stop it – you're making me giggle!' chuckled the young lady. She
seemed to be getting over the tragedy with admirable speed.

From the Coroner's Report into the death of Rik Aitch, 20–22 August 1969

Having heard the testimony of all those who were with this unfortunate
young man at the time of his death, I am quite satisfied that everything
that could be done was done to save him. He was, if I may say so, very
lucky to have his friends with him at the time of his death, and I have
no doubt that, had they not been at hand, he would have passed away
very much sooner.

From the taped diary of Dodo Dixon, 18 July 1969

It must have been something about her giggle, 'cos I thought to myself
for the very first time, 'Jeee-serrs – you're one helluva tasty chick.'

'It wasn't Mike Crane of Locomotive Espadrille was it?' I said. And
as I said it, a noise like a toilet draining comes from the body of Rik on
the floor, drowning out all conversation. 'Ta, Rik – ta very much – just
when I was making headway,' I thought.

'Sorry,' says Dandelion, 'Mike who-did-you-say? I didn't catch that
through the noise. Mike Caine? He's an actor, i'n't he? Met him once.
Ever so *genuine*.'

'Mike Caine? 'Course he's an actor. Brilliant actor,' I said, 'and a
personal friend, as it happens. Far-out bloke. You and me must have

lunch with Mike one day, girl, when you're in town.'

'BLUURGGHHH!' went Rik on the floor – or words to that effect!
– talk about attention-grabbing! – and we all took the trouble to look
down.

'The wretched fellow's gone purple!' said old man Shotterley.

'That's it!' I said, 'I've got it! I've got it!'

'Wot you on abaht?' said Dandelion.

'Purple! *Deep Purple!* – it was the guitarist with Deep Purple who
came second. Jon someone, isn't it?'

'Houseman?' said Dandelion.

'No – he's organ. Well, keyboards actually. Personal friend.'

'Does he begin with V?' she was saying and we were just getting a
really good thing going when Asquith butts in.

'Drugs, was it?' says Asquith.

'Well, I don't know, do I?' I said.

'You and the girl had better search the room top to bottom – every
last inch. The last thing we need just before the festival starts is a
scandal. And if someone could lay their hands on some rubber gloves,
I'll deal with the corpse.'

From the Coroner's Report into the death of Rik Aitch, 20–22 August 1969

I was most impressed, and, indeed, if I may say so, highly *moved* by the
evidence delivered to this court with such very great detail by the
distinguished solicitor Sir Harcourt Asquith, and I would like here and
now to place on permanent record the court's appreciation of the
immense dignity he brought to the handling of his grim ordeal.

From the diary of Sir Clifford Chatterley, 18 July 1969

What a shower! As the unmourned Rik breathed his last – stains
everywhere – and as Dixon and the young lady looked for the whole
shooting-match of pills and powders, I searched high and low for a pair
of rubber gloves, rummaging through every drawer and cubby-hole in
the kitchen, scouring every shelf, even rootling around in the darkest
corner of the larder.

How I loathe poking about in the stubborn detritus of the past! Many of those drawers contained bits and pieces – ribbons, a shopping list, keys, a set of stamps, a locket, a sprig of hair in an envelope, a calendar, five buttons, an address scribbled on a piece of newspaper – that had lain there for half a century, reminders of a time when I was halfway happy. Oh, Connie – why did you throw it away – and all for that burpy, big-bottomed gamekeeper?

But I digress.

I was bustling around, thinking these soppy thoughts, when who should shuffle into the kitchen but Harcourt Asquith, dragging behind him the fully expired body of the ex 'pop' star, looking scarcely more attractive dead than alive.

'I would be greatly in your debt, Sir Clifford,' said Asquith, tugging the body onto the kitchen table, 'If you would be so good as to lay your hands on a variety of common-or-garden kitchen utensils. Let me write you a list.'

From a handwritten list of kitchen utensils presented by Sir Harcourt Asquith to Sir Clifford Chatterley on the evening of 18 July 1969

1 pr Pliers
1 Sharp Knife (Carving)
Cake Icing Dispenser (incorporating pumping action)
Soap, Hot Water, Bucket (large)
1 family-sized packet of large mixed nuts

From the coroner's report into the death of Rik Aitch, 20–22 August 1969

I am perfectly satisfied through listening to the expert medical evidence vouchsafed to this court by Doctors Peppard and McGregor together with a thorough examination of those present that the deceased passed away after choking on a selection of mixed nuts that had somehow caught in his throat. I am also anxious to correct any suggestion there may have been in the mass media of any evidence whatsoever that Mr Aitch had taken any drugs that evening. His body was quite clear of any harmful substances or substances of a suspicious nature, and a full and thorough search of his bedroom, his vehicle and the surrounding premises by the senior officers from the Tevershall police yielded not one iota of evidence to support this malicious allegation.

Melody Maker British Album Top 10 Chart, week ending 29 November 1969

1 (3)   *Shouldn't We Do Something: A Memorial Tribute to Rik Aitch from His Rock 'n' Roll Family and Friends*
        Various Artistes (Firecracker)
2 (1)   *Let It Bleed*
        The Rolling Stones (Decca)
3 (2)   *Locomotive Espadrille 111*
        Locomotive Espadrille (Electra)
4 (5)   *Live Peace in Toronto*
        The Plastic Ono Band (Apple)
5 (4)   *Two Little Boys and other Ballads*
        Rolf Harris (Decca)
6 (9)   *Towards Nirvana in an Oracle*
        Groundsheet Disarray (CBS)
7 (7)   *The Very Best of Bryan Shinn and Friends*
        Bryan Shinn (Harvest)
8 (–)   *Have Yourself a Perry Merry Christmas*
        Perry Como (ROA)
9 (12) *Live and Raw*
        Aking Donut (Firecracker)
10 (–) *Stoned Again 2*
        Excessive Melange (Deram)

(*The figure in brackets indicates last week's chart position*)

From the Coroner's Report into the death of Rik Aitch, 20–22 August 1969

I will end with one final word of warning. If manufacturers of luxury comestibles wish to continue to produce bags of Assorted Nuts, they should take steps to ensure that they are of a size and shape to enable easy swallowing. No bag of mixed nuts, however tasty, is worth a young man's life.

From the taped diary of Dodo Dixon, 19 July 1969

Tragic death, legend struck down in the very nadir of his youth, don't know how the world of rock will recover, God's gained one helluva great vocalist in Heaven, and all that. But it did make a truly beee-ooo-diful start to the Festival, just beee-ooo-diful.

At midday, when the freaks and the chicks and the heads and the hippies had all got their heads round the ticket system – we had a pig estimate of a literally amazing fifty-bloody-thousand, not bad for the first day – and the old guy doing 'one two, one two, one two, can you hear me? One two, one two, can you hear me?' had finally come to an end, we had Jerry Staines of Groundsheet Disarray come on dressed all in white wearing the eye of Vishnu on his forehead and, like, he called for ten minutes total but total silence.

From *Sounds*, issue 68, week ending 27 July, report on Wragby International Rock Festival by Jez Theakston

... Jerry comes on, the White God, clad all in white, head to foot in white, the colour of the clouds, the colour of peace, the colour of all our dreams, yours and mine and Rik's.

'This festival,' he says, 'is dedicated to the memory of a great guy and a great vocalist and, as I said, a great guy and a truly great vocalist. A really great guy, and a really truly great vocalist, one of the greatest all-round guys and vocalists there's ever been – and this festival is dedicated to the memory of him. One helluva great guy and one helluva great vocalist, that's what you were, Rik. Great. So I want you all to give Rik and his memory ten minutes complete and utter silence. Can you do that for me? Can you?'

And we – the audience – who loved Rik when he was alive and love him even more now he's dead – we all shout back as in one voice, 'Yeeaah!' And the White God answers, 'Come on – I wanna hear you say 'Yeah!'

And we raise our voices to the skies above and go, 'YEEAAAH!'

And the White God smiles and he raises both his hands to the heavens and he yells, 'C'mon – put your hands together and feel the beat if you want silence – silence for Rik.'

And we all clap like we've never bloody clapped before. Clapping for silence. Silence for Rik. And then – 'one, two, one two, one two, one two' – they were tuning the sound up for over forty-three hours of beautiful, beautiful music.

From the diary of Sir Clifford Chatterley, 21 July 1969

Why the hell must that awful man drone 'one two, one two, one two, one two, can you hear me, one two, one two, one two' all the bloody time? I was sitting tucking into lunch in the Hall, earplugs firmly in place, quietly cooing over my achievement in avoiding sight or sound of the racket in the grounds when the creep Dixon burst in, all horrid smiles. He bounced up, pulled off the earplugs and dropped his biggest bombshell yet.

'John and Yoko!' he said, uttering the three most vile words in the English language. 'Beautiful news! They'll be arriving by helicopter just before dinner tonight. SplendEEEdo, as my old mum would say! Of course, Yoko's said all the food must be coloured orange, so we'll be having mainly carrots and swedes and bananas and opal fruits, if that's all right by you, squire.'

'Bananas aren't orange,' I said.

'Best get some food dye in, Cliff,' he replied. 'They'll be in the Pink bedroom, don't forget, so best get it ship-shape for them – nothing overdone, mind, they hate anything being made *too* tidy for them – they're very ORDINARY people, John and Yoko, they'd hate to think they were being treated any different just because they're geniuses. Just make sure it's painted orange, eh? Oh, and make sure there's plenty of room for their bag on your bed, that's a love – thanks, Cliff!'

I thought I was going to be sick. The hairy-scaries in *my* bed! 'One two, one two, one two, one two,' went the man again, and back in went my plugs.

From the taped diary of Dodo Dixon, 21 July 1969

Clifford seemed pretty bloody chuffed that John and Yoko would actually be sleeping in his bedroom: not often anything of interest happens at Wragby Hall, I'd say. Funny old bloke, Cliff, but I know he digs me, and that's cool. I've earned his trust, you could say.

While Groundsheet Disarray were playing a truly amazing set (beautiful licks from Rin Tin Tin on lead), Vernon Huff turns up, totally magic as always. Not only is he the greatest Canadian poet of all time and a totally free spirit, but he's also a very, very deep personal friend of John and Yoko. He told me he arrives everywhere in advance of them, just to make sure the Karma is right, and could he have a list of everyone who'd be staying at the Hall tonight, with brief job descriptions, identifying traits, personality disorders if any etc., just so's John and Yoko would know who they're booked to rap with. Vernon said he'd be dropping by the Hall around 18.15 hours, after his set, and, like, it would make him very very very happy if I'd see that all the guests were assembled for John and Yoko's arrival by air at approximately 19.00 hours GMT, just to talk them through their positions, fill them in on how to behave when presented, not forgetting all the dos and don'ts etc. Whatever happened, John and Yoko didn't want the red carpet laid on: they much preferred orange. Sure, Vernon, I said: I'll personally escort you to the Hall after your set, 'cos I'd hate to miss it, I really would. And then he took off his dark glasses and smiled a truly warm smile. 'Merci bien, fellow spirit,' he said, and shook me warmly with both hands. What a beautiful guy.

Poem from *Telegrams from a Childlike Heart: The Collected Poems of Vernon Huff* (Faber & Faber, 1973)

rub your yearning breasts against the body

rub your yearning breasts against the body
of this sad poet
and his dreams
my love

and think of ezra and samuel and walt
before you call a halt
to your touch
my love

and think of me, as sad as they
as you bestride me, every day
hey, hey, hey,
my love
and whisper my verse as i reach my peak
for i love those words that once i speak
-ed,
my love

(*chorus:*)
for i am the prince of darkness and light
and i am the fire which comes in the night
for i am the poet flamed by sorry kisses
and i am the wind whistling through your orifices
my love

From the taped diary of Dodo Dixon, 22 July 1969

'Beautiful, just ... *beautiful* –' I said to Vernon as he came off stage after his sixth encore, no less, ' – the freaks just totally *loved* you.'

'You know, Dodo,' he replied, 'There's a line in one of my early poems – you probably know it – which goes: "Love is the caged goat with the vanilla ice-cream". And that feeling repeated itself very strongly to my soul *aujourdhui, mon ami.*'

'"The caged goat with the vanilla ice-cream"', I said, rolling those beautiful words around my tongue. 'Yeah you're right, Vernon, you're absolutely right.'

'The time now is 18.10 hours,' he said, looking at his watch. 'We have five minutes *exactement* to get to the Hall.'

From the diary of Sir Clifford Chatterley, 22 July 1969

By six o'clock, I had cleared out of the Pink Room and wheeled myself through the thin door to the dressing-room, where I would bed down for the night. I only hoped I would hear the bare minimum of oinks and grunts from the Gruesome Twosome through the adjoining door.

At roughly ten past, just as I was attempting to play the National Anthem on Aitch's abandoned 'electric' guitar, the oily git Asquith knocked at the door to tell me I was expected downstairs for a short talk by a Mr Huff. 'Must I?' I groaned. And out popped the contract from his upper pocket, a gnarled, tobacco-laden finger pointing to Clause 13 (*a*).

From page 9, Contract between Sir Clifford Chatterley and Contrax Inc., dated 7 May 1969

... though any bodily excretions, smears or stains of any sort, type or variety on the carpet situated in the basement (see plan of Hall) prior to the onset of this Contract are the sole responsibility of the PROPRIETOR.

13 (a): If the PROPRIETOR elects to remain resident in the Hall over the duration of the Period specified, he will be afforded due notification of any gathering, meeting, discussion group or conference taking place on said premises.

From the diary of Sir Clifford Chatterley, 22 July 1969

'Aha!' I yelped delightedly, 'No need, then!'

'What on earth do you mean – "no need"?' replied Asquith, 'There's every need.'

'It says here I will be afforded due notification,' I replied, 'But it does not say that I am obliged to attend.'

'Read 13 (*b*),' he said.

From page 9, Contract between Sir Clifford Chatterley and Contrax Inc., dated 7 May 1969

(*b*) at which his presence is obligatory, mandatory and compulsory, even if such a gathering, meeting, discussion group or conference is neither to his taste nor convenience.

From the taped diary of Dodo Dixon, 22 July 1969

Vernon took us through our paces totally bloody brilliantly. The seven of us got it together in the hall (that's in the hall of The Hall – nice one Dodo!) – Asquith, Clifford, my own good self, Vernon and the lovely Dandelion, who's responding with such amazing courage to the wholly tragic etc., death of her former etc. the legendary etc. Rik Aitch, grateful always for a helping hand (or should that be *hands* – only kidding!)

'Good evening, Ladies and Gentlemen,' began Vernon in that same beautiful mellow brown voice that brought us those totally outasight poems 'Let My Body Be Your Umbrella' and 'The Hand of the Poet in Your Back Pocket'. 'As you will know by now, we are all very proud and privileged to be honoured with the prospect of a visit in less than an hour's time from my good friends and fellow poets Mr John Lennon and his good lady Miss Yoko Ono. For your interest, I believe it is their very first visit to a stately home since their recent marriage in Gibraltar, which makes it very, very special indeed.

'As you are about to discover, John and Yoko are very ordinary, real-life human beings, very down-to-earth and with a beautiful sense of humour. They have asked me to say that they very much hope and expect that you will all continue to be yourselves throughout the weekend, even if and when you are actually asked to converse with them. Actually, while we are on that subject, may I earnestly request that none of you engage them in conversation without first being specifically requested to. This is to facilitate their own expressed wish to exchange head-thoughts with as many of you as possible over the course of the weekend: any unnecessary or unrequested conversation can cause interruption to the general vibes, right?

'I will now ask my good friend Mr Dodo Dixon to distribute these specially printed information sheets for your help and guidance. Finally, it only remains for me to say that John and Yoko are very much looking forward to their visit to Wragby Hall, and they sincerely hope to get a chance to speak to each one of you in person. Your co-operation in this matter is much appreciated. Peace.'

Official Information Sheet for those meeting Mr John Lennon and Miss Yoko Ono, year ending 1970

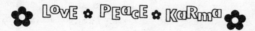

a) John and Yoko are your brother and sister. 'I am you and you are me and we are all together.' Please bear in mind at all times that they do not expect to be treated in any way differently from ordinary human beings.

b) With the moon now in Aries and Saturn enveloping the Magician's scales as the horse's leg enters the wheel of the Giant Astral Cyclist, John and Yoko trust you will wear at least one (1) item of orange clothing about your person at all times.

c) No sardines or shellfish are to be brought into or consumed within the Hall or its grounds. They are bad karma.

d) Use of cameras or tape-recorders is strictly forbidden.

e) Yoko specifically requests that while Jupiter remains in partnership with Neptune words beginning with the following letters:

q   b   p   d

should be avoided in conversation wherever possible.

f) When addressed by John and/or Yoko, answer them perfectly naturally – but *please, please, please* – keep your replies as succinct as possible. They are understandably anxious to fit as many of you in as possible, and time spent in listening to replies is time wasted in reaching out to the next beautiful soul.

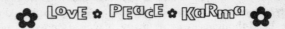

From the diary of Sir Clifford Chatterley, 22 July 1969

The bloated puffball Huff then ordered us out onto the main lawn, where my beloved beech hedges had been pulled up to make a perfectly hideous 'helipad', with grubby sheets and so forth stapled in an 'X' to the turf.

Outside, the sound of the 'pop festival' blaring brahbrahbrahbrah – from the other side of the wood was quite dreadful. Earplug time. There is nothing more loathly than a primitive rhythm.

So hideous was the prevailing noise that the racket made by the approaching helicopter came as a pleasant and comparatively musical relief. After much swirling, the helicopter landed, blowing my hat off as it did so. 'Please form an orderly line, ladies and gentlemen,' Mr Huff yelled through his megaphone at the four of us.

After a few minutes, the blades of the helicopter ceased their ridiculous swirl. Two open Land Rovers painted in all the colours of the rainbow – and, I may say, many wisely rejected from the rainbow – drove across the lawn, creating deep trenches of dirt. 'That's my bloody lawn!' I shouted angrily, at which the shit Asquith dived into his briefcase and pulled out his sheaf of papers: '92(*a*)' he said, pointing at it with his sinister forefinger.

From page 24, Contract between Sir Clifford Chatterley and Contrax Inc., dated 7 May 1969

```
... bandages, though needles and syringes other
than for purposes of medicine are to be provided by
the LICENSEE.
92(a) The main lawn (see MAP) is to be made avail-
able at all times for vehicular access. Maintenance
and repair of the lawn consequent to such access
will be borne by the LICENSEE. The area is to be at
all times kept free of birds, worms and other
animals.
```

From the diary of Sir Clifford Chatterley, 22 July 1969

The idiocy of it all! The doors of the helicopter opened. One Land Rover was stationed directly beneath them, and another, close to, seemed to possess some form of small crane with a net attached. With the greatest of care, as if it contained a shipment of the finest claret, a very large bag from the helicopter was manoeuvred into the net, then heaved into position on the back of the other Land Rover.

'Ladies and Gentlemen,' shouted Mr Huff through his megaphone, 'Please welcome two of the most beautiful souls on this global planet – John Lennon and Yoko Ono!' He began applauding with unwarranted vigour. Judging by his effortful glare, he wanted us all to follow suit. I wondered where I stood legally on the clapping front, and vowed not to move a muscle until I saw the whites of their eyes.

'So where the hell are they? Where *are* they?' I yelled over the noise at Asquith.

'In the bag,' he replied, 'They're in the bag.'

'One two,' came the noise from the distance, 'one two, one two, can you hear me?'

Postcard from Dandelion to her mother, 22 July 1969

Dear Mummy
Today I met John and Yoko they were in a bag for peace so I coudlnt see them and they were asleep so I coudlnt spik to them but they were reely freindly. They are staying in the bag until war ends which is nice. By the way, rik died tragically dont worry I've got a new boyfriend he's luvvly and his names called Dodo.

From the taped diary of Dodo Dixon, 22 July 1969

Faaaar OUT! The truck drove them to the front of the Hall, where we managed to lever their bag and carry them in. You could just about make out the outlines of their heads and maybe their feet but that was all. Then Vernon read them his Poem of Welcome. He said he had written it in 'soft, loving, lovely' words to 'enter like the whispers of the angels' into their sleep, 'steal into their deeper unconscious'. Talk about mellow.

From *Telegrams from a Childlike Heart: The Collected Poems of Vernon Huff* (Faber & Faber, 1973)

this flower i have picked

Written to welcome
my good friends John and Yoko,
Free spirits in a bag,
to Wragby Hall,
in the magical month of July, in the year
nineteen hundred and sixty-nine

this flower i have picked
to remind you of me

this flower i have picked
has a long neck and blue eyes

this flower i have picked
has a dark brown voice

this flower i have picked
wears jeans and deplores injustice

this flower i have picked
wears shades and reads the prophet by kahlil gibran

this flower i have picked
loves too much and shudders at the pain of others

you see
this flower i have picked
for you

                   is

                        me.

From the taped diary of Dodo Dixon, 22 July 1969

The poem was so soulful I don't mind telling you, man, it knocked me backwards and when Vernon recited that amazing last verse – 'You see/ this flower i have picked/ for you is/ me' it knocked me sideways and the tears were rolling down these cheeks of mine, just rolling down. And I have to tell you, even old Cliff was obviously moved, wheeling himself around while Vernon was reading, and grunting in all the right places. So when it was all over and we were totally knocked out and he said, 'Can I go now?' I knew – and he knew that I knew – that he wanted to go into a corner on his own and lose himself in the words and sob and sob and sob and sob for all the sorrow in the world, and all the joy: some poem!

From the diary of Sir Clifford Chatterley, 22 July 1969

The 'poem' was frightful old garbage, tried and tested pardon-me-while-I-vomit stuff. By the end of it I was wheeling myself around with impatience. 'Can I go now?' I barked to Dixon – who to his credit looked simply bored stiff; I could see that he knew exactly what I thought of the whole piss-awful charade.

From the taped diary of Dodo Dixon, 22 July 1969

'We must please ensure that when my good friends John and Yoko awake themselves from their princely slumbers they find themselves in their bedroom upstairs,' said Vernon, 'So we must transport their bag with perfect gentleness up this flight of stairs, at all times ensuring we never disturb their heavenly dreams of Peace for all mankind. Do any of you good people have any idea as to how we might manage their smooth ascension to the upper heavens?'

'We have a dumb waiter in the kitchen,' grunted Clifford. 'That's how I always get up.'

'Please, Clifford – *please*. No man who waits upon another should ever be described as 'dumb' – we are all *humans*, Clifford; we all live and breathe; we all love, we all smell the sweet scent of flowers, we all feel the sun's rays shimmer slowly and surely over our skins; we all die and are then reborn. We are brothers and sisters, and those who are waiters possess many values – of obedience, humility, devotion – denied to those of us suffering above them. So please, Cliff, please – never let me hear you say "dumb waiter" again.'

'Nevertheless,' said Clifford, 'We have a dumb waiter in the kitchen.'

'Who is this little guy? Who the goddamn hell *is* he? Could someone get him outta my sight? I don't want to see him *ever* again! He's getting

right up my goddamn nose! Push him *out* of here, someone! I said *out!*
Vernon seemed a bit cross.

'Vernon,' I said, 'Cool it, brother! A dumb waiter's a lift.'

'A lift?'

'An elevator.'

'An elevator? An elevator? Right. Right. So why didn't you tell me?
Beautiful. So why were you fucking me around, Cliff? An elevator. An
elevator! Great. Let's cool it. An elevator. Jee-zus! Easy, now, easy.'

Vernon started taking deep, deep breaths. 'If these two precious
spirits aren't on that dumb elevator within two minutes, my heart will
just implode from too much caring, d'y'hear?'

From the diary of Sir Clifford Chatterley, 23 July 1969

A most extraordinary night. 'Yeah All Right Yeah Yeah' 'Bang Bang
Lovely World of Peace Bang Bang Bang' and yet more 'One two, one
two, can you hear me, one two' had come drifting into my room from
the bloody festival even with windows bolted, earplugs on and curtains
drawn tight, so I was even more livid at being woken up again an hour
or two later by the sound of mumble-mumble coming from the next-
door room – *my* bloody bedroom you long-haired gits, I felt like
shouting.

I switched on the bedside light. It was 3.15 in the morning, a terrible
time of day, even worse than all the others. Mutter, mutter, mutter.
Trundle, trundle, trundle. Lennon and the Wine Gum have finally
woken up, I thought, and they're celebrating the occasion by emerging
from the bag and tootling about, to buggery with peace.

I switched the light back off and tried to get back to sleep by
counting hundreds of Beatles jumping off the tops of very high
buildings. But the sounds from my bedroom became more and more
animated: not just mutters and murmurs now but raised bloody voices,
and the clatter and crash of furniture and ornaments being moved
around. What the bloody heck are they up to? I wondered, banging my
fists three or four times hard against the wall.

My protests had an immediate effect. A sudden hush descended
upon the house, followed by a scampering like guilty mice, followed by
yet more hush. Once again, I settled back in the bed, patting myself on
the back for silencing the hairy-scaries, determined more than ever to
resume my sleep.

But sleep was not to be. After one minute – two minutes at most –

the murmurs started, and soon they had turned into solid devil-may-care banter. Another few seconds, and the old furniture removal operation was steaming ahead once again. I began to see red. By all means co-habit in a bag, by all means spend your time smooching with a nip while the rest of the world is struggling its damnedest to do an honest's day's work, but there's no excuse – none whatever – to start waking all and sundry by pissing around with the furniture at half past three in the morning. What in hell's name did they think they were they up to?

I'd never be without my glass of water by my bed. With one great glug, I downed all the water, put the open end of the tumbler to the adjoining door and had a jolly good listen in.

He: But it must be somewhere. Have you tried behind the mirror?
She: (*irritably*) Yes of course I have!
He: I only asked!

My immediate impression was that Yoko must have achieved a decent grade two on her elocution course. Her voice sounded quite grand, almost top drawer, and rather older than I had previously imagined.

She: (*indecipherable*) It must be in another room.
He: What d'y'mean, another room?
She: What do you mean, what do I mean, I mean what I say, another room, that's what I *mean*. It must be in another room.

And Lennon's voice, too, was not quite as *common* as one might have predicted, with no trace of that awful Liverpudlian to it. It was more what one might expect to emerge from the mouth of a jumped-up little fellow behind the desk at the bank in Tevershall, perhaps, or from an assistant at Fortnum's, the voice of a counter-jumper, a fellow who has spent his life in merciless pursuit of improving the poor hand dealt him by the Good Lord. And Lennon, too, sounded much older than I had imagined: too many drugs and late nights, I told myself.

She: If I had to guess I'd say the dressing-room.
He: Now she tells us! Hark at her! Come on!

With a start, I realised they were planning to move into my room. I had not the slightest inclination to interrupt their nosey-parkering with any sort of 'scene'. So I nipped back to bed, bravely resolving to feign sleep.

Seconds later, I heard the distinctive squeak and tink of the doorknob being turned, and the adjoining door swung open. One set of footsteps, then another. A Beatle and his wife were prowling about in my room – and there was bugger all I could do about it!

With my eyes tight shut, I set myself on a course of deep breaths.

She: Try the carpet!
He: Why the carpet?
She: Under the carpet!
He: It's too dark – I can't see!
She: I'll draw the curtains – there should be some moonlight. Ah – that's better. I can see you now!
He: Who's in the bed?
She: How should I know?
He: Have a look!

Her voice still had no hint of the nip about it. Likewise, his was miles away from the aroma of long, dirty greasy hair, silly coloured beads and oikish castanets that traditionally lingers around 'pop' singers. The voices, both his and hers, reminded me somehow of a time long, long ago ...

A floorboard creaked near the bed. I felt the gaze of someone upon me. I clenched my eyes ever tighter.

She: It's *him*! Oh my God!
He: Him? Him who?

I felt the covers of my bed being drawn back, but I kept my eyes firmly closed. The sound of muted sobs filled the bedroom. I squeezed open one eye until I could see the back of a woman sitting at the end of my bed, her head bowed low.

I felt my ire rising. Who the hell did they think they were? I half-opened an eye. Slowly, the door to my bedroom swung open a crack, and the light from the landing fell on to their faces.

GOOD LORD! There in front of me, sobbing vigorously, nearly fifty years older but barely changed since the day she said farewell, was the woman I had always loved. And there he stood, as uncouth as ever, naked as the day he was born, but fatter and chinnier and even more self-satisfied, reaching a hairy arm in her direction.

'Unhand my wife, Mellors, you grubby oik!' I snapped, struggling out of bed, wearing only my birthday suit ...

From a confession to the Police by Mr Oliver Mellors a.k.a Thomas, recorded on 23 July 1969

My name is Oliver Thomas. I am the owner and Chairman of the Thomas Supermarket chain, with over 250 stores across the United Kingdom and Europe. It might interest you to know that next month we plan to open a Thomas Hypermarket just outside Boston, Massachusetts, our first such venture in the United States of America. We are widely renowned for the high quality of our produce, and our insistence upon guaranteeing the consumer – what do you mean 'get on with it', Officer? Goodness me, Officer, I was only setting the scene, filling you in about myself, with a brief sketch of the achievements of myself and the company as a whole.

From the diary of Sir Clifford Chatterley, 23 July 1969

I had no doubt it was him. How many times had I watched him advertise his ghastly chain of 'supermarkets' on the telly, dressed in that horrid cheap suit with that over-red carnation, tossing his ghastly 'thumbs-up' sign to Housewives Everywhere?

From a confession to the Police by Mr Oliver Thomas, recorded on 23 July 1969

In 1967, all of us at Thomas supermarkets, staff and management alike, were proud to be selected for the Highly Commended category in the Queen's Award to British Industry. Partly on the strength of this accolade – but I *am* getting to the point, officer, I *am* getting to the point.

From the diary of Sir Clifford Chatterley, 23 July 1969

'What do you want here, anyway?' I asked, 'And why are you burrowing around like that? Clear off this minute, or I'll call the police!'

'You know what I want, you old bastard,' replied Mellors, 'I want my inheritance, that's what I want!'

'I – I – I don't know what on earth you are talking about,' I blustered, 'What's he getting at, Connie? I sometimes find these coarse accents awfully hard to decipher, don't you know?'

From a confession to the Police by Mr Oliver Thomas, recorded on 23 July 1969

Partly on the strength of this accolade, we were awarded the principal catering franchise at Gatwick Airport. Two days of my working week is devoted to overseeing this operation in a personal capacity, fine-tuning it for the benefit of customers and shareholders alike. Accordingly, Officer, it has developed into a very smooth-running affair affording welcome returns for the shareholders. I should add here that my wife, Mrs Constance Thomas, supervises our Fine Wines, Spirits and Beverages facilities at the airport, though she generally feels the need to sign off from her duties around midday.

Early in the morning of July 22nd 1969, I had occasion to be informed by the senior officer in Freight Transfer that a bag containing Mr John Lennon and Miss Yoko Ono in transit from Amsterdam to Wragby was temporarily delayed in a room off the VIP lounge, for which THOMAS SUPERMARKETS enjoyed exclusive catering rights. Realising a unique opportunity, I summoned my wife without further ado.

From the diary of Sir Clifford Chatterley, 23 July 1969

'You know what he wants, Clifford,' said Connie, her eyes straying to my manhood.

How old was she now? Seventy? Seventy-one? In so many ways she looked lovelier than ever, yet still she was in the smarmy grip of that flabby oaf.

'No idea, Connie. And I'd be pleased if you would ask him to kindly leave the house – or 'premises' as I believe they call it in the – ahem – *catering* industry.'

From a confession to the Police by Mr Oliver Thomas, recorded on 23 July 1969

We discovered the bag containing the above-mentioned personages at the location of which we had been earlier apprised by the senior officer. It was a large freight bag sitting upon a luggage trolley with no notable markings other than a large brown label bearing the inscription:

LENNON/ONO – WRAGBY

Listening at the bag, Mrs Thomas and myself could hear the breathing of two human beings, both apparently asleep. We wheeled the bag to a left-luggage locker of a size to ensure a snug fit. We were careful to pick a selection of Thomas own-brand products and place them in a corner of the locker. This high-quality premiere selection included one of our very popular ready-cooked chickens, two Mars-style Thomas Bars, a Packet of Thomas own-brand 15 per cent Swiss Muesi and, from our renowned delicatessen counter, a large packet of Thomas Ready-sliced Salami, Smokey Bacon flavour. Having seen to it that the couple in the bag would be in no danger of starvation, we took it upon ourselves to turn the key in their left-luggage locker, just to be on the safe side.

We then removed the large brown luggage label, placed it on a similar bag from Freight Handling, Placed it on the trolley and obtained accommodation for ourselves therein. Twenty minutes later, we felt ourselves being transferred to a helicopter bound for Wragby Hall.

We greatly regret any distress and/or embarrassment suffered by Mr Lennon and Miss Ono from our thoughtless action and would now wish to offer them our sincere apologies, together with the apologies of our staff and shareholders.

From the diary of Sir Clifford Chatterley, 23 July 1969

And then, as I reached for my crutches, my pillow slipped and the bugger caught sight of it.

'I'll be having that, thanking you kindly, Sir Clifford,' he said, grabbing at the envelope beneath where the pillow had been, fifty years in the catering business having done little to rub the edges off his uncouth manner.

'No you damn well won't!' I spluttered, giving him a good few swipes with a crutch, 'Give it here!'

'Argh! Urgh! Oof!' he replied, vulgarity itself. But still I could not dislodge the envelope from his hairy proletarian arms.

'I don't like your general attitude, labourer!' I said, swiping him again and again, 'If there's one thing – '

'Ooof!'

'I can't stick – '

'Ouch!'

' – it's an uppity member of the below-stairs class!'

'Urfgh!'

'SSSSHHHHH!' It was Connie, bidding us be quiet. Outside the door we heard the clear sound of footsteps.

What if they were discovered in my presence? Dixon would raise hell that they weren't the Wine Gum and Husband, I would be seen as conniving in the subterfuge, Asquith would declare my contract null and void, and all that cash – and Wragby itself – would be pissed down the drain!

'Quick! Into the bag!' I whispered. The three of us – me on my crutches – then rushed through the adjoining door and Connie and Mellors clambered into the wretched bag. It was then that I glimpsed the envelope still in his sweaty hands. 'You're going nowhere without me!' I hissed, and threw myself in too.

From *Melody Maker*, issue 1764, 25 July 1969

WRAGBY WROCKS – 6

Tony P. Scaggs finds his brains totally blown out on the final day at Wragby

The morning started at 10.30 with a dynamic set from Black Zebra Cushion which recalled the late Incey Spider at his heroic best, a cacophony of intellectual pyrotechnics and sheer bloody honest-to-goodness brilliance which made Jim Hendrix look like, well, Jimi Hendrix. What was it Friedrich Nietzsche said about noise? I forget now, but, whatever it was, BZC were right up there with it, ironically hammering our eardrums for all they were worth so's we could find their imperishable message of urban disintegration pounding through our entire bodies, not just our heads. Frankly, I put their guitarist Jimmy Shoehorn up there with the all-time greats Alvin Lee and the (tragically) late Skid Roe not to mention the God Clapton whose next album incidentally promises to be a thorough-going trip. To my mind, Jimmy Shoehorn doesn't just play the guitar, he really and truly *plays* it, so that by the end of the set nothing is left of it except – ironically – what was always there in the first place. Their version of the seminal 'My Babe (Is My Babe)' must surely now be counted as definitive, and if the howl of sheer incarcerated pain that is their new album 'Don't Give Me No Don'ts' (Apple) doesn't bring the war in Vietnam to an end, then nothing will, though, ironically, lead singer Jeff Boxx claims it's not intended to be so much a scorching howl of pain against the Vietnam War as a gentle and loving tribute to his new chick Maisie who now plays with the band on tambourine and occasional castanets.

Up next were Aspirant Pickle, five tons of raw powerhouse post-

Proustian bluegrass to my mind influenced by the foghorn rhythms of Gentile Headache and borrowing ironically from the original heavy missile tones of Heads, Hands and Feet in their late-Jamesian phase, before the tragic death of Ace Kirk after accidentally eating a dinner service two years ago come November. Bloody marvellous set, lads, with totally but totally compelling Leavisite vocals from Tom Rash that made my heart leap up my throat and out through my nostrils.

By now it was getting on for noon, and the legendary Vernon Huff, poet, visionary, thinker and general all-round bloody genius came on and nearly 100,000 people stood and cheered like crazy. 'Friends,' he said, 'I wanna to read you a poem. And during that poem, something kinda beautiful is gonna happen. During that poem, a bag is going to be brought on the stage. And that bag, friends – that bag is the most beautiful bag in the world. Because in that bag are the two most beautiful people in the world because in that bag, Ladies and Gentlemen are, yeah, I'm telling you – John Lennon and Yoko Ono!'

The heads went out of their heads, recalling the amazing ovation they had given Friday's set by Sean O'Evil on his first comeback gig since the tragic death of drummer Bo Palmer after his car crashed into another car when they were both driving in the same hotel swimming-pool six months ago. And then, when the applause had died down, and the land lay wrapped in silence like the dewy shroud of an ironic corpse, Vernon recited his beautiful new Poem. And we sat. Mesmerised. Literally.

From *Telegrams from a Childlike Heart: The Collected Poems of Vernon Huff* (Faber & Faber, 1973)

is this my bag (for john and yoko)

is this my bag
oh gracious dreamer
audacious schemer
satellite beamer
from london to lima
(peru)
i wish i knew
i wish i knew

oh how
i wish
i knew

is this your bag
oh childlike hoper
tenacious coper
utopian groper
all-over soaper
sitting on your sofa
drinking cofa
or tea
with me
i wish i knew
i wish i knew
oh how
i wish
i knew

is this their bag
oh sacred lovers
underneath covers
butterfly hovers
you know we are rovers
like all the others
and their mothers
i wish i knew
i wish i knew
oh how
i wish
i knew

now i know
this is OUR bag
our bag of invention
of no condescension
of sublime ascension
of so much to mention
of an end to all tension
when i sit on a bench on
my own
away from home

and now i know
john and yoko
oh how
oh now
i know
ono

From *Melody Maker*, issue 1764, 25 July 1969

Around the most moving point in Huff's great verse-poem – truly a
'Wasteland' *de nos jours* – a large iron bed was wheeled on, with that
world-famous bag upon it, the most blessed bag in the whole entire
universe of Planet Earth and beyond. The heads in the crowd popped
wide open, screaming – some even crying – with joy at the return of
this great modern genius and his lovely lady from the East. Not since
Wittgenstein first published his innermost secret thoughts in his truly
mind-expanding Tractatus Philosophicus and Paul Groggle of Flat Tyre
played the opening bars of his epic concept album Journey Through
the Bleached Bends of the Mind on what was to prove to be his last gig
before slumping forward in bed, vomiting into his early morning tea
and then drowning in it has anything ever met with such tumultuous
acclaim from a wholly (and holy) responsive audience. 'Ladies and
Gentlemen, boys and girls, freaks and freakesses, please rise,' said
Vernon Huff as he reached the bittersweet end of the poem. And all
around the grounds of Wragby, heads and freaks, lovers, headbangers,
chicks, lost souls, flower children and sheer unadulterated hippies rose
to their feet. 'And now please raise your right hand towards this bag –
the most loved bag in the world, right now – and repeat after me:
'John and Yoko ...'
'*John and Yoko*'
'We thank you for being here today'
'*We thank you for being here today*'
'We thank you for being our ambassadors for peace'
'*We thank you for being our ambassadors for peace*'
'And we ask you to continue to spread your philosophy of baggism'
'*And we ask you to continue to spread your philosophy of baggism*'
'To shock and upset and horrify the older generation, the Establish-
ment, into re-evaluating our whole concepts of love and peace'
'*To shock and upset and horrify the older generation, the Establishment, into re-*
evaluating our whole concepts of love and peace'

'So that someday, somewhere, we may all live as one'

'*So that someday, somewhere, we may all live as one*'

'Amen.'

'*Amen.*'

'And now, friends,' he concluded, 'I will call on Mr Dodo Dixon to open the bag, so's to let John and Yoko receive your love on a more person-to-person basis – Dodo, please open the bag!'

From the taped diary of Dodo Dixon, 23 July 1969

But as Vernon ordered me to open sesame and the freaks in the crowd all went into one almighty hush, I noticed there was one helluva lotta activity in the middle of that bag, gasps and sighs and oofs and heavy breathing and limbs pumping about here there and every-bloody-where – right bang in the middle of the stage! So I leaned over and whispered in Vernon's ear, 'They're making love, Vern!'

'Pardon me?' said Vernon.

'John and Yoko – they're doin' it – sex or whatever – look !'

And we both looked at the bag, which by now was going every-whichway – up and down and round and round, the grunts getting louder and more furious. 'Better wait 'til they're done, eh, Vernon?' I said.

But he replied, 'Cool it, Dodo. Leave this to me.'

So, like, he walked over to the microphone, looked deep into the eyes of the hundred thousand heads and said, 'Friends, you've heard John and Yoko preach, "Make Love, Not War", right?'

'Yeah!' went the heads.

'Well, friends – that's what they're doing right now, for us, for the world, for the … *globe*, right now, this minute, LIVE at WRAGBY!!!'

They all went W-I-L-D, and over the noise Vernon said to me, 'Open the bag, now Dodo – it's what John and Yoko want.'

'Eh?'

'Open it, Dodo,' he said, as if he really meant it. So I grabbed at the top of it and with one great tug it fell wide open.

Naked pensioners horrify hippies

St John Ambulance treats record numbers for shock

MANY pop-music fans expressed themselves 'shocked and bewildered' yesterday when a bag they had believed to contain Mr John Lennon and his second wife, the Japanese performance artiste Miss Yoko Ono, was opened to reveal three near-naked pensioners involved in a fist-fight over what appeared to be a small cache of documents.

'It was obscene,' commented a woman who gave her name only as 'Dandelion', who had been close to the front of the 100,000-strong crowd at the time, 'And a heck of a lot of people were shielding their eyes.'

Other festival-goers demonstrated their horror at the spectacle by pelting the three elderly combatants with discarded beer-cans, handfuls of turf and abandoned sandwiches. 'What they did was disgusting, absolutely disgusting,' said Jeff 'Loonpants'

Simmons, 24, 'and they deserved to be punished for it – that's the only language these people understand.'

A representative from the National Viewers and Listeners Association, who was present to monitor the Wragby Festival, said he had received a 'staggering' number of complaints from festival-goers. 'A lot of them were only teenagers and were very upset by this flagrant display of nudity from a generation which really should have known better.'

An on-site counselling service for victims of post-trauma syndrome attracted a record number of clients, many of them in tears. The three unknown nudists, believed to be in their mid-seventies, are helping the police with their inquiries. Meanwhile, Mr and Mrs Lennon have been discovered, still in their original bag, locked in a left-luggage locker at London Airport. They were reportedly unaware that anything had occured. 'They are heavily into medication,' explained an assistant last night.

Mr and Mrs John Lennon

AN APOLOGY

Owing to a misprint (July 24th), the word 'medication' appeared in our report yesterday. This should have read 'meditation'. We apologise unreservedly to Mr and Mrs Lennon for any embarrassment inadvertently caused to them and their families.

From the taped diary of Dodo Dixon, 23 July 1969

There was Sir Cliff, lying naked – not a pretty sight – on the floor of the stage, clutching at a brown envelope while this other old bloke is thumping him and trying to grab the envelope off of him. Blimey O'Reilly! There was an old lady in there somewhere too, but I've tried to block it out my head!

The crowd was screaming and booing and yelling and hurling beer bottles left right and bloody centre because even someone right out of their skulls could tell that these three old bats certainly weren't John and Yoko, No Way José.

'Gerremoff stage,' I called to the roadies. With the bottles sailing past our heads we managed to drag the three of them away – but not before they had torn the envelope into a hundred little pieces, all scattered over the stage. 'Who's on next?' I yelled, and the old soundcheck guy looked at his sheet and said in his posh bored voice, 'Frozen Misery'.

'Well – get 'em on,' I said.

'They haven't changed into their jeans yet.'

'Well do some one-two's then!' I yelled at him. 'Anything to keep this lot in order.'

'One two, one two, one two,' he said over the speakers. Soon the bottles died down, and along came hush. As we delivered the old folk into the hands of the pigs, I glanced back at the stage. In that hush before Frozen Misery came on, the soundcheck bloke was picking all the torn bits of paper neatly off the stage and carefully putting them in his pocket.

The police inquiry was the most frightful bore. 'This envelope you mentioned,' said the officer (jumped up little prig with poor teeth), 'What exactly did it contain, sir?'

'No idea,' I said, 'Absolutely no idea. And now we'll never know. Awful shame!'

'I'll bloody murder you, Chatterley!' said Mellors, his fury revealing the coarseness of his origins.

'Am I to take it that *you* know what it contained, then, Mr Thomas?' enquired the PC.

'I've got a fair idea,' said Mellors.

'But you'll never be able to prove it!' I laughed in his face.

'Now, now, gentlemen,' said PC Prig. Meanwhile, Connie was fast asleep, having sought consolation from her hip-flask after her recent ordeal.

A policeman in his early teens or younger strode in. 'Excuse me, sir,' he said to PC Prig, 'But there's a bloke outside who said he's the soundcheck man at the festival. Says he's got something important to show us.'

PC Prig sighed testily. 'Show him in.'

A middle-aged man came in, holding a sheath of papers. I recognised him immediately from the newspapers. And – worse – I recognised what was in his hand.

'John Thomas!' exclaimed a tearful Mellors, squeezing all the melodrama out of the moment, as one might have expected from his ill-mannered type. 'My own John Thomas! My son! It's been thirty years!'

'Okay, sir,' said Prig to the newcomer, 'Let's hear your story, shall we?'

From a statement to the Police by Sir John Thomas, 23 July 1969

After I was moved on from Charing Cross, I became mobile – a tramp, if you like, picking up the odd job, here or there. A month ago, I was walking along Dean Street, Soho, past some offices, when I saw a postcard in their window.

Recruitment postcard in the window of Contrax Inc., 22 June 1969

REQUIRED

Unemployed Man with Clear Speaking Voice
To say 'One-Two, One-Two, One-Two'
Into A Microphone
For Five Days, End of July
at world famous
WRAGBY HALL FESTIVAL
OXBRIDGE DEGREE AN ADVANTAGE

From a statement to the Police by Sir John Thomas, 23 July 1969

It was the words 'Wragby Hall' that caught my eye. I had never been there, of course, but it was the one place in the world that had overshadowed my life. Wrecked it, you might almost say.

I was led to the office of a Mr Dodo Dixon, a young man with long hair. I didn't take to him.

'What do you think of Rock?' he said.

'Rock?' I said.

'Rock music,' he said, 'What do you think of Rock music?'

'Nothing at all,' I said, 'No interest whatsoever.'

'Far out,' he said, 'Just what we want. You get so many one-two men who just want to hang out with the stars and can't keep their minds on the job. And you can count to two?'

'Certainly.'

'Let's hear you.'

'One – two.'

'Cool! You'd be surprised at the people who can't manage it. What's your name?'

'Thomas John,' I said. With a past like mine, I have learnt not to draw attention to myself.

'Welcome aboard, Thomas John!' he said, 'We're a crazy crew, but you'll get to like us.'

It was a tedious job, listening to that dreadful racket, day in, day out, repeating 'one-two, one-two, one-two' in every available interval. Only once had I managed to steal away into the wood nearby. You can imagine what I was looking for. And sure enough I found it: a few sticks and stones where once a gamekeeper's hut had been, and there, on an old birch tree, a carved inscription.

Carved inscription from a silver birch in the grounds of the Wragby Estate

From a statement to the Police by Sir John Thomas, 23 July 1969

And below it, another, clearer inscription, presumably added on at a later date.

Second carved inscription from a silver birch in the grounds of the Wragby Estate

From a statement to the Police by Sir John Thomas, 23 July 1969

It must have been fifty years since they were scratched, but still those inscriptions bore the power to enrage! For a few hours, I barked 'One-TWO! One-TWO!' with a sense of anger seething through my voice. Eventually Dixon sensed something was wrong and told me to 'Cool it, Man', so I took myself in hand.

And then came today. When the bag was brought on, I treated it with the same mixture of disdain and indifference I had reserved for the rest of the festival. Normally, I wouldn't have bothered even to look from backstage at the 'entertainment' on offer, but as it was meant to be Lennon and Ono in the bag, I thought I would treat them to a quick glare of my deepest contempt.

But the spectacle that met my eyes was among the most vile I have ever encountered. One second there was a bag on stage. The next second, there was my father, who I had not seen for thirty years or more, wrestling naked with another naked old man whilst my mother, also naked, looked on in terror. Perhaps to distract myself from the unseemly sight, my eyes found a focus on the brown envelope over which they were squabbling. What could be so powerful as to have reduced two elderly men to such grotesque humiliation? When they were led off stage, leaving the envelope and its contents all in shreds, I vowed to find out. Repeating 'one-two, one-two, one-two' as instructed into my microphone, I picked up all the shreds from the stage floor. Throughout the time Frozen Misery were blaring away, I sellotaped those shreds together again. And I was utterly flabbergasted by the result.

From the diary of Sir Clifford Chatterley, 23 July 1969

'Let's hear it, then,' said PC Prig.

'Surely no need, officer,' I stammered. 'It's transparently bogus.'

'Bogus my foot,' piped up Mellors, 'it's as real as my arse.' Muck will out, methinks.

'But it's so scruffy, officer,' I protested. 'Quite inadmissible, I feel sure.'

'I said, "Let's hear it",' snapped Prig.

And my heart sank like a stone.

The sellotaped document handed to the Police by Sir John Thomas, 23 July 1969

Being the Deathbed Confession of Mrs Olive Mellors, witnessed by Sir Clifford Chatterley and Mr Baxby Sturgeon, Solicitor, and signed in their presence by Mrs Olive Mellors shortly before the occasion of her death.

My name is Mrs Olive Mellors. I am shortly to die.

I was born of farming stock in the village of Tevershall in 1874, when Mr Disraeli first came to power. 'Never trust a man with a beard,' I remember my father saying. He was right, you know, but did I listen?

In 1891 I met Jack, a ploughman by trade. I was a servant-girl at Wragby Hall. Jack cut a dash at the springtide dance. I lost my heart to him. He wore a beard. My father warned me ag'in him, but I ignored his advice. He used to quote me the old country adage, 'Marry a man with a beard, and your son will be bearded too.' But I didn't listen to a word of it. We were married on a wet day in the winter of 1892: Mr and Mrs Jack Mellors.

Jack was a drinker and a reprobate. He'd go off gallivanting with other women, he'd drink, and when he came back he'd knock me about something terrible. I got in the family way that spring. I told myself if it were a boy, I'd never let him take on like that. One night in a fit of temper, I told Jack as much. He just laughed in my face, saying any son of his would be the same as him, to every last drop of his blood. 'His name will be Mellors and he'll be a Mellors to his fingertips.'

All through that long spring and hot summer, I grew to fear for the babe in my womb. Whene'er Jack came back, he'd lurch in, stinking of beer, burpin' and belchin' and hollerin' somethin' terrible, and he'd place his great big dirty hand on my stomach. 'That's *my* boy,' he'd say before rushing off to be sick o'er the kitchen table.

That wasn't what I wanted for my son. Not a bit of it. I wanted a lad who'd grow up neat and tidy, a lad who wouldn't drink and wouldn't philander, a lad who'd treat me as a woman should be treated, with dignity and respect, not someone to knock me around and beat me black and blue, as his father liked to do. What chance had any son of Jack Mellors ⌐ the child of his blood, brought up under his roof, subjected to his revoltin' ways? If the lad were not of his blood, or even if he were brought up in the house of another, away from Jack's influence – well, then he might escape that fate. Otherwise he would be doomed beyond salvation.

I never planned it. However awful the deed may seem, I never planned it.

Chance played its hand. The lady of the Manor, Lady Cecilie Chatterley, a more charming lady you'd never hope to find, was also heavy with child at the very same time. Being but a chambermaid, I rarely saw her ladyship, but she was good and kind, taking a special interest in my progress, asking me how I was feeling, ordering me not to overdo it on the cleanin' front, and what-have-you. But never did I breathe a word to Her Ladyship, nor to another soul, of my fears for my wee babe, my fears about that Mellors blood.

On a bitter cold morn in the eighth month of my pregnancy, her Ladyship happened to hear that our cottage had a dreadful rotten roof and was leaking. One mad night Jack had swapped the tiles for beer with the publican. Her Ladyship summoned me to her. She insisted the cottage was in no fit state for a woman heavy with child. 'From here on, you will reside in the Hall,' she said. 'I will tell Wilberforce to make ready an attic room.'

Such was her kindness – and see how I repaid it: sometimes I think I was driven by demons.

Our two babes were born on the very same night, within hours of one another, mine in the attic room, Her Ladyship's downstairs in the Pink Bedroom. I have since heard that this is often so when two pregnant women are beneath the same roof. Even at this late stage, and with her own worries, Her Ladyship's kindness knew no limit, for she sent her midwife's assistant to assist at my birth. I had been hopin' against hope for a little girl, but I remember those terrible words as though it were yesterday. 'It's a boy, Mrs Mellors!' I cried and I cried. What hope would there be for the precious bairn? No hope at all! 'My dear, you are tired,' the midwife's assistant said to me. 'You must get a good sleep.'

I fell into the deepest of sleeps, my baby in my arms. When I awoke it was to the sound of the midwife, Mrs Studholme. Her Ladyship would very much like to see me, she said, for she wished to congratulate me on the birth of my little boy. In a fluster, I placed a nightgown around myself, lifting my son, still asleep, from the bed. Already, I fancied I could see in his face the savage, pagan look of Jack Mellors. Where was Jack? Even at that moment I knew he would be out bartering our baby's rattle for a kiss and a cuddle with the local trollop.

Was my action so very selfish? I did it for my son, you must understand. Full of the deepest foreboding, I held the babe in my arms and walked slowly downstairs towards the bedroom of Her Ladyship. With my left hand, I knocked on the door of the Pink Bedroom. There was not a sound, so I knocked again, this time a little harder. Still no sound, so I gently pushed the door open, and tip-toed in.

Lady Cecilie had fallen asleep, the dear. My first impulse was to leave the room, but then I thought how much it would please her Ladyship if I were to take a peep at her own wee babe. Now, the Pink Room has a door which leads through to a dressing-room. That door was open, so I imagined the babe would be in there, fast asleep. Ever so softly, I crept into the dressing-room. There in the cot, his head cushioned by the tufts and frills of a fine linen pillow, lay the new-born babe, the infant who would one day inherit the baronetcy of Chatterley, together with the magnificent Hall and all the estate of Wragby. And then I glanced down at my own poor little mite. He looked so much the same, but his life would be so very different! At that moment, I felt nothing but sorrow, deep, deep sorrow.

And then it came to me! Brought up in Wragby, my babe would have a chance – a chance of education and immense wealth, but also a chance to shake off the blood of the dread Jack Mellors! But what of the other babe? Well, he could be well loved and cared for by me. He already had the best start in life of the two of them, for he had not a drop of the Mellors blood coarsing through his body.

Without further ado, I took the silken robes off the Chatterley babe and the cotton robes off my own. Once I had dressed each in the other's robes, I put my babe in the Chatterley cot, and held the Chatterley babe close to my breast. Before I left the dressing-room, I placed a kiss on the forehead of my baby in the cot, for I knew that I would never be able to kiss him again, not as long as I lived. Then I stole back upstairs with the Chatterley babe and pretended to be asleep until Mrs Studholme came into the room.

'Have you not visited Her Ladyship yet, Olive?' she said.

'I must have fallen back to sleep,' I said.

'Quick, quick!' she said, 'And for mercy's sake, don't forget to take your little baby! Does he have a name yet?'

'Oliver,' I said.

'Why, that's a grand name!' replied Mrs Studholme, 'Now downstairs with you both – let's not keep her Ladyship waiting!'

I entered the Pink Room for the second time that morning. Her Ladyship was sitting up in bed, the sweetest smile on her face. My baby was already at her aristocratic breast, drinking deeply of her milk. I had never seen Her Ladyship look so happy.

'Oh Olive!' she exclaimed, 'We are mothers together! How is your little chap? Do let me see him! My goodness, isn't he adorable? You must be so very proud!'

It all seemed so natural, so very, very natural.

'And have you thought of a name for your little fellow, Olive?'

'Yes, ma'am. I thought I would call him Oliver!'

'A lovely name – and do you know, in a funny way, I think he *looks* like an Oliver! And I shall be calling my little fellow Clifford! Clifford Chatterley – it has a ring to it, don't you agree? It is a name to live up to, you might say!'

Suddenly, the babe in my arms began to whimper and mewl. 'Your little Oliver is thirsty!' laughed Lady Cecilie. 'Sit down here on my bed and let us suckle our babies together!' And so we sat there, the Lady and her servant, each of us feeding the other's baby.

In the May, we christened the Chatterley boy Oliver: Oliver Mellors. I loved him as though he were my own. Well, I did and I didn't. He was a dear until he was five or six years old, but then he started to copy Jack Mellors – smashing plates against the wall, arm-wrestling the cat, always carrying on about himself and oh how manly and *rugged* he was. I wanted to tell him, 'Oliver, your father is a toff, he's the 9th Baronet, you're no child of the soil.' But of course it was too late for any of that.

I never lost my soft spot for the lad who was really my own. I remained a cleaner at Wragby until he was seventeen, and I would see him almost every day, running this way and that, though I don't suppose he ever knew my name.

Did I do wrong? My own boy grew up to inherit Wragby Hall, whilst the real son of Wragby, poor little Oliver, became only a humble gamekeeper. Oh, when Sir Clifford – as he had become – married Lady Constance, I was there at the gate of the church with all the other folk from the village, waving and cheering; but no one could have realised that the tears I shed were not those of a loyal servant but of a mother. A few years later, after poor Cliffie had been so badly injured fighting for his country, a miracle seemed to occur and Lady Constance grew pregnant. I was a grandmother! Oh, how I inwardly rejoiced! But then the village began to talk: the baby, they said, was not Sir Clifford's. It was the child of Oliver Mellors.

'Is this true, Oliver?' I said over one Sunday lunch.

'Tis true, mother,' he replied, practising his arm-wrestling, his left arm against his right.

'Oh, Oliver,' I sighed.

As usual, his right arm won, humiliating the left by squashing it into the remains of the Yorkshire pud. What could be worse for a woman than to have her son cuckolded by her ward, and to have to stand by in silence?

Months later, after the scandal had become common knowledge, Lady Chatterley departed from Wragby. I heard through Oliver that the baby had arrived, and that he was to be called John Thomas. Meanwhile, my poor Clifford was left alone at Wragby, without the comfort of his mother. It was then that I began to regret my impetuous act. Would he not have been better off humble but happy? Had I not made the most terrible mistake?

Two days ago, the doctor informed me that I had only a short time to live. I called a solicitor, Mr Baxby Sturgeon, and informed him that I wished to make reparation for an awful misdeed. I explained the position to him. Accordingly, he persuaded my darling boy, Clifford Chatterley, to be present while I have been making this last confession. I hereby ask the forgiveness of Clifford, of Oliver, and of Oliver's boy, John Thomas. I entrust my darling son Clifford with the task of imparting this news to the others. There is no point keeping anyone in the dark any longer. There is no source of misery that is not bound by a secret. It is better that everyone should know the truth, for then an ancient wrong may be righted. Oliver and John Thomas may have the Hall that is rightly theirs, and Clifford may move to humbler surroundings, there to enjoy a life of good hard work and rustic peace.

This is the last testament of
Olive Mellors, mother of Clifford.

'May the Lord have Mercy upon My Soul'

witnessed by:
Sir Clifford Chatterley (né Mellors)
Mr Baxby Sturgeon, Solicitor.

From Detective Constable Pringle's Official Police Report into the Wragby Hall Affair, 19 August 1969

At the conclusion of my reading of the testament of Mrs Olive Mellors, Sir Clifford Chatterley (né Mellors) commented:
'I am ruined!'
And Mr Oliver Thomas (né Chatterley, a.k.a. Mellors) commented:
'The Hall is mine!'
Mr Oliver Thomas (né Chatterley) then added: 'Twenty-four hours, Chatterley – twenty-four hours! That's the time I'm giving you for clearing your stuff out of MY HALL!'
Sir John Thomas then commented: 'I am not John Thomas Mellors after all. I am a true Chatterley! When my mother had her ... liaison ... with the gamekeeper, she was in fact ... liasing ... with the real 8th Baronet of Chatterley! There was NO SCANDAL!'
The noise created by these last two words proved sufficient to wake

up Lady Chatterley, who commented:

'What's happening?'

At which Mr Oliver Thomas (né Chatterley) commented:

'It's as I said, Connie – I've been a Chatterley all along! Wragby is OURS!' Lady Chatterley then commented:

'But I HATE Wragby,' before resuming her sleep.

From the diary of Sir Clifford Chatterley, 23 July 1969

My secret had been discovered. I was Mellors and Mellors was Chatterley. My breeding was rock bottom, the lowest of the low, whilst the sordid Mellors was a damned Baronet. And as with my breeding, so with my future, which had now slipped inexorably down the slide into a slum dwelling in Tevershall at best. How the hell had Mellors discovered my secret? No one but Baxby Sturgeon, my wretched mother and myself had known the foggiest, and Sturgeon and the old bat were now dead and buried. 'Who told you?' I barked at Mellors, 'Who the bloody hell knew about it?'

From Detective Constable Pringle's Official Police Report into the Wragby Hall Affair, 19 August 1969

'Who told you? Who the bloody hell knew about it?' commented Sir Clifford Chatterley (né Mellors) to Mr Oliver Thomas (né Chatterley).

At this point, the door to the Inquiry Room flew open. In walked a lady of middle-aged appearance.

'I did,' she commented.

'And who are you?' I enquired.

'I am Joy Greenley,' she commented, 'and I know everything.'

From a statement to the Tevershall Police by Miss Joy Greenley, 23 July 1969

... and so following six months of in-depth research into the Chatterley phenomenon in 1958–9, I knew – and I *alone* knew – that his father was not a Mellors but a Chatterley – and that he, John Thomas, was in fact the rightful heir to Wragby Hall. I resolved to inform him of the good news, and at the same time to discover more of his upbringing for the purposes of my book.

We met at Beachy Head on January 1st 1960. The moment I mentioned I knew he was the child of Oliver and Constance, he went berserk, screaming at me and threatening me with my life. 'But you don't *understand*!' I said, for I wished only to reassure him.

'I understand only too well – you are out to wreck my life and my career!' he yelled back. I got out of the car. He chased after me. We tussled. I fell. He left me for dead and ran away.

At his trial, I had no wish to let him off the hook. I had no wish to make his life easier by telling the world – as I had tried to tell him at Beachy Head – that he was in fact the true heir to Wragby Hall, and that there was now no scandal in his family, as Lady Chatterley had simply run off with the true Sir Oliver Chatterley. So I kept it to myself, and let him face ruin.

But I too was ruined by the trial. No editor would publish me. No university would employ me. I had no money. I had no home. All I had was my precious secret. A few months ago, penniless and working as a cleaner, I saw Oliver Thomas on the television. He was advertising his chain of supermarkets. This gave me the idea of offering him my secret in return for a large sum of money, money that would allow me to resume my life as a highly reputed biographer. I wrote him a letter in which I hinted at the truth – a truth he had never suspected. He agreed to meet me. I found him a very smooth, mature, almost refined and very conservative man, very different from the way he was portrayed by Lawrence in *Lady Chatterley's Lover*.

From a statement to the Tevershall Police by Oliver Thomas, 23 July 1969

To be honest, I found Miss Greenley a most attractive woman, almost boyish-looking, with the get-up-and-go and first-rate business sense I often associate with her fellow countrymen. I had seen her nine years previously, in court, of course, but the Old Bailey lighting hadn't been kind to her.

At first, we talked straight business. She told me she thought she could lead me to the ownership of Wragby Hall; if she succeeded, I would have to agree to give her £50,000. Well, it struck me as an improbable proposition, so my initial response was to laugh. But then I said, OK, then – you're on. That was when she brought out the contract. I like a hard head in a woman. As it entailed payment only upon results, I signed.

She told me of her researches, and of how she had spied Chatterley and Sturgeon emerging from the nurse's house bearing a piece of paper, and how that paper was more likely than not some sort of confession. If I got my hands on that piece of paper, then Wragby would be mine. I was excited, very excited, for I felt sure I could outwit Chatterley.

'One last thing,' she said. 'Just for me, would you read this out in your old voice – your old gamekeeper's voice?' And she passed me a copy of the Lawrence book with the passage marked. So I did.

From *Lady Chatterley's Lover* by D. H. Lawrence

'Dunna ax me nowt now. Let me be. I like thee. I luv thee when tha lies theer. A woman's a lovely thing when 'er's deep ter fuck, and cunt's good. Ah luv thee, thy legs, an' th' shape on thee, an' th' womanness on thee. Ah luv th' womanness on thee. Ah luv thee wi' my ba's an' wi' my heart.'

From a statement to the Tevershall Police by Oliver Thomas, 23 July 1969

And when I looked up, she had fainted.

From a statement to the Tevershall Police by Joy Greenley, 23 July 1969

It was the very first time in my life I had been able to appreciate to the full the true power and beauty of literature, for this was indeed Mellors, here with me at last.

'Oh, Oliver!' I said.

'Oh, Joy!' he replied.

From the diary of Sir Clifford Chatterley, 23 July 1969

'It's all very well you cooing away at one another in that revolting fashion,' I interrupted, 'But what about poor Connie here?' I pointed to the slumbering body, clutching vainly at the empty bottle of Thomas's Own-Brand Scotch, 'What about her feelings, eh? You two should be ashamed of yourselves, carrying on like that.'

There was a knock on the door of the Inquiry Room. Enter the dread Dodo Dixon accompanied by his young lady friend, a wodge of notes in his hands.

'Great news, guys,' he said, 'I am engaged to be married to Miss Daniella Lacloche! Come on, Dandelion, give them all a twirl!'

'Dandelion' then twirled around in her mini-skirt to the applause of the assembled company.

'And just so's we're all on Cloud Nine, I'm going to distribute a few of these notes among our friends, the marvellous Boys in Blue, just to celebrate the dropping of all charges, if they know what I mean, eh?'

'Very thoughtful of you, Sir,' said PC Not-Quite-Such-a-Prig, scooping the £20 notes with both hands and thrusting them into his back pocket. 'Very thoughtful indeed.'

From out of nowhere, John Thomas rushed up to the young lady. 'Did you say Lacloche? ' he said, 'Miss Daniella LACLOCHE?'

'Too right,' she replied, 'But my friends call me Dandelion.'

'And when were you born?'

'Twenty-first of April, 1950, cheeky! I'm nineteen!'

'And what was your mother's name?'

'Lacloche, of course!'

'Her Christian name?'

'Floella.'

'My God, girl – you're my daughter!'

'So you're my father!'

'And if she's your daughter,' said Mellors, 'then she's my grand-daughter.'

'So you're my grandfather! And Lady Chatterley is my grand-mother!'

'And you,' said Dixon to Thomas, 'Will be my father-in-law! And –' he added, drawing out a pocket calculator, 'I will inherit Wragby!'

'Friends . . . ' The face looming around the door belonged to Vernon Huff. 'I guess this calls for a poem.'

And at that the room emptied.

Announcement in the classified advertising section of the *Tevershall Free Press*, 13 August 1969

May it henceforth be known that from this day of Our Lord the

THIRTEENTH day of AUGUST in the year NINETEEN HUNDRED AND SIXTY-NINE the gentleman appertaining to the name of MR OLIVER THOMAS shall by rights and duty fermented through his birthright attain to his true and former name and title of SIR OLIVER CHATTERLEY, resident of WRAGBY HALL in this our county of DERBYSHIRE and that his son JOHN THOMAS MELLORS, also resident of WRAGBY HALL, shall by rights and duty fermented through his birthright attain to his true and former name and title of SIR JOHN THOMAS CHATTERLEY and FURTHERMORE may it henceforth be known that from this day of Our Lord the THIRTEENTH day of AUGUST in the year NINETEEN HUNDRED AND SIXTY-NINE the previous bearer of the title of said address and baronetcy, formerly known as SIR CLIFFORD CHATTERLEY will regress through the rights and duty fermented through his birthright to his true and former name and title of MR CLIFFORD MELLORS, now resident of 5, GAMEKEEPER'S COTTAGES, WRAGBY. All and any enquiries pertaining to this matter should be addressed on this day or subsequent days to the offices of ASQUITH HARCOURT AND CO, SOLICITORS, NEW FETTER LANE.

From the Guest Directory of The New Wragby Hall International Leisure Hotel and Conference Centre, 1992

Welcome to the Wragby Hall International Leisure Hotel and Conference Centre. Wragby Hall has been the home of the Chatterley family for over 150 years now, and many famous writers, artists and statesmen have passed through its portals. These include, of course, the great English novelist David Herbert Lawrence, who immortalised the Hall and its beautiful estate in his celebrated work, *Lady Chatterley's Lover*.

We are proud of our fine tradition of service to our guests. To endeavour to assist you in every way during your stay we have compiled this directory of information.

You will find overleaf details of all of the services and facilities we provide along with opening times of our splendid Sons and Lovers Four Star Restaurant. And why not start your evening with a relaxing visit to our famous Queenie Leavis Cocktail Lounge, where our cocktail waiter will be pleased to serve you a range of over 250 exotic choice tipples from our extensive cocktail menu.

Whether you are travelling on business or are here simply for pleasure, it is our aim to make your stay as comfortable and enjoyable as possible. Should you require any further information or assistance, please do not hesitate to contact any member of the management team.

We trust that you thoroughly enjoy your visit to Wragby Hall, and hope we have the pleasure of welcoming you again in the not too distant future.

Guests are requested to vacate their rooms before 11.30 a.m. on the day of departure.

Sir John Thomas Chatterley
Hotel Manager

Accounts

Accounts may only be forwarded for payment if arrangements have been made in advance and confirmed by the owners.

Bedroom facilities

All our bedrooms are equipped with tea- and coffee-making facilities and a mini-bar. Please fill in all beverages consumed from the mini-bar on the available form and pass it to reception for scrutiny on the evening before your departure. Local police accommodation will be made readily available to any guests failing to comply with this request.

Cocktail bar

The Queenie Leavis Cocktail Bar is open from 10.00 a.m. through until midnight on every day except Sunday. Situated just off the entrance hall this is the perfect location for a relaxing drink either before or after your meal. House specialities include:

Scarlet Trousers: Fresh Tomato Juice, Campari, Ribena, Vintage Red Wine, Creme de Cassis and Tizer, served with Ripe Loganberries in a Heart-shaped Schooner.

Naked Self: Amaretto, Curacao, Egg White, Gin and a hint of Campari with Fruit Accompaniment.

Smouldering Sense of Deep Injustice: Noilly Prat, Grenadine, Beef Stock, Vodka, Pimms, Fresh Cream and Kahlua shaken and served in a long Glass with sponge Fingers.

Class Overthrow: Crème de bananes, Pepsi Cola, Pernod, Baked Beans, Sloe Gin, Cointreau served with straws and thrown over a Hollowed Pineapple.

Entertainment

Entertainment is provided in the cocktail bar each evening between 18.00 hrs and 21.00 hrs by former Sixties singing star Vernon Huff, playing a selection of songs for the young at heart. He is also happy to play your requests.

Hotel services

Should you require any further information please contact Mr Clifford Mellors on the Porter's Desk (ext. 305), who will be pleased to assist you. Please – no tipping.

Laundry and dry cleaning

Soiled bedlinen should be cleaned and laundered by guests themselves. Mrs Constance Mellors, housekeeper – and 'other half' of our excellent old husband-and-wife team! – will conduct her inspection at 10.00 a.m. on the day of departure.

Restaurant

The Sons and Lovers Restaurant is open to residents and non-residents. Guests are requested not to speak with their mouths full.

Sexual Congress

Guests are requested to refrain from sexual congress whilst on the premises as it may give offence. Colour televisions are provided in all bedrooms, and also in the Games Room, located on the lower ground floor.

Shoe cleaning

Dirty shoes should be handed to Mr Clifford Mellors at the Porter's Desk (ext. 305) before midnight. He will clean them and return them to your bedroom by 7.00 a.m. the following morning. Again, please – no tipping.

Sightseeing

Guided tours around the grounds of Wragby Hall may be arranged through Reception (ext. 403). Our world-famous facility, The Lawrence Memorial Hut, is free to residents of the Hall. It is open from 10.00 a.m. – 5.30 p.m. throughout the year, except for Christmas Day and Boxing Day, when it is closed. Guests may also pick up a token from Reception (ext. 403) to exchange for a free circuit on the renowned Chatterley Wheelchair. Alternatively, a footpath map detailing the sights and scenes of the world-famous 'Lady Chatterley's Way', with historic footnotes by Professor Hoggart, is available at a modest price from the Herbert Bookstall situated to the right of the Front Desk. Please do not pick the flowers.

Transcript of a speech delivered by HRH Princess Margaret at the opening of The D. H. Lawrence Memorial Hut, Wragby Hall, 5 September 1972

My Lords, Ladies and Gentlemen,

It is now over forty years since the untimely death of David Herbert Lawrence. He is now widely acknowledged to be one of the very greatest of all our English writers and a tremendous source of pride to Nottingham, Tevershall and surrounding areas.

And it is a full fifty years since Mr Lawrence first drew inspiration from this shady nook in the heart of the English countryside to pen one of his most memorable and best-loved novels, *Lady Chatterley's Lover*. Today, it is taught in schools and universities the world over, and continues to inspire young and old alike to a fuller appreciation of the world and all that it has to offer.

The many leading literary experts present today have been kind enough to tell me that, over half a century ago, on a spot roughly where I am standing now, D. H. Lawrence first set eyes on the 'goings on' in the makeshift gamekeeper's hut which is today housed in this magnificent Memorial Exhibition.

And it was what he saw on that clear summer's day that first gave rise to his delightful and informative novel.

As you can see, a very great deal of care and attention has been spent on recreating in exact detail the very look and feel of the gamekeeper's hut.

To my mind the figures of the gamekeeper, Mr Mellors, and his companion, Lady Chatterley are entirely lifelike and convincing, a triumph of the waxworker's art. When I press this button, you will note that the figures begin to move up and down, up and down, a brilliant recreation, involving great mechanical ingenuity, of one of the most memorable scenes in the book.

(*HRH Princess Margaret presses button. Applause.*)

Note too, just to my right-hand side, how the admirably lifelike effigy of D. H. Lawrence himself sits peeping through a window of the hut on to the famous couple, pen and notebook in hand. And when I press this button –

(*HRH Princess Margaret presses button*)

– you will see him start to scribble, scribble, scribble.

(*Applause*)

I hope this may serve as a reminder to all visitors to Wragby that no book comes into existence without a very great deal of effort and extensive research. Over the years, our hard-working novelists have contributed much to our national heritage and we salute them for it.

(*Applause*)

I am much impressed, too, by so many of the fascinating exhibits, fashioned from real-life incidents that made the book so enchanting: the stuffed chicks, for instance, and the exotic plaster-casts.

And for schoolchildren who are being taught how men of toil lived in the early part of this century, I know the model of an Edwardian colliery will prove an invaluable and illuminating aid.

Finally, may I repeat how delighted I am to be opening this D. H. Lawrence Memorial Hut at Wragby Hall. I hope that from it this and future generations may derive much benefit.

Applause as ribbon is cut. Her Royal Highness then takes her place in Sir Clifford's wheelchair, and makes a triumphal circuit of the exhibition, pushed by the Lord Lieutenant of Derbyshire, Sir Oliver Chatterley, and his wife, Lady Joy.